A PERILOUS ALLIANCE

The Ursula Blanchard Mysteries from Fiona Buckley

* available from Severn House

A PERILOUS
ALLIANCE

Fiona Buckley

CRÈME de la CRIME

This first world edition published 2015
in Great Britain and the USA by
Crème de la Crime, an imprint of
SEVERN HOUSE PUBLISHERS LTD of
19 Cedar Road, Sutton, Surrey, England, SM2 5DA.
Trade paperback edition first published 2015
in Great Britain and the USA by
SEVERN HOUSE PUBLISHERS LTD.

British Library Cataloguing in Publication Data

Buckley, Fiona author.
  A perilous alliance. – (A Tudor mystery)
  1. Blanchard, Ursula (Fictitious character)–Fiction.
  2. Murder–Investigation–Fiction. 3. Great Britain–
  History–Elizabeth, 1558-1603–Fiction. 4. Detective and
  mystery stories.
  I. Title II. Series
  823.9'14-dc23

ISBN-13: 978-1-78029-076-8 (cased)
ISBN-13: 978-1-78029-559-6 (trade paper)
ISBN-13: 978-1-78010-672-4 (e-book)

All Severn House titles are printed on acid-free paper.

Severn House Publishers support the Forest Stewardship Council™ [FSC™],
the leading international forest certification organisation. All our titles that
are printed on FSC certified paper carry the FSC logo.

Typeset by Palimpsest Book Production Ltd.,
Falkirk, Stirlingshire, Scotland.
Printed and bound in Great Britain by
TJ International, Padstow, Cornwall.

This book is for Susan and David,
Long-standing friends, with whom I have shared so many happy times.

ONE
Retreating to Sussex

All I wanted was a quiet domestic life.

After many years of a life that was only inter-mittently domestic and hardly ever quiet, I desired nothing more than to live in my two houses of Hawkswood in Surrey and Withysham in Sussex – although these days I rarely visited the latter, preferring Hawkswood – and look after my small son Harry; to make occasional journeys to Buckinghamshire where my married daughter Meg lived, and to take care of my household.

I most certainly did not wish to remarry. I had had three husbands and an unwanted affair that was forced on me. Offers were made from time to time but I refused them all, being content with widowhood. The life I now desired was not only peaceful but single. And in 1575 I thought I had at last attained it.

Towards the end of that year, the steward who had been looking after Withysham suddenly died. I was then living, as usual, at Hawkswood, which I loved because it was a beautiful house and also because it had once belonged to my third and most beloved husband, Hugh Stannard. I did not go to Withysham myself to arrange a replacement but sent Hawkswood's steward, Adam Wilder, into Sussex to find and install a replacement. Adam, tall, grey-haired, with years of experience of looking after Hawkswood, could be trusted with the task and in his absence, my excellent manservant Roger Brockley could well take over his duties.

Adam was back before Christmas, saying that he had found a competent new man, named Robert Hanley, in whom I could have every confidence. We kept Christmas pleasantly at Hawkswood just as usual, but as the new year began, and I started to think about a celebration for little Harry's fourth birthday, I realized that the years were slipping by at a surprising rate. It was a very long time since I had last seen Withysham, and this was neglectful. It had been granted to me by Queen Elizabeth herself, in return for services I had been able to render to her, and it was ungrateful of me to ignore it.

And then my plans were interrupted by yet another unwanted proposal of marriage.

It was the fourth since my dear Hugh's death in 1571. Offers had to be expected, of course, for I was a well-off widow, still – just – of childbearing years, and well connected. The latter was not supposed to be widely known, but it *was* known, all the same. I was therefore a catch. But a year had gone by since my refusal of the third approach and I had concluded that word of this had got round and that now I would be left in peace. Then Captain Yarrow arrived at Hawkswood.

Captain Yarrow was the deputy constable of Dover Castle and I had met him in 1573 when I was involved in another of the diplomatic adventures which had for so long been part of my life. This had begun almost by accident when I first came to court, as one of Elizabeth's ladies, and was in need of money and glad to undertake an unusual assignment. Since then, I had often acted as a secret agent for Elizabeth, which was the reason why recent years had been so very unquiet and had taken me out of the domestic world so often. But I had now withdrawn from such work, for it could be dangerous and I had grown tired of it – and besides, there was Harry to consider.

Yarrow's arrival seriously annoyed me.

There was nothing really wrong with the man. He was a widower, whose wife had died of lung congestion five winters before. He had three sons, aged twelve, fifteen and twenty, and brought the eldest one with him, apparently to provide a testimonial to his good character as a husband and father. He was certainly well off. His position at Dover Castle was well paid; he was trustworthy and he was a humane man in his way when it came to questioning suspects. I had seen a demonstration of that.

He was small in stature but wiry and active and he was a

brilliant marksman. He was highly respected by his men, to the point that some of them feared him. He had a couple of oddities, in that he had a high-pitched voice for a man, and a high-pitched giggle to go with it, and he did embroidery as a hobby. That alone should not have been off-putting; some of the finest professional embroiderers in the land are men. Perhaps it was the combination of the needlework and the voice. But whatever my reasons, I did not like him. Even if I had wanted to marry again, I would not have considered Captain Yarrow.

He proved hard to get rid of, however. Having invited himself and his son to Hawkswood, he seemed determined to stay and was impervious to any hints that it was time they both left. They talked persuasively to me of the pleasant accommodation the captain had at Dover, and the beauties of his own country home in Kent, of the agreeable society I would move in and how welcome all my present companions would be.

Well, most of them. As well as Roger Brockley, my closest household members were Brockley's wife Fran, my personal woman (I still often called her Dale, which had been her maiden name), Sybil Jester, who lived with me as my companion, and who was a widow like me though a little older than I, and an aged Welshwoman called Gladys Morgan who had attached herself to me long ago when Brockley and I had rescued her from a charge of witchcraft. Gladys was not an attractive character, since she disliked washing herself, was bad-tempered and had in fact been arrested for witchcraft all over again after she joined my entourage, because of the lurid curses she had thrown at people she disliked. She had also provoked local physicians by being better at brewing successful herbal medicines than they were. Yarrow said that he couldn't agree to accept Gladys.

I could tell that he wouldn't give way on this and finally managed to use Gladys as the means of dislodging him. Where I went, she went, I said firmly. It worked. He and his son at last took themselves off, disappointed.

Their presence had disturbed me so much that I had had two bad migraines during their stay. Brockley, glad to see me downstairs again after the first one had subsided, had looked at me with serious grey-blue eyes, wrinkled his high, gold-freckled forehead, and said: 'I cannot like the effect these guests are having on you, madam.'

During the second attack, two days later, Dale, her slightly protuberant blue eyes anxious, and the pocks of a long ago attack of the smallpox standing out as they always did when she was upset, brought me a soothing potion (brewed by Gladys) and said candidly: 'Ma'am, if you marry that captain, you'll spend half your life having migraines.'

Gladys had already offered to give them a distaste for Hawkswood by putting purges in their wine, but I had told her that the last thing I wanted was to have the pair of them being ill and tied to my premises accordingly. Now, Sybil, standing worriedly beside Dale at my bedside, simply said: 'Dear Mistress Stannard, don't do it.'

'I don't intend to do it,' I said, waspishly, not because I was angry with Dale or Sybil but because an invisible demon had just struck me over the left eyebrow with an invisible hammer. 'It's just so hard to convince *them.*'

I was touched by the concern of my people, and more grateful than I can say for the drawbacks that made Gladys so unacceptable to Yarrow. I have never bidden guests farewell with greater enthusiasm.

The day of the Yarrows' departure was when I decided that Harry's birthday, which was in February, should be celebrated in Withysham, deep in Sussex, a healthy distance from both Dover and London, as I remarked to Brockley.

'It's not that far, madam,' he observed. 'Getting to Sussex won't really be an obstacle for anyone who really wants to find you.'

'I know,' I said. 'But it just *feels* as though it is.'

It was January, but after one short spell of snow, the weather had cleared and by the final week of the month, it was frosty but dry. The roads would be passable. We set off at once.

I would have left even sooner, had I been present at a meeting of the Royal Council, which took place about a week before I started for Withysham. I got to know about that later, when Sir William Cecil, Lord Burghley, gave me a detailed description of the proceedings.

Not that moving faster would have done me much good. Brockley was right. Having to travel into Sussex was no problem to anyone who really wanted to find me.

The meeting in question took place at Whitehall Palace, which is less of a building than a small town in its own right. To get from one part of it to another frequently means coming out into the open air and crossing a courtyard or two. Because of the frosty weather, all those attending the meeting arrived, to a man, in cloaks of velvet or heavy wool, with lavish fur trimmings: ermine, sheep fleece, black bear from the Continent, and in the case of Lord Burghley, the silky, curly fleece known as astrakhan, imported expensively from Russia. As the queen's Treasurer, Cecil usually considered that for someone in his position, too much ostentation looked like a form of boasting, but weather like this excused any kind of luxury that kept a man warm.

'But there was a good fire in the conference chamber,' Cecil told me. 'Everyone shed their cloaks with a sigh of relief and the servants took them away and we settled round the table and picked up our copies of the agenda in a cheerful fashion. A mood which lasted,' he added drily, 'approximately five minutes.'

Cecil was a serious man, grave of face, with a wispy forked beard that he sometimes pulled at when worried (which was often), and a permanent anxiety line between his eyes. But he did have a quiet sense of humour and if he had a startling announcement to make, he usually did so tactfully. He was not given to melodrama.

It was the Secretary of State, Francis Walsingham – no, *Sir* Francis, since he had been knighted shortly before the previous Christmas – who threw the firework into their midst. Ignoring the agenda that lay in front of him, he rose to his feet and said: 'Gentlemen, before we even consider the official business of the day, there is something else, of vital importance, to discuss. I am sorry to report that somewhere in court circles there is a spy. Someone in a position to be well informed has been in touch with Spain and France, and not to our advantage.'

There was a silence, before the Earl of Leicester, Sir Robert Dudley, said: 'In what way?'

'Her majesty,' said Walsingham, 'has good reason to regard both nations as potential enemies. Both are strongly Catholic and both would like an opportunity to impose their religion on us. France also has an interest in Mary Stuart's claim to our throne. That is based, as you are all aware, of course, on the Catholic insistence that our queen's mother Anne Boleyn wasn't lawfully married to King Henry the Eighth because his previous wife was still living. Mary Stuart of Scotland was formerly a queen of France – and a very popular one. The French back her claim. Meanwhile, our relations with Spain are so uneasy that they no longer have an ambassador here! Our best protection so far has been the fact that France and Spain are hereditary foes. But as an additional safeguard, we have wished to impress both with the idea that we are a strong nation, well able to defend ourselves. For this reason, we have – again, as most of you know – tried to let it be known abroad that our navy is greater than it actually is.'

Round the table, there were nods. Everyone knew about that particular stratagem.

'It hasn't been too easy,' Walsingham said, 'since the embassies are the usual conduit for this sort of thing and, as I have just said, the Spanish embassy is currently closed. But through the French embassy, and the work of agents in both countries, we had, we thought, convinced them that we have at our disposal, one hundred and seventy ships, with more being built. Our agents now report that both governments now know that we actually have only seventy vessels ready for use. This is serious, not just because it is now clear to both Spain and France that we are a weaker nation than we wanted them to suppose, but also that someone in England is passing damaging information to them. Are there any theories on who our spy could be?'

There were shaken heads and anxious faces. There were people of Spanish and French nationality at the court but most of them were there because they were out of favour in their own countries, and had taken refuge in England. Few, in any case, were likely to be privy to the sort of information that was now being leaked.

My lord of Sussex, Thomas Radcliffe, finally remarked: 'Well, there are other ways to deal with the dangers posed by these two powers. A strong alliance with one would neutralize both of them. None of us want, or would trust, a treaty with Spain, and I therefore urge – as I have done before – that we should seek a treaty binding England and France to come to each other's aid if either is attacked by Spain, and back the treaty up by a physical bond of marriage.'

Robert Dudley, bristling, said: 'We have been into all this half a dozen times already, Sussex. You want the queen to marry and provide the land with an heir, and you did your very best not so long ago to encourage a marriage between her and a French prince. It fell through and thank God for it. How you can consider thrusting her majesty into a marriage she does not want, and risking her life in childbirth now that she is over forty, I can *not* understand.'

'Gentlemen, gentlemen,' said Cecil pacifically. 'I have given this very matter much thought and am in fact awaiting a reply to a letter I recently despatched to King Henri of France.'

'Without our knowledge?' snapped Sussex.

'Hardly that, since most of you agreed long ago that a marriage alliance between England and France would be desirable. I have thought of a way to provide such an alliance without putting the queen at risk. In writing to King Henri, I was testing the water, as it were. And privately. With a spy at large in the court, discretion seemed desirable.'

'Would your new scheme provide an heir?' demanded Sussex, glaring at Dudley. 'It's an heir that England desperately needs. And the queen is not so opposed to the idea of marriage as you imagine. I have talked with her several times on the subject. As for her age, she is healthy, and many women bear a first child when they are past forty, with perfect success. In some matters, we must trust in God.'

'I would prefer to trust in building up our navy – and raising an army – as soon as possible and making sure that no one passes any more secret information to unfriendly powers!' Dudley blazed, and Walsingham remarked: 'England will be in serious straits if she ends up with neither a queen nor an heir. Or no queen and an heir in a cradle. Her majesty's well-being is the well-being of us all.'

Pacifically, Lord Burghley said: 'Pending the result of my correspondence with France, I think we should set about smoking out our hidden spy. I am conscious of his existence and intended to speak of it today, except that Sir Francis did so first. I urge every one of us to consider how the spy might be discovered and I recommend an extraordinary meeting in a few days' time to discuss our ideas. We should now turn to the rest of the agenda. There have been too many complaints lately about counterfeit coins and it also seems that the gang of Algerine corsairs that two years ago made a stronghold for themselves on the island of Lundy, in the Bristol Channel, are still defying all our efforts to remove them. We need to pursue coiners with more energy and sanction a further plan for an attack on Lundy . . .'

Our journey to Withysham could not be hurried, since we had a baggage cart with us, and we also needed to take the coach that Hugh had once used. Neither Sybil nor Dale were good horsewomen, while Gladys was too old to ride at all and of course we had Harry with us, and his young nursemaid, Tessie, and also Netta, a maidservant who was married to Simon, one of the grooms I wanted to take, and who was expecting their first and much longed-for baby. All six were packed into the coach. I preferred to ride my black mare, Jewel, but those of us who were on horseback had to limit ourselves to the speed of the wheeled transport. All the same, by making an early start and taking regular breaks to rest ourselves and our horses, we reached Withysham in one day. We arrived just as dusk was falling but I had sent Simon on ahead and we came through the short tunnel of the gatehouse arch to be greeted by eager barking from the Withysham dogs, candlelit windows and a smell of cooking and on the doorstep, a dignified figure dressed in a smart black suit and wearing a gold chain of office, waiting to greet us.

'Master Robert Hanley, at your service,' he said. 'Welcome to Withysham.'

Once within, we found bright fires, hot water and good food, and beds ready prepared. Adam Wilder (who had stayed behind at Hawkswood to look after it in my absence) had made no mistake when he hired Master Hanley.

My Sussex home is very different from Hawkswood, which is a big, gracious house built of light grey stone, with ample windows, a great hall, two charming parlours, and beautiful grounds including not only an orchard and the usual kitchen and herb gardens, but also a lake, a patch of woodland, a formal flower garden and the rose garden which had been the joy of Hugh's heart. Withysham, however, had once been a women's abbey, until the queen's father King Henry put an end to the monasteries. It had ample stabling and a good many spare rooms but it was smaller than Hawkswood and less well lit, with narrow, lance-shaped windows. It too was built of grey stone but it was darker and the walls were thicker than at Hawkswood and where the rooms were panelled, the panels were of dark oak.

At Hawkswood, the panelling was all of a light golden brown, matching its wide and beautiful main staircase – though the stairs could not be polished. They would have looked even more beautiful if they had been, but Hugh said that they were polished when he was a boy, and his mother had once slipped on them, and fallen so badly that she lost a child she was then expecting. They had been left alone since then.

Withysham also had very modest grounds. There was one little flower garden; otherwise, there was a kitchen garden, a group of fruit trees – too small to be called an orchard – and four paddocks. In one of them, Roundel, the dappled mare I had had before Jewel, and her last year's foal, together with a couple of trotting mares, also with foals, were at this time of year taken out for exercise each day by a groom. When spring came, they would be turned out in it to graze and be company for each other. All of them would have further progeny in the summer, and their growing colts from previous years lived out in two of the other paddocks, though they had shelters and in winter they were provided with better fodder than winter grass.

By law, Hugh as a landowner, albeit a modest one, was

supposed to keep trotters as they are well-bred, stylish animals and King Henry had been determined to improve the standard of horseflesh in his realm. Because Hugh wasn't a major landowner, he didn't have to maintain a stallion, but he kept a couple of breeding mares instead, and when on our marriage I brought Withysham to him, he promptly transferred them thither because he didn't like them. As his joints worsened, he found them uncomfortable to ride, and he disliked driving them as well. Between the shafts, he said, they were show-offs.

'Why did the old king have to inflict trotters on everyone?' he would say, and did say, quite often. 'Give me a nice easy ambler for the saddle and a solid workhorse for pulling things. He should have simply ordered us to keep tall horses and left it at that!'

As we rode in, I saw that a groom was leading the trotting mares patiently round the paddock. He was running while they, with their high-stepping action, looked as if they were about to take off into the sky. Hugh would have groaned at the sight of them.

And suddenly, I was missing him, aching for him, and the years since his death seemed to vanish. It was though I had only lost him yesterday. And people had been at me to marry again! Never, I thought, feeling the tears prick my eyes. Never, never.

After being used to Hawkswood, I usually felt somewhat confined when I visited Withysham, but I did like its serene atmosphere. Perhaps the centuries of prayer and contemplation it had known before King Henry intervened had left their memory in the stone of its walls. This time, it began to soothe me as soon as I stepped over the threshold.

I must not wallow in the past, I told myself. I spent most of the next two days playing with Harry, noticing that he was surely going to grow up looking like his father, my second husband, Matthew de la Roche, but hoping he would not grow up to think like Matthew. I had once loved Matthew de la Roche to desperation point but I had never known any peace with him, for he was an enemy to Queen Elizabeth.

After our marriage, we lived in France, but I left my little daughter Meg, the child of my first husband, Gerald Blanchard, whom I had lost to smallpox, in England. I returned to England when Meg needed my help. While there, I heard that Matthew was dead and later I married Hugh. When I learned that the report of Matthew's death was a lie, Hugh and I were settled together and I chose to stay with him.

Only after Hugh himself was gone did Matthew and I come briefly together once more. Harry was the result of that. But there was nothing now between Matthew and me. I was glad to have Harry but I rarely thought of his father. It was Hugh I mourned, and always would, when anything such as the sight of the trotters reminded me of him.

But it was time, I said to myself, to let Hugh go. I should let the tranquillity of Withysham gently bury the past. I should not let the sight of the trotters continue to be painful reminders. Trotting foals always sold well and I decided to adopt the sensible attitude that they were assets.

I had things to do. I had already sent word to Meg and her husband to let them know that for the time being I would be in Sussex. Meg, herself the mother of a small son, must always know where I was to be found. I had sent a message also to Sybil's daughter, Ambrosia, who was married to a schoolmaster in Cambridge. Sybil too considered it essential that Ambrosia should know her whereabouts.

Now, however, I must send word of my arrival to the uncle and aunt who had brought me up and who lived at the big house in Faldene, a village not far away. Anyone else who wanted to see me would have to go to the trouble of tracking me down.

I found myself very pleased with the move and decided to prolong my stay, perhaps through the spring and summer. For nearly a week, I enjoyed Withysham undisturbed. And then, on the sixth day, towards nightfall, an outbreak of barking from the dogs and the echoing rattle of wheels and iron-shod hooves from the gate arch drew me to a window. From which, to my astonishment and dismay, I watched a crowd of horsemen followed by two big coaches, each drawn by four horses and each with an all too familiar coat of arms painted on its doors, arrive on my premises. A baggage wagon followed them, creaking.

The coaches were so big that the gatehouse tunnel was only

just wide enough for them. One belonged to Sir William Cecil. The other belonged to Sir Francis Walsingham. They both travelled by coach if they needed to make journeys, for Cecil suffered from gout and Walsingham from attacks of diarrhoea. In addition, at the head of the riders who had led the way in was a figure I recognized instantly. He had no trouble with his health and loved to be in the saddle. He was mounted on a spectacular, snorting, head-tossing blue roan stallion, and he was the queen's Master of Horse, the Earl of Leicester, Sir Robert Dudley.

If these weighty men were calling on me in person and en masse, it was ominous. It would – it must – have something to do with Elizabeth and most probably was linked to the fact that she and I were related.

King Henry had not been a faithful husband. During his marriage to Queen Anne Boleyn, he had had an affair with one of her ladies in waiting. With my mother, in fact. I was not legitimate, but Elizabeth and I were half-sisters.

TWO

A Suitable Alliance

Cecil, Walsingham, Dudley and their respective entourages amounted to a considerable crowd to inflict on a modest manor house like Withysham, but to be fair to them, they knew that quite well. Our stabling was adequate, but food could have been a problem and accordingly, they had brought two cooks with them, and a good supply of provisions.

I was thankful, for although I had brought my own chief cook, John Hawthorn, with me to Withysham, travelling in the baggage cart along with our own supplies of viands, he would have been hard put to it to deal with such an influx of guests without more help than the junior cook and the two kitchen maids who worked at Withysham permanently. Since he was autocratic and temperamental, this didn't stop him from being resentful when his kitchen was taken over and I was faintly amused to see that he somehow managed to look relieved at the same time, which was quite a feat. My amusement *was* faint, however. I was too worried about the purpose of this intimidating invasion.

It was not discussed that evening. Sybil and I supped with our guests and conversation was general. Cecil told me that, as I must have realized, they were there on the queen's business but did not propose to explain it until the next morning, and the others nodded agreement. Sir Francis Walsingham, tall, dark and cadaverous as ever, added that the matter concerned would take time to discuss, while Dudley, also tall and gipsy dark but with a sparkle about him that made him quite different from Walsingham, entertained us all over supper, with amusing anecdotes of his work as the queen's Master of Horse. Some of them concerned the difficulties of running a stud and his problems with a recalcitrant mare who didn't approve of the stallion presented to her and made her opinion clear in several unpleasant ways. Walsingham, who had puritanical attitudes, looked disapproving but the rest of us laughed. Walsingham was one of the queen's most trustworthy men but I never really liked him.

After that, the conversation shifted to more general matters, such as the prospects for next season's harvest, some alterations being made to part of Hampton Court Palace and the shocking fact that the nest of pirates which had established itself on Lundy Island and regularly raided the Cornish coast to attack shipping and capture slaves was still there.

'They have cannon on the cliffs,' said Walsingham angrily. 'They sank two of our ships when we last tried to attack them, with much loss of life as well as the ships! We can't spare either!'

In the morning, however, we would talk business and I lay awake for a while that night, considering how to dress. That I was the queen's sister might have something to do with all this and from that point of view, since I was already sure that whatever they had come to say, I didn't want to hear it, I might do best to appear simply as the lady of an ordinary manor house. On the other hand, to dress in royal style was like putting on a suit of armour.

In the end I compromised. I discarded the hood edged with genuine oyster pearls that Hugh had given me one Christmas, and instead put on a pretty but less costly hood edged with fresh-water pearls, and asked Dale to arrange my hair so that the hood concealed nearly all of it, though I did this with some regret, for it was dark and glossy, with no trace yet of grey, and I was rather proud of it.

I also dressed in my favourite colours of cream and tawny, which were not spectacular, but my tawny overdress was of the finest wool and my cream kirtle was a silky damask. When in the past I had gone on risky assignments for the queen, I had had hidden pouches stitched inside my open overskirts, where I could carry such thing as picklocks, money and a small dagger. But I did not need such things today and my skirts were weighted only by heavy embroidery. Gold embroidery in this case.

For jewellery, I just had a pendant consisting of a big yellow topaz encircled by fresh-water pearls, set in gold and hung on a plain gold chain. I had three pairs of earrings to match the pendant, and I put on the smallest. My ruff was elegantly edged with the same tawny as my overdress but it was smaller than the latest fashion. In any case, I disliked the big ruffs which were then in vogue. Dale held up a mirror so that I could examine the total effect. I was walking my sartorial tightrope with some success, I decided. Except that my eyes, which were hazel, looked dark and had small lines round them. They looked like that when I was wary – or afraid.

But whatever awaited me downstairs must be faced. A dab of lavender perfume and I was ready. With Sybil, discreetly dressed in dark blue, as my attendant, I went down to join my visitors in Withysham's small hall.

It was an austere place, with its stone walls and narrow windows. I had tried to soften this monastic air by hanging up a lively tapestry of a hunting party, riding out against a millefleurs background of green leaves, and by spreading a small Turkey carpet, with a red and blue pattern, over the table, where I kept a set of silver branched candlesticks. The candles had been lit in readiness, for the morning was dull. But the place still seemed austere, as though it retained a memory of the days when it had been the nuns' chapterhouse. I rarely used it from choice.

My visitors were there ahead of me, all three of them, plus a secretary with a notepad. Sybil and I joined them at the table, and then Walsingham began to speak.

I listened in silence, feeling my mind harden as I did so, as though a wall were being built within me, that I was supposed to scale, or jump. I felt, in fact, very much like a horse confronted with an obstacle it knows it can't surmount.

When Walsingham had finished, I opened my mouth and said one word.

Hugh had once told me that he had heard that somewhere in the world there was a language that had no word for *no*. I wondered how on earth people could live without that most useful little word. I couldn't have dealt with this situation without it; that was for sure.

'No,' I said. There was a silence, so after a while I said it again, more strongly. *'No!'*

After a further pause, Dudley said in a conciliating tone: 'There is no disparagement, you know. Gilbert Renard is royal by blood. His father was King Henri the Second of France – though he was not yet king at the time. In fact, Renard is the result of an adventure when his father was only seventeen. He was recognized as Henri's son and was granted the rank of Compte, and has an estate of some size. At least, he had. His lands were confiscated in 1572 at the time of the St Bartholomew's Eve massacre of the Huguenots, when Renard revealed considerable sympathy for them, tried to help survivors and quarrelled with his half-brother King Henri the Third, and with the French queen mother, Catherine de' Medici.'

He paused, and Walsingham took up the tale. 'That was when he came to England and was made welcome at our court. On my recommendation, because of his support for the French Protestants. He had managed to save some money from the wreck of his fortunes and has bought a small house in Kew.'

'Not far from my own house,' Dudley put in. 'I know him quite well as a neighbour.'

'Lately,' Walsingham continued, 'he has corresponded with the French king and has indeed made two brief journeys back to France to talk to him and to the queen mother, and it seems that he has been forgiven. He is to have his lands returned to him, or most of them, anyway. The queen mother is apparently holding on to a couple of productive vineyards!'

'She would!' remarked Dudley.

'But his chateau and his farms and two other vineyards are to be his again,' said Walsingham. 'Mistress Stannard, it really is a suitable alliance.'

Beside me, Sybil stirred restlessly. I knew what she was thinking because it was what I was thinking too. I drew a deep breath. 'I have said, time and again, that I don't wish to remarry. I have refused offers!' It seemed only a day or two since, with such difficulty, I had shooed the Yarrows out of Hawkswood. I felt tired.

'But those offers were not as politically important as this,' said Cecil. The line between his eyes had become a deep furrow.

'Ursula, this is for the queen. And it is true – we are *not* offering you anyone unsuitable. He is about three years younger than you but that, surely, is not important. He is pleasant-looking and seems amiable; he says he is willing for you to spend part of each year in England – indeed, he will wish to visit his own English home sometimes. He has been married before but his first wife died in 1570, of a summer fever. Where his chateau is, the summers can be very hot. He suggests that you and he should make your visits to England during the summer.'

'He has no children,' Dudley said. 'Not living, anyway. I believe there were two that died in infancy. You won't have to be a stepmother.'

'And it *is* for the queen,' said Walsingham. 'Mistress Stannard, England is not just an island of rock, surrounded by sea; it is also a religious island encircled by Papist countries. The Spanish have the Netherlands as well as Spain; France is only just on the other side of the Channel. It is sheer good fortune that they happen to detest each other. That gives us our chance. For the safety of this realm, England should create a strong alliance with one of those powers, to create a bulwark against the other. The obvious way to bring all this about is through a marriage. One attempt to arrange a match between our queen and a French prince has already fallen through and time is going on. Her majesty is now forty-two years of age. It is not a good age to embark on marriage for the first time. Childbearing has risks.'

I knew that. And I would myself be forty-two in May.

'As much as anything,' said Dudley, 'we are here to ask you to help us to protect the queen. She means so much to us all, to the country at large and to us, here present, personally.'

'I know,' I said. I was well aware that the queen's safety meant a great deal to them, for heaven only knew what their position would be if she were to die and a Catholic invasion followed. In Dudley's case, she meant even more than that. He and the queen were not lovers in the physical sense, for all the rumours that had been spread about them. I knew her well enough to know that. But they loved each other, just the same. I knew that too. If anything happened to her, it would break his heart.

'But you are the queen's sister,' said Walsingham. 'You are not much younger than she is but you have already borne children successfully.'

I was silent. To my surprise, Harry's birth had been easy. But Meg's had not, and there had been two other pregnancies that came to nothing. One of them had nearly killed me. I remembered, all too well, the pain and the fear and the exhaustion, the oppressiveness of the overheated chamber, the useless intoning of a priest, the smell of my own blood. Death in childbirth is no easy way to go.

Walsingham had more to say and though he was not very good at sounding beguiling, he made the attempt. 'You are not legitimate but you are recognized in a quiet way as her majesty's kinswoman. The same applies to Count Renard' – he used the English form of the word *compte* – 'and his relationship to the French royal family. A union between the two of you would not be the same as one between our queen and a French prince but it would be near enough. It would be a marriage between two people who are both half-siblings to reigning monarchs. It would be a physical bond, undertaken to seal the treaty that would be signed on the day of the wedding. And it would save the queen from sacrificing herself.'

He stopped for a moment, looking at me gravely, letting his meaning sink in. Then he said: 'If she were to marry now, she would be taking a serious risk, far more serious than you would. Such a marriage might produce an heir, yes. There are those on the Council who keep on repeating that – my lord of Sussex for one. But it might also leave England defenceless with no queen and no heir either. You could protect her majesty and England alike from those dangers.'

'This has all been discussed in Council,' Cecil said, and it was then that he repeated to me what had been said at that recent meeting, of which I had known nothing. At the end, Cecil said: 'The reply from King Henri, giving his consent to such a marriage and assuring me that Count Renard has indeed been reinstated to his original position in France, arrived the day after that meeting. I was relieved. I have long considered that the queen ought to marry, but I have begun to realize that perhaps, yes, the time has gone by when it would be really wise.'

Dudley had been watching me, I think with more understanding than either of the others. He said: 'You are not a slave, Mistress Stannard. We have no slaves in England, in which we are unlike the Ottomans of Turkey and Algiers, whose corsairs last year relieved us of two valuable ships and all their crews. You cannot be forced to wed. The queen once ordered me to marry Mary Stuart but I refused and nothing happened to me except that I was coldly treated by her majesty for a while. You are being asked, not compelled. But we beg you to consider. The queen and the realm of England have need of you.'

'And if I refuse and her majesty herself risks marriage and dies,' I said, 'I could be blamed. And would blame myself. Yes, I see.'

'Ursula should have time to think these matters over,' said Cecil to the others. 'All this has been sprung on her very suddenly. I suggest that we adjourn this meeting and gather again tomorrow morning to discuss it further. Ursula may well have questions she wishes to ask.'

'If I marry a French count and go with him to France, I might be regarded as a bigamist,' I said. 'In the eyes of French Catholics, I am still married to Matthew de la Roche. They do not recognize the fact that my sister annulled our union.'

'I think not,' Cecil said. 'The French royal family are prepared to accept you as a bride for the count. King Henri certainly made no allusion to de la Roche. They seem to have forgotten all about him. And no one has ever, I understand, challenged the right of de la Roche's elder son – the one born to him when he believed *you* to be dead, and he entered into another marriage – to be his heir. I have no anxiety on that score.'

I thought I had seen a chance of escape, but it had slammed shut in my face. I now felt not only tired; I seemed to be drowning in exhaustion. Again and again I had tried to escape from the world of politics and diplomacy; again and again I had been dragged back. But this time it was worse. It might endanger my life or it might not (one of the happy things about my marriage to Hugh, one reason why I felt so safe with him, was the fact that he could not sire children). But if it didn't threaten my life then it would be *for* life, instead.

Yet I had been given reasons for agreeing, reasons that were real and strong. I heard myself say: 'Very well. I'll meet the wretched man. I'll go that far. But I make no promises.'

THREE
Uninvited Guests

'Y ou don't want to marry this man, madam. I know you don't,' said Brockley. He had a slight but down to earth country accent and just now it was very down to earth indeed. '*Why* have you agreed to meet him?'

'I felt I had no choice. The matter is too important,' I said.

I had left my guests and withdrawn to a small parlour at the rear of the house. It had a pleasant southward outlook over fields towards the distant downs and immediately in front of it was the smallest of the four paddocks. Just now, Tessie was watching and laughing while Simon gave little Harry a ride on Bronze, one of our quiet all-purpose horses, steadying him with one hand and leading the horse with the other.

Now that Harry was almost four, I thought, he ought to begin riding lessons in earnest. I had been planning to buy a small pony for him. I intended Brockley to be his instructor. If my life were about to be turned upside down as my uninvited guests wanted, what would happen now to all these pleasant plans?

I had told Adam Wilder to make my visitors at home in the bigger, more formal parlour and provide wine and snacks for them. Then I sent Sybil to fetch the rest of those whom I regarded as my close household. She returned very quickly, bringing – not to say being dragged by – Brockley, Dale and Gladys, all anxious to know what had transpired downstairs. When I told them, their faces all expressed various degrees of alarm and disapproval.

Sybil said diffidently: 'What the mistress says is true. It was difficult for her to refuse even to see the man.'

'Simply to agree to meet him has committed me to nothing,' I said. 'He will make a visit to Hawkswood, that's all. We're going back to Hawkswood at once, by the way. Sir Francis feels that it is a more suitable place for such a . . . a high-level encounter.'

'Sounds as if this Frenchie count might have doubts himself,' remarked Gladys. 'Might think we're not good enough for him, eh? If it comes to anything, what happens to us?'

'You come with me wherever I go,' I said. 'All four of you. That's final.'

Gladys grinned, always a depressing sight, since the few teeth she still had were no more than brown fangs and made her look as feral as a strayed hound. 'That's how you got rid of the Yarrows, indeed,' she remarked.

Dale said miserably: 'I don't want to go to France. I hate France.' She had good reason for saying that. On one of my assignments, I had taken her there and being an ardent Protestant and quite incapable of hiding her opinions, she had been arrested for heresy. She hadn't forgotten.

'We'll worry about all that later,' I said. 'Perhaps Count Renard won't like me at all and that will be the end of it.' I used the English form of his title, as my visitors had mostly done. 'Or perhaps,' I added, trying to infuse something like enthusiasm into my voice, 'he and I will look at each other when we meet and know that we were made to be man and wife.'

'Let us hope so,' said Brockley. But as he spoke, he looked at me in a penetrating way that told a different tale. *You know that nothing of the kind is going to happen*, his eyes said, *and so do I.*

Once, a long time ago now, Brockley and I had come near to being more than lady and manservant. We had very nearly become lovers. Only nearly. Nothing actually occurred and never would, but a rapport had nevertheless sprung up between us. We were, so often, in touch with each other's minds.

Briskly, I said: 'We had better prepare for the move back to Hawkswood. Delay would be pointless.'

We did delay a little. We said farewell to our visitors the following day, and the day after that was Harry's birthday, which we celebrated by playing games with him and serving a special dinner. But the following day, a Friday, we left before dawn and were back at Hawkswood by late afternoon. None of us were cheerful about it, especially Brockley. Roundel, the pretty dapple grey mare I had had before Jewel, would have her new foal in the late spring and since I had mentioned to him that we might well be still at Withysham then, Brockley, who had once been a groom and still thought like one, had been looking forward to superintending the happy occasion.

'We don't know how all this will turn out, madam,' he said hopefully to me. 'Perhaps we shall find we can go back to Withysham in the spring, after all. I have taken the liberty of mentioning the possibility to Master Hanley – just as a possibility, no more. But we may as well keep our original plans open, until we're sure they have to be changed.'

I had the feeling that he was trying to build up those plans like a seawall in the hope that they would hold back what he saw as an advancing tide of trouble. I saw it the same way, and made no protest.

We were expected at Hawkswood, as Simon had once more been sent galloping ahead to announce our coming. We found, however, that new events had taken place in our absence. There was a strange pony tethered outside the stable so that its dirt-stained legs could be washed in the open air. It was an odd-looking animal since it was dapple grey from head to loins while its rear end and tail were the smooth dark grey of iron. But I had no time to wonder about it for the moment we appeared, Ben and Joan Flood, the two under-cooks we had left there to feed the household, came running out to meet us. They were excited and both talking at once, so that it was a few moments before any of us could make out what they were saying.

'Gently, gently, one at a time,' I said, or rather, shouted, over their confused voices.

Eventually, the word *Ambrosia* emerged from the babble and they were not referring to any kind of comestible.

'My daughter!' said Sybil, who had been listening with her head out of the coach window. She opened the door with an agitated thrust. Sybil was calm by nature, always helpful yet never obtrusive, but now, she was all wide-eyed alarm and distracted exclamations, and shut her skirts in the coach door as she scrambled out. I had to release her. 'She is here?' Sybil demanded of the world at large. 'And in trouble? Dear God, what's wrong?'

'Oh. *Mother!*' cried a frantic voice, and out of the door behind the Floods erupted a young woman who rushed towards Sybil and flung herself into her arms.

I had not seen Mistress Ambrosia Wilde for years but I would have known her at once because of her resemblance to her mother. Both had slightly splayed features, as though, in early youth, their heads had been slightly compressed between chin and scalp. The effect was rather attractive than otherwise, but the long eyebrows, the broad nostrils, the wide mouths, were distinctive. Ambrosia, though, had two other exceptional beauties. Her colouring was like her mother's, but Sybil had had hardships in her life which had dimmed the shine of her brown eyes and put grey into her dark brown hair. Ambrosia's hair, which at the moment was unconfined by any cap, was glossy and abundant, and her eyes were as bright as diamonds.

Though just now, as she ran to her mother, I saw that they were also tired. The two of them clung together, with Sybil patting her daughter's back and murmuring words of comfort, while Ben and Brockley started to unload luggage and the rest of us dismounted or climbed out of the coach. Eventually, everyone moved indoors and into the great hall, where we learned that Sybil's message concerning our move to Withysham had missed her. She had already set out to find her mother, and told no one where she was going.

'I was with my in-laws and oh, the trouble they are making for me!' Ambrosia told us, tearfully. She had fled from them in secret and in due course had arrived at Hawkswood, riding a pony – the one I had noticed having its legs washed – and alone, with neither maid nor groom, to find her mother not there.

'And she was that upset, not finding Mistress Jester here, ma'am; we hardly knew what to do with her,' Joan Flood told us. 'She'd been staying at inns on her own all the way from Cambridge and you know what some inns are like when it's a woman alone; she'd had to argue to get accommodation at all, and fend off – well, you know – *and* pay extra! She's got

hardly any money left. Well, we did know where you were and would have sent her on to you, except that just then, Simon got here.'

'Well, we're all here now,' I said, taking charge, while Sybil steered Ambrosia to a settle and sat down with an arm round her. 'So, what is all this about?'

'Yes. Where is your husband?' Sybil asked anxiously, and then looked with concern at her daughter's creased grey gown. 'My darling, you look quite distracted!'

'I *am* distracted! John is dead – he complained of a bad headache one night and went to bed and never woke up! He was dead at my side when I woke next morning! And now his family want me to marry a cousin of his; they say it will be convenient and will keep his money in the family. John didn't just have a schoolmaster's pay; he had property too, that was left to him, and he willed it all to me and the family don't like that, and they've taken my sons! My twin boys!'

She was crying bitterly now. 'They've been sent to York, so far away, and put in the care of my sister-in-law Eliza and her husband and my parents-in-law say I can't have them back until I agree to marry this cousin and I don't like him and I *won't* marry him, I *won't*, but I want my boys back! I had three other babies and none of them thrived but these have; they're four years old and lovely and healthy and they ought to be with me and I need help! My parents-in-law made me stay in their house after John died, so that they could go on at me and stop me from going to York after my boys. I had to get away at night, creep to their stable and saddle Irons all alone . . .'

'Irons?' said Sybil irrelevantly.

'My grey pony. He's iron coloured,' said Ambrosia. 'And he's strong and can go all day. I got away on him before dawn and rode through most of the next day. I couldn't go to York – I know where Eliza lives in York, but I would never find the way there alone, only *they'd* expect me to make for it and give chase. I thought of coming here instead; I knew how to get here because I've visited so many times. And I wanted to find you, Mother. Oh, Mother, please, please help me!'

I had told the Floods to provide some food and drink for

us all and at this moment, Brockley and my steward Adam
Wilder brought the trays in, a welcome sight.

They had provided wine as well as ale, and food in the
form of chicken legs and small apple pies and a dish of nuts.
The Floods were always anxious to please. They were of the
Catholic persuasion and once had been caught up in a Catholic
scheme which could have done me harm. Hugh was alive then.
We had forgiven them and kept them, for they were excellent
at their work, and since then, they had striven to be perfect
employees in every possible way. The wine was a good one
and the chicken legs were hot, having gone on to the spit the
moment Simon arrived with the news of our approach. I felt
that hot food and strong wine were what Ambrosia needed
and needed badly.

Unobtrusively, I sighed. I had gone to Withysham for a quiet
life, but Life seemed determined to turn into a ghastly series
of just one thing after another. Here was someone else with
matrimonial problems, and something would have to be done
about them, I supposed.

As Brockley and Wilder handed things round, I said: 'Well,
Lord Burghley owes me one or two favours just now and he
is a lawyer. He will know whether what your in-laws have
done is legal or not, Ambrosia. If not, we can take action.'

Ambrosia, sipping from her glass and already calmer, said:
'I would be grateful, oh, so grateful. But . . . Mistress Stannard,
how is it that Lord Burghley should owe you favours? Though
I know you know him; I have heard much from my mother,
over the years, of your many exploits.'

'Many of them I undertook to please him,' I said. 'Though
it's true that just now I'm resisting his latest request. He's
trying to marry *me* off – he's nearly as bad as your in-laws!
Before too long, a French count called Gilbert Renard is likely
to visit me here to offer me his hand and heart – for political
reasons. I don't know when he'll be here, but soon, I fancy.'

'Next week, madam,' said Adam Wilder, offering me the
platter of chicken legs. 'He has sent word. He won't be bringing
a big entourage – just a groom and a valet, I understand. We
can expect him on the Saturday, I believe.'

*   *   *

'What I'm doing,' said Jerome Billington, the principal Hawkswood forester, 'is called coppicing. It can't be done with all trees, but with these here hazels, if you cut them down at the right stage, they'll sprout again from the stump and you'll get some good new wood that makes things like hurdles – very useful, very saleable. You can do it with alder and chestnut as well – better stand well back, ma'am. She'll be coming down any minute now.'

The two men who were working the saw, stripped to the waist and shiny with sweat even though it was February and the morning, though bright, had started with frost, paused for a moment to look at the tree they were cutting. It had already been stripped of its branches, which lay in a heap some yards away, and it had been cut to weaken it on the side where the woodsmen wanted it to fall. The men spoke briefly to each other and then resumed their work with the saw. The tree swayed and fell, precisely where they had decided that it should. And I had learned a little more about the work of what was now my own woodland.

In Hugh's day, I had had little to do with the farm and woodland, and hardly knew Billington. I had had much to learn since Hugh's death. This morning, I was out in our little wood, where Billington was busy, interesting myself in forestry work and I was there because I was running away from my own feelings. The count was due to arrive today and I was full of an inner rage, which was at least half fear. It burned so fiercely in me that I had come out to the wood straight after breakfast, without even pausing to discuss the day's meals with John Hawthorn, as I certainly should have done. I was so overstrung that I had snapped unjustly at Dale when she did my hair that morning, and had had to bite back a sharp remark that I nearly made to Sybil. I felt I was hardly fit for polite society.

I was dreading, so much, the approaching advent of Gilbert Renard.

I'd been dreading it for days, even while I made preparations for it. I had had rooms made ready for the count and his servants, and since those chambers had not been used since the Yarrow party left Hawkswood the previous summer, I was

having fires lit in them every day to disperse the chill of winter. I had overheard Phoebe and Margery, the two maids who had the task of laying, maintaining and clearing the extra fires, grumbling about it when they thought I couldn't hear them, and from this I knew that they did not relish the prospect of my new marriage any more than I did. They were normally the most willing of servants and had never before complained about anything, in or out of earshot of their employer.

Phoebe, who was forty, portly and conscientious, had strong opinions on the duty of employees to do as they were told, and Margery, who was only seventeen, was always nervous of giving offence, for she came of a large family and had had to leave home to make way for younger siblings. They must be feeling strongly.

I didn't blame them. I felt strongly, too.

Since returning from Withysham I had also sent John Hawthorn to buy extra supplies so that our hospitality would lack nothing. I had had windows cleaned and rugs brushed and furniture polished and I had written a letter to Cecil, asking him what the legal position really was concerning Ambrosia's children.

I had given Simon a rest from travel and let him keep his pregnant wife company while I despatched one of our other grooms, Joseph, to London with it. Arthur Watts, the senior groom, was no longer young enough for long journeys and I considered our newest groom, Eddie, who was only sixteen, to be too young for responsible errands such as this. Joseph, who had been at Hawkswood since he was fourteen, was now a competent twenty-two, fair-haired, stolid, taciturn but good-humoured, and well able for the task. I made sure he had a good horse. 'You can take Redstart,' I told him.

The horse was one of the reasons why I had taken young Eddie on. In Hugh's later years, we had had some financial problems and had reduced our stable, but this sometimes caused inconvenience and lately I had acquired a couple of horses for general use, and hired an extra groom to look after them. One was a piebald called Magpie, a weight carrier who could if need be cope with Adam Wilder or my cook John Hawthorn. Adam was not fat but he was over six feet tall,

while John Hawthorn was a very heavy man indeed. The other
was Redstart, a leggy chestnut with a good turn of speed.
Joseph should make good time to Cecil. I expected him back
at any moment.

My new purchases hadn't filled up the stable; as at
Withysham, we had plenty of spare stalls, left over from our
more prosperous days. I had told Arthur Watts to make them
ready. Another of the preparations for the guest I didn't want.

Now it was Saturday, just over a week since my return to
Hawkswood, and a messenger had brought word yesterday, to
confirm that Count Renard would be with me shortly after
noon. In an act, I suppose, of rebellion, I had chosen to spend
the morning in the woods, dressed for out of doors in February,
in a warm, plain wool gown with no ruff or farthingale, and
a good thick shawl. However, the morning was slipping away.
I could not prowl about in the wood, asking Billington artless
questions, any longer.

While he talked to me, Billington had been watching me
thoughtfully. He was a squarely built, flaxen man, rather like
an older version of Joseph, though not so silent. He was at
the moment respectably dressed in a brown working shirt and
old breeches. He had a calm and competent manner and I
knew that Hugh had thought highly of him.

'He's a good man,' Hugh had said. 'Good at his work and
likes his work. His forebears were mostly foresters just as he
is. He's got a son to follow him, who seems just as happy to
fit the same pattern. The Billingtons seem to breed true.' He
had laughed. 'And there's nothing subservient about any of
them. Billington tells me what needs doing in my woodland
and I listen respectfully and give him a free hand.'

That calm lack of subservience was in Billington's eyes
now, as he nodded to his men to start cutting up the branches
and the tree trunk, but kept his gaze on me.

'This be a worrying time for you, ma'am,' he remarked. He
had the same country accent as Brockley, though Brockley's
was far less marked. 'Is that why you came out here today,
to inspect your trees? You've not done so before.'

Taken by surprise, I hardly knew how to answer. He did it
for me. 'I know why, ma'am. You're worried. We all know,

everyone here and at Withysham too, I dare say. And we all think the same. That it's for you to say. No one else. You can't be forced.'

'It's complicated, Billington. More than you realize.'

'Perhaps. But the queen, blessed majesty though she is, can't dispose of your person at will. It belongs to you.'

'She once ordered the Earl of Leicester to marry Mary Stuart,' I said.

'But he didn't obey, did he?'

'No,' I agreed.

'And he's still the Earl of Leicester. He ain't in the Tower – nor headless, either. Ma'am, the queen has many powers but she ain't a Barbary Corsair. You ain't her slave.'

'I know. Thank you, Billington. You're right, of course. In the end, it's my decision.'

Only it wasn't. Not quite. Not if the queen not only wanted me to consent, but needed it.

But time was passing. I thanked Billington and his men for letting me watch them at work, turned away and set off, slowly, towards Hawkswood House, my home, my place of safety, which was about to be invaded. As I entered the courtyard, I saw Brockley there, looking about him anxiously

'Madam! I wondered where you had got to. I've seen them from an upper window. They're early. They're coming now.'

FOUR
First Impressions

I could already hear the approaching hoofbeats. They were coming at speed. Then they were there, a group of riders pounding in through the gate arch. In the lead was the man who was presumably Count Renard, for he was riding a tall bay stallion, a mighty animal with white-ringed eyes and foam round its bit. Its accoutrements were elaborate, a scarlet leather bridle with silver studs and matching scarlet reins, scalloped, with silver edgings. The count pulled his steed to a dramatic halt in the middle of the courtyard and his companions pulled up behind him.

I had understood that he would be bringing a personal man and a groom. The personal man was probably the one in clerkly black, riding a roan gelding. Behind him, however, was someone Cecil had not mentioned, a self-evident chaplain with a heavy jewelled cross swinging against his chest. Judging by the white hair I could see beneath his cap, he was not young, and perhaps because of this, he had a quiet mount, a steady-looking brown mule. He would be a Catholic chaplain, I supposed. Well, the Floods would like that; no doubt they would want to share any Masses that he said in my house.

Behind these two came two grooms on sturdy cobs, one of them leading a pack mule. They all remained in their saddles while the count swung himself athletically to the ground. He was of middle height, I saw, elegant in his dress, which consisted of a blue doublet and cap, tawny hose above highly polished boots and a tawny cloak in gleaming velvet. On his right hand he wore a great ring with a square-cut ruby in an ornate gold setting. He pulled off his cap and I saw that his hair was light-coloured, somewhere between brown and fair, and that his eyes were light blue. It was not colouring that appealed to me; I had always preferred dark-haired men. This

man's eyes were also disconcerting in that they were very
round and slightly fixed, like the eyes of an owl. Despite
his obviously capable horsemanship, he did not have the
complexion of an outdoor man, but was fresh-skinned, pink
and white with no trace of tanning.

He said: 'I seek the lady Mistress Stannard. I believe I am
expected.'

In the plain dress and shawl I had used for roaming through
the woods, of course, I didn't look in the least like the mistress
of Hawkswood. Feeling that I was probably not making an
ideal first impression, I said: 'I am Mistress Stannard. I have
been outdoors this morning about the business of the estate.'

'Your pardon, madame! I did not realize.' He swept me a
low bow. 'I trust we are welcome, for we are happy to be
here.' He had a pleasant voice, and his English, though
accented, was otherwise excellent.

I was still conscious of having been taken at a disadvantage,
and felt flustered. I looked round. Wilder had come out of the
house now, along with Sybil, and Arthur Watts had appeared
from the stables. I hurried into speech. 'Please, everyone,
dismount. This is my steward, Wilder. Watts here is my senior
groom and will show you where the horses are to be stabled.
Brockley is my personal man but he will help with the horses.
This is Mistress Sybil Jester, my gentlewoman . . .'

I was too voluble but I had no idea at all of how I should
welcome this stranger who was in fact so very unwelcome.
His companions now got down from their saddles and he made
them known to me. The clerkly man was his personal attendant,
as I had surmised, but was apparently also something more.
'This is Pierre Lestrange, my man and also my friend. He is
the son of my mother's steward and we were virtually brought
up together. I look on him as a brother.' He was asking me,
or warning me, not simply to dismiss Lestrange to the servants' quarters. 'And this is my chaplain, Father Ignatius.'
Both Lestrange and the chaplain bowed to me.

The count didn't bother to introduce his grooms, who were
in any case already leading their mounts away, accompanied
by Watts and Brockley. I said: 'I am scarcely dressed for
receiving visitors. You came before you were expected, sir.

Please excuse me for a short time. Wilder, please take our guests to the great hall and provide refreshments. Sybil, please go and change as well, then come to the hall. You and your daughter will dine with us, of course.'

I made my escape somehow, to dress in a manner that would make me look more like the mistress of the house and to snatch a hasty and belated word with John Hawthorn, who met me as I went in and was reassuring. 'All is in readiness, madam, have no fear. You went out so early this morning that I had no chance to consult with you but we did talk yesterday, if you recall. I have a leg of mutton on the spit as you wished, and if you can hear agitated noises from the poultry yard, Ben Flood is out there killing a couple of chickens. That speckled hen that seems to have given up laying will do very nicely, chopped up and cooked with pine nuts, and the other one can be served jointed and fried with the pepper sauce you like so much. The bean stew is ready and only needs heating. We haven't discussed the sweet course, but I suggest bread and butter pudding with saffron, and almond fritters. Master Wilder has already chosen the wines, subject to your approval. Dinner may be later than usual, as I expected your guests to arrive later. But it will be all it should be, I assure you.'

'Dear Hawthorn, you're a marvel. Now I must dress properly. Where is Dale?'

'Here, madam,' said Dale, appearing at my side.

Ambrosia, hurrying down the stairs, smiled at me and said: 'Do let me help. I've been watching from a window. I thought the count looked *very* handsome! Isn't it wonderful how people always arrive to catch one unawares? I can brush things and hand things, if Dale doesn't mind.'

'You can marry the count yourself if the queen doesn't mind,' I said sourly. 'Yes, come upstairs with me, both of you.'

Ambrosia had her mother's ability to be useful without being intrusive. In a very short time, she and Dale had me washed and brushed, my hair tidily crimped under the hood with the fresh-water pearl trim, and they were buttoning and tying me into a peach-coloured silk gown over a pale blue kirtle with silver flowers embroidered on the kirtle and on the big peach silk over-sleeves. With all this went a ruff and farthingale wider than I normally preferred, but fashionable. Sometimes, one had to be, and I had suitable items in readiness.

Sybil looked in just as I had made ready, to collect Ambrosia and hurry her into changing as well. 'We must look elegant if we are to dine with Mistress Stannard and the count.'

Dale and Gladys were to eat upstairs, with Tessie and Harry. Dale, though, put on a fresh hood in case she should by chance come face-to-face with the count. Gladys didn't seem inclined to take the trouble but I ordered her out of sight until she had removed the awful patched and stained brown gown which was her regular choice of garment, and had put on the respectable dark blue dress and white ruff that I had given her for the previous Christmas and which she always had to be nagged into wearing.

Eventually, Sybil and I went to the hall to find our guests enjoying the wine and the meat patties that Wilder had provided to bridge the gap until dinner. I noticed that Lestrange had indeed not retired to servants' quarters but was at his master's side. They all smiled at us and Sybil and I smiled back. Then we all sat or stood about, rather ill at ease, making stilted conversation on harmless topics. There was an atmosphere of constraint, and no one referred even obliquely to the reason for this visit.

I found that Pierre Lestrange and Father Ignatius spoke good English just as their master did, and congratulated them on this. Meanwhile, the count and I kept glancing at each other, taking silent stock of our possible future life partners, but aloud we limited ourselves to exchanging platitudes about the fortunately dry weather (so nice that the roads weren't muddy) and Father Ignatius made a little jest about a tricky point of English grammar.

Presently, there was a break during which the guests were shown to their rooms and were given warm water and towels so they could wash before dinner, which was considerably later than usual, and didn't appear until dusk was imminent.

As it was a social occasion, it was reasonably successful. Wilder had chosen my best wines to go with it and they had a relaxing effect on everyone's tongues. Some jokes were told and there was a discussion about the differences between French and English cuisines. Lestrange helped to wait on the count and seemed to enjoy the jokes. Father Ignatius, who was quite a lively soul, told us amusing tales of their journey from London, including one about an innkeeper who claimed to speak French and kept trying to talk to them in that language. 'And it was oh so much an embarrassment; we couldn't understand a word he said!'

The count himself turned out to be well read in both French and English. Indeed, things went so smoothly that I sent for Tessie to bring little Harry in to share the dessert course with us, and though Harry, a typical four-year-old, stared blankly and rather rudely at the stranger who was so obviously the chief among the other strangers, and had to be nudged into making a bow, the count spoke admiringly of his good looks and healthy air, and congratulated me on my son by quoting a poem I did not know, though I thought myself knowledgeable about English poetry.

'You have a lovely child,' he said to me. 'Have you come across the poem by George Gascoigne – "A Lover's Lullaby"? *Sing lullaby as women do, wherewith they bring their babes to rest; and lullaby can I sing too, as womanly as can the best.* But I will not go on, for it is a long poem and not all of it cheerful, and those first lines say what I mean so well.'

'But I know that poem!' said Ambrosia. 'My husband was a schoolmaster and he loved poetry and used to read it to me as well as to his pupils. I don't know it by heart but the poem goes on to say how the lover's youthful years must be stilled to sleep with lullaby because age and grey hairs have hold of him now, and his face is lined. I found it very moving.'

'You are a lady after my own heart,' said the count, laughing and bowing gallantly to her across the table. 'We must talk more of poetry before I leave.'

Sybil, seated next to me, clicked her tongue softly, clearly thinking that Ambrosia should have kept silent and not drawn the count's attention away from me. As far as I was concerned, she was welcome to seduce and run off with him at her earliest convenience. Only, I could recognize Gallic gallantry when I saw it, and knew that it meant little. Gilbert Renard was here

on political business, business with me, and Ambrosia, no
matter how knowledgeable she might be about poetry, could
not be more than a passing distraction.

When the meal was finished and cleared, the count spoke
quietly to Lestrange, who left the hall and returned with a
lute. 'Can we offer you some music?' he enquired. 'I see there
is a spinet here and my lord count is a fine exponent of that
instrument. I can accompany him with this lute.'

The count had clearly sent Lestrange for the lute, but he
now made polite disclaimers. He was overridden with equal
politeness by Sybil and myself. The fire was made up, we
gathered round it, and our guests began to play. But after a
while, I saw Brockley in the doorway, signalling to me, and
murmuring that some important matter must have arisen, but
please, let the music not be interrupted, I went to him. 'What
is it, Brockley?'

'Something I think you should see, madam,' said Brockley
grimly.

He led me out of the hall, and out through the kitchens into
the courtyard. There was a door straight from the hall into the
courtyard but evidently he didn't want it to be obvious where
we were going. He picked up a lantern in the kitchen, and guided
me across the yard to the stable block and the tack-room.

Inside the tack-room, there was a table, benches and wooden
mounts where saddles could be put for cleaning, and on the
wall were hooks for bridles and driving harness to hang on,
and long, thick pegs to accommodate saddles not in use.
Brockley, lantern in hand, went straight to the hooks and lifted
a bridle down. I recognized it at once, for it was of red leather
with silver studs. It was the bridle worn by the count's bay
stallion.

Brockley carried it to the table and set it down with the
lantern beside it. 'Madam, come and look at this.'

He was pointing but at first I couldn't understand what he
meant. Then he jabbed at something with a forefinger and I
saw. The curb bit which formed part of the bridle was of the
usual pattern, meaning that it had cheek-pieces on either side,
to give the bit good leverage, and that the part inside the
horse's mouth was arched in the centre, so that the bit would

turn when the rein was tightened, and give the rider still more leverage for controlling the horse. What was different about this example was the height of the arch. Once I had grasped what Brockley wanted me to see, I gasped.

'But that would bruise the roof of a horse's mouth! It's enormous!'

'Quite,' said Brockley, again in that grim voice. 'I haven't ventured to try and examine that stallion's mouth – it's a vicious animal and would probably have my hand off at the wrist – but I hardly need to. You're right, of course. *Also*,' he added with emphasis, 'although I haven't been close to the animal, I think I saw blood on its flanks when its groom was leading it to the stable. Our noble count uses his spurs rather freely, in my opinion.'

'If the horse is very difficult to manage . . .' I said hesitantly, but Brockley snorted.

'Stallions can be difficult, yes, of course, but if they're handled right they can also be the best of partners – trustworthy, intelligent, willing. This horse has obviously been mistreated and from the way I saw the count pull up when he came into the courtyard this morning, I think most of the mistreating has been his. Oh, I've seen worse than this, I grant you, in my soldiering days. I was infantry but we'd sometimes help with the horses. There was one so-called noble knight had a curb bit like this – only in his case, the bit was twisted, like a screw – with sharp edges to the thread.'

'But that . . .!'

'That horse always had bloodstained foam round its mouth when I saw it being ridden,' Brockley said. 'And it had a very savage temper. In the end, it threw its master and trampled him. I can't say I mourned him much, but his squire had the horse's throat cut. The animal was probably almost impossible to handle by then, anyway. It had become a killer.'

I shuddered.

'This isn't that bad, but it's quite bad enough.' Brockley's face was grave. I could see his lines of worry, even by lantern-light. 'Madam,' he said, 'do not marry this man.'

FIVE
Welcome to Hawkswood Inn

The next day was a Sunday. I and most of the household went to church in Hawkswood village as usual, but my guest said that with my consent, his chaplain would say a Catholic Mass in his chamber for him and Lestrange and the grooms.

'I am no religious fanatic. I quarrelled with my family because I advised tolerance towards the Huguenots. But I like to worship in my own way, nonetheless,' he said to me.

He added that if any in my house were of the Catholic persuasion, he would be happy to let them attend, with my permission, of course. I said yes, Joan and Ben Flood were, and were welcome to join him if they chose. Ben did so, though Joan to my surprise did not.

The day was wet and Brockley remarked that he wished we too had a chaplain in the house, to save us from riding in the rain. Dale, as I expected, disapproved intensely of Mass being said on our premises. I told her not to think about it but she shook her head at me and said that if I married the count, we'd all have to think about it. We should have no alternative.

'I will deal with that, somehow, I trust,' I said grumpily. I was worried and not just for religious reasons. Brockley's lantern-lit face in the tack-room as he warned me against this marriage kept returning to my mind.

The day seemed long. After worshipping in our respective fashions, everyone dined and then passed the afternoon in indoor pursuits. Sybil and I did embroidery; Dale brushed my clothes, Brockley got together with Adam Wilder over some accounts, Ambrosia and the count played backgammon and talked about poetry. The count and I had some conversation about poetry as well. What we did not have conversation about, was marriage. He didn't mention it and I had no desire to bring the subject up. He might have been any guest, making a short sociable stay.

On Monday, the household routine claimed my attention. It was washing day. On the ground floor, next to the kitchen, where water could be heated in quantity, there was a room set aside for baths, which on every other Monday became a laundry. A small room adjoining it had a table for pressing and a little hearth for heating irons, and rope lines were slung just under the rafters so that in bad weather things could be dried there, with the fire to warm the air. In good weather we used a small walled drying yard.

Monday, in contrast to the previous day, was dry and breezy, with the high grey sky that doesn't mean rain. However, washday as usual filled the house with steam and the smell of soap and fogged all the windows. The work needed all the pairs of hands it could get and I always helped. I had also decided that I must finally deal with the problem of Gladys' dreadful brown gown. When I had finished helping to wring sheets, I took her up to my chamber.

'Gladys, *why* do you keep wearing that terrible dress when you have much better ones? Look at it! Food stains everywhere – patched elbows – I can't bear the sight of it any longer. It needs a wash, only it probably won't survive one. Put on something else and give me that one. I'll get rid of it!'

'I'm fond of it. I like it 'cos it's brown. I like brown. And it's warm and it fits, look you. I've had it years.' Gladys was sullen.'

'That's obvious! Sybil and I will make you two new ones to replace it – light brown worsted for warmer weather; dark brown wool for winter. And I'll have some new ruffs made for you, too. That dress that you've got on now will be turned into dusters.'

'Here, whose gown is this? I don't want . . .'

'Don't *argue*, Gladys. I insist that . . . Yes, Dale, what is it?'

Dale, who had just entered the room a little nervously, having no doubt heard the edge on my voice, said: 'Ma'am, our visitor has gone out into the grounds. Mistress Ambrosia

is showing him about. I think the smell of washday has driven
him there.'

'Good. But you needn't have come to tell me that . . .'

'I didn't, ma'am. I really came to say that we now have
another visitor. He has just ridden in and Wilder has put him
in the East Room to wait for you. His name is Christopher
Spelton.'

'I've never heard of him!' I said crossly. 'What is happening
to this house? First Ambrosia arrives out of the blue, then we
have the count and his entourage; now this man . . . on washday
too! I might as well run Hawkswood as an inn! I could hang
out a sign!'

Sheer irritation made me warm to my theme. 'A fine heraldic
inn sign! Field, vert. Or, two hawks in flight, side by side,
dexter, holding in its talons a covered dish; sinister, holding
in its talons a goblet. Below, a single hawk in flight, bearing in
its talons a tester bed. That may not be quite the right way to
word the blazon but it's understandable, at least. And above,
in gold letters, the words WELCOME TO HAWKSWOOD
HOSTELRY! Oh, very well, I had better see this man, I
suppose. Where is he from, Dale, did he say?'

'The court, ma'am. From my lord Burghley.'

'From Cecil?' That was different. I went, in haste.

Stepping off the staircase, I heard voices from the hall and
paused to glance in, in case the unknown Master Spelton had
been moved from the East Room, which was our name for
the larger of Hawkswood's two parlours. He was not in the
hall, however. If Ambrosia had shown Gilbert Renard round
the garden earlier, they had come back inside, however soapy the
hall smelt (it did) and however fogged its windows might be
(they were). Ambrosia, very nicely dressed, was perched on
a window seat, and Gilbert Renard was seated at the table and
writing. Just as I stopped to look in, he halted in his task to
say to Ambrosia: 'I can't be sure I remember every word of
Gascoigne's poem quite right but I'll do my best.'

'I do like the poem as far as you've recited it to me. Please
do write all you can recall.'

'Your wish is my command,' said Renard. He dipped his
quill, and began once more to write. The quill spluttered and

a blot flew on to the page. 'Though I fear *that* wasn't by your command! My apologies, madame!'

Heavy handed with a quill as with a bridle, I thought, and walked on.

In the East Room, standing by the window, sipping a glass of the wine that Wilder had no doubt provided by way of refreshment, and looking out into the flower garden, where a few crocuses were making patches of white and gold and purple and the green shoots of daffodils were poking through the soil, was a short, balding man, plainly dressed, with dusty boots. I said: 'Master Spelton? I am Mistress Stannard.'

He turned at once and bowed. 'At your service, mistress,' he said. He sounded as if he meant it. It was not mere gallantry and the smile in his brown eyes was genuinely friendly. 'I have brought you a letter from my lord Burghley,' he said. He handed it to me.

Though I knew it was from Cecil, the sight of the familiar seal still sent a lurch through my stomach. I expected to hear from him, of course, because I had written to him about Ambrosia's troubles, but perhaps it would not just concern Ambrosia; perhaps in some way it would release me from my own dilemma, from the queen's need of me. Perhaps . . .

I broke the seal.

No. The letter hoped that Gilbert Renard had arrived safely and settled in for a visit and that we were enjoying each other's company. Then it recommended that Ambrosia should avoid getting entangled in the law. The law would be abysmally slow, Cecil said. Mistress Jester would do best to advise her daughter to reconsider the marriage offered by her present in-laws.

Love matches are not always successful. My daughter Anne's love match with the Earl of Oxford has proved a sorry disaster. I am advising all my friends who have unmarried daughters to betroth them quickly, before they marry themselves off and choose badly.

Ambrosia would not thank him for that, I thought.

The letter had more to say, but it had nothing whatever to do either with Ambrosia or the count. It informed me that my French husband, or rather, ex-husband, Matthew de la Roche, was dead.

I am well aware that you were once lied to concerning the death of Matthew de la Roche, Cecil wrote. *This time, I assure you that it is true, and I also assure you that regardless of any agreement you may or may not reach with Count Renard, you are free to travel or send an emissary to France, to enquire into the facts for yourself.*

Our information is that de la Roche was travelling in France, raising funds for the cause of Mary Stuart as he so often did. He fell foul of some Huguenots in a hostelry where a first-floor room was being used as a card room. De la Roche and his companions were at one table; a group of Huguenots at another. They overheard some of the talk between de la Roche and his friends and a quarrel broke out. One of the Huguenots challenged de la Roche to a duel. Swords were drawn. The landlord, hearing the uproar, rushed up the stairs, followed by his wife and a serving man. The landlord tried to interfere but his wife and servant dragged him out of harm's way. Meanwhile, de la Roche had sustained a wound to the chest and died of it an hour later.

So Matthew was dead. And, as before, most opportunely from the point of view of Cecil, Walsingham and the queen. The rest of the letter consisted of conventional hopes that I was in good health; the usual platitudes.

Would I be told the same lie twice? Perhaps not. Perhaps, this time, it was true that Matthew was dead. Later, I supposed, I would mourn for him but for the moment, all I could feel was doubt and a vague, aching regret for all that might have been, if only he had not had that absurd obsession with Mary Stuart. Only, then, I would not have known Hugh. I would not have Hawkswood. It was all too difficult. I folded the sheet and said: 'Do you know what is in this letter?'

'The gist, Mistress Stannard. I was not present when it was dictated, but my lord Burghley told me. Mistress, here in private, we may speak freely. I am aware that you are not all you seem. Lord Burghley has told me much about you. You have in the past carried out secret tasks for the queen. I do the same.'

By this time we had seated ourselves on the comfortable settles with which the room was furnished. From the corner of his, he smiled at me. 'Officially,' he said, 'I am a Queen's Messenger with the added duty of acting as interpreter for Sir Francis Walsingham and my lord Burghley when they have dealings with the French, here or in France. I speak the French language well. But sometimes, I have other, more private, tasks. I have two at the moment and am on my way to France to carry them out. As you may be going to marry into the French royal family, you have a right to know of certain matters, so Lord Burghley says. If you are to enter a political marriage, you ought to understand its political context. He assures me that your discretion can be trusted.'

'I have no wish to be privy to anything I need not know,' I assured him, but he smiled again and shook his head.

'My lord Burghley bid me tell you all. He said, Mistress Stannard must know exactly what she is doing before she gives her consent to the marriage.'

Indeed? I thought. It sounded as though Cecil had a conscience about the way I was being used. As well he might, considering the way he had used me in the past. Master Spelton was continuing.

'My first commission,' he explained, 'is to encourage feelings of friendship between King Henri and the French queen mother Catherine de' Medici, and our own Queen Elizabeth. That I can do openly. But my second mission is contradictory – and therefore confidential. I am to encourage the Protestant leaders in France – the Huguenots – to uphold their rights and to feel that they have friends in England. Our queen needs as many friends as she can who dislike Spain as much as she does and that is certainly true of the Huguenots. It is said that even King Henri now feels that more tolerance towards French Protestants could be wise. That is why the quarrel between Gilbert Renard and his family has been mended, if somewhat reluctantly on the queen mother's part, I believe. Similarly, certain French princes who have been out of favour because they feel that Huguenots may be better company than Spain, are now being reinstated – as Count Renard has been. I am to make contact with them and try to build diplomatic friendships between them and Elizabeth. Unknown to King Henri or his mother, of course.'

'I see,' I said, somewhat distractedly. A faint sound had caught my attention. The door of the room was closed but I was seated nearer to it than Spelton. I put a finger to my lips, rose and darted to the door. I jerked it open. There was no one there. I shut the door again and came back to my seat.

'I thought I heard something. Soft footsteps and then something brushed against the door . . .'

'Such as an ear?' said Spelton quietly. 'Your own ears are keen, Mistress, and the world is full of inquisitive ones. But I can hardly suppose that Catherine de' Medici would plant a spy in your home. I think you imagined it.'

'I hope so.' I was doubtful, however. I was not given to imagining things. I *had* heard something, I said to myself. Aloud, I said: 'I can't suppose that any of my household would listen at doors! Which only leaves the count and his men, but why on earth should they want to eavesdrop on me? The count is here to propose marriage to me, and with the goodwill of the queen behind him, too.' I sat back with a sigh. 'No, perhaps it was just someone passing by, close to the door, and brushing against it for a moment. Anyway, I couldn't see anyone. Never mind. Master Spelton, there is something I want to ask you, if I may.'

'By all means. What is it?'

'Would you undertake a commission for me – if time allows? If you know what is in the letter you have brought me, you know that it speaks of the death of one Matthew de la Roche, formerly my husband. His home is – or was – a chateau called Blanchepierre, in the valley of the Loire. I want to be sure that he is really dead. Could you find out for me? He was a well-known man; it need not be difficult.'

'But of course. I would be happy to do that for you.'

'Thank you,' I said. 'I would welcome absolute certainty.'

Yes, I would, even though, at heart, I already knew the tale was fact this time. I had sensed it, smelt it, somehow in the wording of Cecil's letter. Even yet, it seemed, I had harboured a small, thin hope that Matthew's existence might defend me against marriage with the count. That hope was finally gone. It would no longer be bigamy even to the most rigid of Catholics.

'Do you intend staying here tonight?' I asked. 'Or are you riding straight on?'

'I meant to deliver your letter, beg a meal and then ride on, but my mare has a loose shoe on her off fore. You have a smithy in the village, I believe. This afternoon I will lead her there and have it seen to. Then, if I may, I will rest here tonight and set off again in the morning. The ship I am to take from Dover does not sail until the day after tomorrow, in the evening. May I do that?'

I said yes, as any good hostess must. I called Phoebe to arrange a bedchamber and show Master Spelton to it, and then went to talk to Sybil. It would be best, I thought, if she were the one to tell Ambrosia of Cecil's reply.

I found Sybil lending a hand with hanging out the wash. She frowned, however, when I said what I wanted. 'The letter from Lord Burghley was to you, Mistress Stannard, in answer to one you wrote to him. I think it would be better if you told her. Let her read the letter for herself, if you think it right, and explain anything she might not understand. Then she can come to me for comfort.'

'Where is she now?' I said. Ambrosia had not come to help with the wash.

'Out in the garden again, I think. Still showing the count round the grounds. After dinner, you could ask her to walk with you instead! I don't think she should be spending so much time in the company of the count. Has he spoken to you yet? About . . . well, you know.'

'No. No, he hasn't. Very well. After dinner, then.'

Ambrosia came for the walk quite willingly. But as we sauntered through the rose garden and the woodland, I told her of Cecil's unpalatable recommendations. She said nothing until we had emerged on the far side of the woodland, and reached the lake.

Hawkswood's little lake was always kept well stocked with fish; fresh trout was always at my command. The breeze had dropped and the water was still except for the trout rings here and there. I found a fallen log and the two of us sat down.

'I don't like the man they want me to marry,' said Ambrosia

flatly. 'And that's that. I don't think he will be a good stepfather. He wants to send my boys away to "learn manners in some good household". Well, it's often done but I don't want to do it and if I did, it wouldn't be yet. They're only four! Anyway, I just don't like *him*.'

'What's amiss with him?' I asked her.

'He's fat, for one thing. And he's a schoolmaster like my first husband. I don't like fat men and though I did love John, I was never really at home as a schoolmaster's wife. I was so used to the pie shop and . . . and arranging supplies and cooking and serving customers and doing accounts and all the things that go with running such a place and I missed it. My parents-in-law just want to keep John's money and property in the family. They want to get their hands on it.'

'We must talk to your mother,' I said. 'She and I must find you someone else. Once you're married, you can't be pushed into marrying this man you don't like. The boys might well be handed back to you then and anyway, you'd have someone to help you fight for them.'

Ambrosia looked at me and smiled. It was Sybil's smile, always notable for its sweetness. 'I was right to come here,' she said. 'Though I fear I was not welcome at first.'

'Your mother's daughter would always be welcome,' I said firmly. 'Only, I have troubles of my own just now. As you know.'

'Yes. I am sorry. To feel as though one is being forced . . . well, I know all about that.' We were silent a moment and then Ambrosia said: 'There is a little island in the middle of your lake. What is that – something – on top of it?'

'Probably the remains of last year's moorhens' nest,' I said. 'Or perhaps they've started building again. They nest there. We don't mind them. They don't eat trout – just water insects and seeds and the like.'

'I wish I were a moorhen,' said Ambrosia with sudden passion. 'Life seems so simple for them.'

'I agree,' I said with a sigh.

SIX
A Sense of Injustice

I woke the next morning to a sense of deep unease.

It came from more than one source. One, obviously enough, was the fact that Christopher Spelton had spoken to me of a secret mission that Cecil thought I was entitled to know about, and I was still sure that someone had been listening at the door, though for the life of me I could not imagine who or why. It was wildly unlikely that anyone in my household would behave so improperly and I couldn't think why the count would want to do such a thing or order anyone to do it for him. Yet the certainty was there.

My other source of unease was private and personal. The fact was that advantageous matches, certainly matches of value to her majesty the queen, could not be reasonably refused on the grounds that I preferred dark hair to light hair, and the man was rough in his handling of a high-spirited and probably all but unmanageable stallion.

But today, that match would be, must be, discussed. The count would surely not put it off any longer. Though I wasn't going to raise it myself. Absolutely not. I knew now, for certain, that I did not want to marry him, and I was filled with a sense of injustice, because I had been forced into a position that I did not want, even feared, and one that would affect my whole life – for the rest of my life.

I was late to breakfast and everyone but Renard had come and gone before me. I could see no sign of either Pierre Lestrange or Father Ignatius. I ate alone with the count, while his round blue eyes gazed into mine across the table, and when – not at all to my surprise – he asked me to walk in the garden when we had finished, I agreed.

There was no point in procrastinating. The moment had come. He was going to talk of marriage. What else was he here for?

I was, however, relieved to see the stocky figure of Christopher Spelton appear at the door with a pair of laden saddlebags over his arm. Any delay to the inevitable was welcome.

'I must just speed a parting guest on his way,' I said as I rose from the table. 'You have breakfasted, Master Spelton?'

'I have, Mistress Stannard, sometime earlier. Many thanks for your hospitality.' The nice brown eyes smiled at me. 'My mare is already saddled. She now has four sound shoes. I had her reshod all round yesterday afternoon.'

'A wise precaution before a long ride,' I said. 'I must see you off.'

'I wish you a safe journey, Master Spelton,' said Renard politely. They had met at dinner the day before and I gathered that they already knew each other slightly, having come across one another at court.

In the courtyard, I watched Spelton mount and reached up to shake his hand in farewell. 'I wish you success in all you undertake,' I said as he adjusted his girth. He had already checked the curb chain on the (reasonable) curb bit. He was a careful horseman. 'Take good care of yourself,' I added.

'That I always do. We live in a dangerous world, Mistress Stannard, as you no doubt know. You should be wary too.' He hesitated and then said: 'I know who Count Renard is, Mistress Stannard. I mean, I know he is the man that the queen wishes you to marry. I knew beforehand that I was likely to find him here. No doubt my lord Burghley would say it was none of my business but as you know, since it emerged at dinner yesterday, the count and I have met. I don't know him well, and I've never heard anything against him. He is quite popular in court circles and I haven't a morsel of a right to speak as I am doing, but I do urge you to consider carefully before you accept his proposal. For some reason, I just don't take to him. If that is an impertinence, forgive me.' He grinned suddenly. 'I expect that Lord Burghley *would* think me impertinent and probably not forgive me.'

'Even Lord Burghley wants me to be sure about what I am doing,' I said. 'Or he wouldn't have asked you to tell me of your confidential mission. There is no impertinence. I feel as you do, as a matter of fact, but my position is difficult.'

'May God give you a good deliverance,' said Spelton, sincerely, and then he was gone and I went back indoors, feeling as if a good friend had just taken leave of me.

Count Renard was just rising from the table. 'We might ride together after our walk,' he said. 'Would you like that?'

'Not with you on that stallion!' I said, trying to be bright and friendly. For the queen's sake, I must try to like him. 'He might excite my mare. We don't want her coming into season unexpectedly.'

His eyes sparked and I knew I had made a tactical error. I should not have mentioned anything which related in any way to sex. He had misinterpreted what was actually a plain down to earth statement as a semi-invitation.

'We will find you something else to ride,' I said, still brightly. 'There's plenty of choice.' For a moment, my reluctance to walk or ride anywhere with the count forced its way to the surface. 'I do have one or two household duties,' I said. 'I must see to them first.' I was procrastinating after all, though I knew I should not. 'I will join you very soon,' I said.

'Very well, madame. When you have interviewed your cook and scolded the maids for carelessness, you will find me in my room. A tap on the door – and I will come out to you. We will stroll out together and then we will ride. Ah, when we are married you will have no such household tasks to concern you. My chateau is well run. You will have nothing to do but enjoy life.'

Yes, he meant to speak of marriage and I shrank from it. His smile was pleasant but it stirred nothing in me. Once more, I remembered that savage curb.

He went upstairs and I sought out Hawthorn to settle the day's menu. After a lengthy discussion – which I dragged out for as long as possible – I took myself upstairs as I usually did after breakfast, just to see if the routine work there had been properly done.

The first thing I saw when I reached the upper landing was Joan Flood standing at the door of Renard's room, with her left ear against the panelling.

Well, that was one mystery solved! No, I hadn't been imagining things when I was talking to Spelton, and it was now clear that there really was someone in my household who had taken to listening at doors! At least it disposed of any suspicion against the count, and that was a relief. But to catch Joan doing such a thing . . .! Furious, I grabbed her by the arm, shook her hard as she started to squeal, and hauled her along the upstairs gallery to my own chamber, at the far end. Once inside, I shut the door, pushed her into a chair and stood over her.

'Just what do you think you're doing, listening at guests' doors?' I was so angry, I was shouting. 'There can hardly be two eavesdroppers in one house so I take it that it was also you who put an ear to the door yesterday when I had what *should* have been a private conversation with Master Spelton. I knew I heard someone out there!'

'But I didn't!' Joan was gaping at me, eyes wide and appalled. 'I didn't! I don't know what you mean! I wouldn't . . .! I didn't know you had a private conversation with Master Spelton! If anyone eavesdropped on you then it was that sneaking Lestrange. He creeps about in silent shoes. I don't like him.'

'Rubbish!' I said. 'There can hardly be two of you at it! I'd have thought you'd approve heartily of the count and his entourage,' I added sardonically. 'Seeing as they're all Catholic.'

Joan looked completely stricken, understandably, for I had never before gibed at her or Ben concerning their religion, even though it had once led them into conspiring against me. I had let it go, even granted permission for them to attend the count's Mass under my roof – which Joan had actually declined to do. I also knew quite well that she and Ben sometimes heard Mass at another house and I had never interfered; never tried to find out which house it was. I was not myself, I thought.

She was a small, nervous woman with stringy hair and I had never heard her answer anyone back before, but she did it now and in a surprising way, for her. 'There's other things besides religion,' she said with dignity. 'This is a good house and Ben and I appreciate it. Ma'am, I have to tell you, what I heard just now was . . . well, I think you should know. It's true I didn't understand much of it because it was in French, but I did catch . . .'

'Joan, be quiet!' Indignation seized me once again. 'How

dare you behave like this! Eavesdropping on the private conversations of my guests – when you can't understand them
anyway! And I don't believe it wasn't you doing the same
thing to me and Master Spelton yesterday!'
Joan began to cry, but I persisted. 'Whatever you heard,
either time, is private – you understand? It must never be
repeated to anyone, not even to me or to your husband. And
what were you doing up here anyway? You have no work here
– you are employed in the kitchen!'
'Don't shout so, ma'am, please don't shout at me! I came
up to put clean sheets in that cupboard there, to save Margery
from doing it; they're heavy and you know what washday's
like!'
This made sense as Joan had a helpful nature and often lent
a hand to her fellow servants. I said: 'I've no objection to that,
but . . .' It suddenly occurred to me that there was a very
pertinent question that so far I had failed to ask. '*Why* did you
put your ear to the count's door?'
'Because of his *valet*, ma'am!' Joan raised her voice in
passionate protest against my anger. 'That Pierre Lestrange.
Padding about everywhere . . . you must have noticed how
you can never hear him coming. Yesterday I was up here too,
with those towels that dry quickly, putting them away in that
same cupboard, and I swear I saw him come out of your room,
though I had my head in the cupboard and only glimpsed him
through the crack where the hinges are.'
'You saw Lestrange come out of *this* room?'
'Yes, ma'am!'
'Joan, this won't do. You're making up stories to excuse
your own snooping and though I hate to remind you, you have
a questionable past. You once schemed against me. I don't
believe this tale; I don't believe *you* . . .'
I was *not* myself. I would never normally have been so
downright and obstinate and I wasn't surprised when Joan's
sobs escalated into a loud wail, whereupon, the door was flung
open and in marched Ben. I glared at him. 'What is this? Since
when have you had permission to stride into your employer's
bedroom – a *lady*'s bedroom! – without knocking!'
'I heard my wife crying. No one makes my wife cry in my

hearing without I want to know why!' Ben, who was short like his wife, had a bald head and watery pale-blue eyes and though he was less timid than Joan, he was normally very respectful towards me. Just now, however, the pale eyes were flashing, which was rare. Today, no one at all seemed to be themselves.

Joan proceeded to tell him why she was in tears. I interrupted her. 'This time,' I said, cutting the whole wretched scene short, 'I will take no action. But there is to be no more of this snooping. I will deal with any velvet-footed valets who require it. Go away now. Both of you. Back to the kitchen.'

I was very angry but I didn't threaten to dismiss them, in case I actually had to carry out the threat. I really didn't want to lose them as they were most gifted as cooks and John Hawthorn, who valued their skills, would have been furious with me.

And then, after all that, I had to face reality and walk in the garden with Gilbert Renard and let his courtship begin.

Which, of course, was exactly what happened. We strolled about in the rose garden while Renard said, in gentle tones, that now that we knew each other a little, there were things that we must discuss. I made myself say that I understood. First of all, though, said Renard, he wished me to know what he had to offer me. He then began to talk to me about his chateau in France and the kind of life his wife would have there.

'The place is most beautiful. It is in good vineyard country. It is called the Château d'Oiseaux because it stands high up on a hillside and there are birds all around it. It was taken from me when I showed sympathy for the Huguenots and I feared it would be sold but I do have friends among some sections of the royal house and perhaps they hindered that. At any rate, my steward has kept in touch with me always and no one has disturbed him. He has continued with his duties and even taken *my* orders, secretly, you understand. There is a good staff and you would have nothing to do for all can be left to him. The mistress of my house will not have to wring sheets or berate servants herself. Now that my land has been restored, we can live there like a prince and princess. Harry shall have a beautiful pony of his own; he is of the right age now. The chateau looks down into a valley which all belongs to me. There is a village down there, and vineyards, and believe me, my wine is second to none. My people are experts. They create a smooth, dry light red wine that will delight you. And also . . .'

It went on and on. Later we went back to the house to change for a ride. I had Bronze, the amiable gelding whom I had had for years, saddled for Renard. I was sorry to see that the count was as ham-fisted with a quiet horse as with his temperamental stallion.

On the way back, he said: 'Ursula – may I call you that? And will you, henceforth, call me Gilbert? Ursula, you have listened, and smiled and asked questions now and then but what are you thinking? We need to come to the point. I say it myself but I represent a valuable match. Will you accept it? Will you marry me? We can hold the ceremony at will. I already have a licence.'

While we had walked and ridden, something had clarified in my head. 'I have a visit first to make to court,' I said. 'I shall go tomorrow. When I return, I will answer you.'

SEVEN
Playing the Queen

lizabeth's court was a highly mobile affair, moving regularly from one to another of her palaces along the Thames. Cecil always kept me informed of its where-abouts, and at present it was at Hampton Court. For the first time ever, though, I was not sure whether Elizabeth would see me. She would guess why I had come and perhaps she would not want to discuss the count – or his proposal – with me. She had given her orders and to her, that might well be that. I set out, accompanied by Brockley and Dale, and tried to talk cheerfully as we rode, but I knew that they too were anxious. They understood the situation.

In fact, she did grant me an audience but my heart sank when I realized how public it was going to be, for I was shown into the main audience chamber, where I found her enthroned on her dais, huge brocade skirts spread round her, a vast open ruff at her neck, and a dozen ladies and courtiers standing round her.

'I fancy I know why you are here,' she said as I rose from my curtsey. 'It concerns Count Renard, does it not? Am I right?'

'Yes, your majesty,' I said, nervously.

She bit her lip. I studied her, recognizing, because blood does speak to blood, that beneath the shield of her pale pointed face was an uncertain, even a frightened woman. Her golden brown eyes were more expressive than her face and gave the secret away. I waited.

'Some matters are private,' she said at last, and rose to her feet to descend the three steps from her dais. 'Follow me.'

I did so, inwardly sighing with relief. We passed through a door behind the dais and entered a much smaller room, lit by a stained-glass window that cast a mingling of crimson, azure and gold over the black and white tiled floor. Here there was another dais but there was also a long settle against one wall. I was familiar with the place, for she and I had talked there before. She had similar arrangements in her other palaces. They allowed for a kind of intimacy. Elizabeth sat down on the settle and signalled to me to join her.

'You have doubts about this marriage,' she said without preamble. 'Again, am I right?'

'Yes, majesty.'

'We can be sisters while we are alone. I knew you would not want this. I can only say that the service I ask of you is important. We need a close alliance with France. The French need it too. We must both defend ourselves against the growing might of Spain, and a strong bond between us would serve us both well. But we need an alliance that is truly strong; not just a matter of a treaty on parchment – though there is such a treaty, of course. It has been drawn up and is waiting to be signed, as soon as you and the count are declared man and wife. And that is the point, of course. Parchment on its own can be chopped up and cast into the fire but marriages are more resilient.'

I waited, silently, and once more, my heart sank.

'You have understood? We need a link of blood to back the treaty up,' Elizabeth said, looking at me, I thought with both pleading and compassion. 'You and the count are the best possibility that we have. It would help if there were children too. They couldn't be my heirs, of course, but they would still be a living bond between England and France, and therefore valuable, part of the bulwark that both parties need to build against Spain.'

'Yes,' I said despairingly. 'Yes, I see.'

'Are you asking yourself, why am I not to be the bride? Ursula, I . . . I . . . have very good reasons for fearing to hazard myself in the dangerous lists of wedlock. That is why I have offered the French a substitute – my half-sister. Not legitimate but still, my half-sister. They in turn offered a substitute; not a legitimate prince of the house but still, the son of a king of France. It was the best compromise we could reach.'

She gave me a wry smile. 'Let me make a little play on
words. I am asking you to play the queen! To be a pretend
version of me. So that, as if in a game of cards, the English
nation does *not* have to play the queen, and risk her life in
the process.'

I wanted to protest about the sacrifice she wanted from me,
but I had no reason strong enough to outweigh her reasons
for it. She was only asking me to exchange my life at
Hawkswood for a life of luxury in France. I would still be
able to visit Hawkswood. Most women would have thought
it a good bargain.

She gave me a small, rueful smile. 'I am a woman, like
you, Ursula. I am not without the natural desires of a woman.
There are – there have been many – times when I have longed,
yearned, for things that most women take for granted. But
time and again, fear steps in the way. Ursula, I *dare* not offer
myself. Children? My mother nearly died in bearing me. My
first stepmother, Jane Seymour, died when she gave birth to
my brother Edward. My last stepmother, good Catherine Parr,
married Admiral Seymour after my father's death and did not
survive having his daughter. The daughter died too, a little
later. Childbirth is perilous. And I am no longer young. If I
die attempting to provide England's heir, then where will
England be, even if the baby is a son, and lives?'

I remained silent. *I don't want to marry again* sounded like
the whining of a spoilt child, compared to Elizabeth's desperate
need. And the fact that the count was hard on his horses didn't
necessarily prove that he would treat his wife badly.

'There is no point in taking the risk,' Elizabeth said.
'England can't be ruled by a babe in a cradle, and protectors
turn into usurpers in the blink of an eye. Besides, I have other
reasons to dread marriage, things I will not discuss.'

Still I kept silent. When she was two years old, her father
had had her mother beheaded and when she was eight, as
though he meant her to understand fully what he had done to
her mother, he executed his young fifth wife, Catherine
Howard. To Elizabeth, marriage and death must be two sides
of the same coin. There was no need for her to explain that,
for I knew.

'But you have married three times,' she said, 'and borne children safely. For you, it will be different. Ursula, the man is wealthy, now that his lands have been returned to him. He will give you as good a life as you could dream of, and England will be the safer even though – as some of the Council, especially Lord Sussex, keep saying – there is no direct heir. I must consider another way of providing for my country's future. But you could well be very happy. I am not asking you to live in a hovel with a beggar! Ursula, there are matters in which I will not command you, cannot command you. I can't send you to the Tower just because you don't want to marry! I could cast you out of my favour, of course, but you want to live a private life anyway and I doubt, my dear sister, if you would suffer much because of that. But I ask you, dear sister – *please!*'

It had been a cloudy day so far but the sun chose that moment to come out, and the colours that the stained glass splashed over the floor and over us blazed bright as heraldry. For a moment, Elizabeth was transformed; from a queen who was also a frightened woman into a celestial being of glittering colour and power, far beyond all human weaknesses, whose orders must be obeyed without question.

What was I to say, or do? I went on being silent for so long that Elizabeth was finally the one to speak. 'Is there someone else, Ursula? Do you have any other alliance in mind?'

I shook my head. I still felt bonded to Hugh but Hugh was dead. And although my manservant Roger Brockley and I had a deep regard for one another and a unity that at times almost amounted to reading each other's minds, it was not physical. Ours was a friendship that mirrored the queen's own friendship with Robert Dudley, which was also deep but not physical. It was not the sort of thing to be put into words. To the world, to the queen, I was free to remarry. It was not a matter of did I want to do so, not now, not after hearing what Elizabeth had to say. It was more a matter of could I reasonably refuse?

We rode home, Brockley and Dale and I, through a day which was now sunny and bright but there was no brightness in me. In my chest, my heart was as heavy as a stone. I had told

the Brockleys what had transpired and they were silent, recognizing, as I did, that there was no escape. My quiet domestic life was over. I must become Gilbert Renard's countess and pretend to like it. Oh Hugh, my dear, dear Hugh, why did you have to die and leave me exposed like this? When the chimneys of Hawkswood came in sight, tears came to my eyes, as though I were facing bereavement. Which, in a way, I was.

Dale at that point said hesitantly: 'It may work out well, ma'am. You may be very pleased with your new life.' But Brockley kept silent and I knew well enough that Dale did not believe what she had said. Brockley had no doubt told her all about the way the count mistreated his horse. She was trying to encourage me; that was all.

Then silence fell again, until at length we clattered into the Hawkswood courtyard. Our approach had evidently been observed and it looked as though most of the household had gathered there to greet me, which was gratifying, until I realized how sombre all their faces were.

'What is it?' I demanded. 'Is it Harry? Is something wrong with Harry?' I don't remember dismounting. I was simply out of the saddle and standing on the cobbles as if by sorcery.

Then I saw that Ben Flood was crying. Through his tears, he said: 'Harry is well, ma'am; he's in his nursery with Tessie. It's my Joan. She's dead. She fell downstairs.'

'*Fell downstairs?*'

I found myself leaning against Jewel's warm dark shoulder. I needed support. I couldn't take this in. It was all getting beyond me. Gilbert Renard. The queen's need; the queen's command. My dread, my reluctance, Brockley's warning . . . Spelton's veiled hints! . . . And now this. I was like an army confronted with multiple enemies, all at once. 'What do you mean?' I said.

Gilbert Renard was there among the throng, along with Pierre Lestrange and Father Ignatius. The three of them now came forward, and even through my confusion, I noticed and resented that Renard's manner suggested that in his mind, he was already my husband and the man in charge at Hawkswood. I had been addressing Ben, but it was Renard who answered.

'She fell down the main stairs, from top to bottom,' he said. 'She slipped at the top and – just fell.'

'I hadn't had them polished!' said Sybil earnestly. 'We never do that, just because it could make them slippery. They were just as they always are!'

'Yes, they were!' That was Ambrosia, pale with horror.

'Aye, just as always and none of us ever fell down them afore!' declared Gladys. Whenever there was a crisis of any kind, Gladys had something to say, even if it was pointless.

She and Sybil had a point this time, though. The main stairs were wide and shallow, running straight, with no bends in them, and a stout banister. Hugh had told me of his mother's accident in the days when they were polished, and so I had made a point of seeing that they were not. I considered it important, for servants sometimes used them when carrying luggage or piles of linen up and down. The back stairs were steep and narrow and had an awkwardly sharp curve.

Adam Wilder, stepping forward in turn and unobtrusively putting himself ahead of Renard, said gravely: 'I was in the hall. I heard her cry out and I heard her fall. Gladys heard her too. I ran to see what had happened and Gladys came after me. We found her lying at the foot of the staircase. Her . . . her neck was broken. There was no doubt about that. She must have died at once.'

Simon was waiting to take Jewel from me. I moved from the patient support of her shoulder and threw him my reins. 'Where is Joan? Where has she been laid? I want to see her,' I said.

Renard said: 'In your absence, madame, Master Wilder conferred with me and we decided to lay her in the small spare room that isn't often used, the one at the top of the house. Master Wilder had it dusted.'

'Let us go there,' I said.

It was an attic chamber under the roof. Its ceiling sloped almost to the floor at one side and there was little space for furniture. There was a clothes press – an old one with scratches on it where a cat had once sharpened its claws – and a single tester bed, not made up. The room had been dusted, as Renard had said. A sheet had been spread on the bed and Joan lay on it with an old linen coverlet over her. Wilder drew it down. She lay on her back, hands folded over her heart. She was still dressed although someone had removed her ruff and shoes.

Despite the lack of space, Ben Flood, the Brockleys, Wilder, Renard, Father Ignatius and Lestrange had all crowded in with me. Sybil and Ambrosia were in the doorway and Gladys, who was lame nowadays and slow on stairs, had come last of all and was peering from behind them.

Ben, wiping his eyes, said miserably: 'It happened less than an hour ago. Master Wilder and Gladys got to her first, but from the kitchen we heard her fall; we were there only seconds later. She was lying in such a heap . . . she was dead!' His voice went up, into a cry of grief.

'It must have been quick,' said Wilder comfortingly. 'She can't have suffered much pain.'

'Turned a somersault, we reckon,' said Gladys helpfully. And then added, without any noticeable change in her voice: 'Funny, ain't it, look you! Joan Flood gets into trouble, listening at doors, and next day she falls down the stairs and breaks her neck.'

We all turned to gape at her. Ben let out an anguished sob. 'What do you mean?' I snapped. 'And what do you know about Joan and her . . . her . . . eavesdropping?'

'You shouted at her,' said the count, sounding more amused than anything else. 'Loud enough, I would think, that they must have heard you in Hawkswood village! And she shouted back.'

'And she talked of it herself, down among the servants, after you'd done frightening her,' said Ben angrily, to me. 'Everyone knows, all of us.'

'I gathered,' said the count, 'that the poor woman had been listening at my door and must have overheard me talking, in French, to Lestrange, on the subject of some clothes he thinks I should replace. As far as I'm concerned, she was welcome to listen at my door all day and all night. She'd hear nothing harmful, even if she could understand our tongue! From what Lestrange and I both overheard, when you caught her at it, it seems she saw Lestrange looking for you one morning, madame. He knocked at your bedchamber door, and when there was no answer, ventured to look inside, and she saw him. For some reason it made her suspicious of us.'

'I should not have looked into your room, madame,' said

Lestrange contritely. 'My master wished me to find you, and it sounded urgent, but I know I should not have done it. I apologize.'

'I wanted to talk to you privately,' the count said to me. 'I expect that to Lestrange, I did sound as if the matter were urgent. But you were always so elusive – busy with your washday and then with Master Spelton.' He smiled at me in a conspiratorial manner. *Were you trying to evade my proposal?* said his round blue eyes.

Er . . . well . . . yes. Although if I remembered rightly, he had spent quite some time writing out poetry for Ambrosia. We had, perhaps, been shy of each other.

At that moment, Gladys cleared her throat. We turned towards her and she said: 'There's something else funny, seems to me. I *thought* I saw it when we found her, all in a heap and her clothes all pulled about. When we got her ruff off, I saw it again. See here.'

She moved to the bed and tugged at the neck of Joan's dress. Adam Wilder, outraged, tried to pull her back, exclaiming: 'Stop this, Gladys! You're always making trouble . . .' but I shook my head at him and went to Gladys' side, the others crowding after me.

What Gladys wanted to show us were three small bruises. They were dimly bluish, just where Joan's neck joined her left shoulder.

'*That* don't look like what'd happen however many somer-saults she turned falling down the stairs,' said Gladys.

'What are you saying, Gladys?' demanded Brockley.

'Ain't they fingermarks? Don't they look like that to you?' Gladys sounded quite fierce.

'Oh, really! *Really!*' Adam was spluttering. 'We can all guess what they are!' His face had gone puce. 'If a married lady can't sport a love-bite or tw—'

'Don't talk like that! Don't talk of such things! It's not decent and it's my Joan, my poor beloved Joan and those things are private . . .!' Ben was nearly hysterical.

'Cover her up,' I said. I glared at Gladys. 'Stop this at once. You shouldn't make foolish comments or pretend that . . .

private, ordinary things . . . are sinister. There's no point in creating trouble out of thin air.'

'I'm sure she meant no harm,' said Renard. 'She's a poor old soul and they do say things, you know.' He tapped his forehead expressively.

'Here, you needn't talk about me like I wasn't here! And I'm no poor old soul half out of my wits!' said Gladys belligerently.

'Gladys, be quiet!' I said. 'I have seen enough. Let us all go downstairs.'

Most of the rest of the household was gathered at the foot of the staircase, staring and whispering. I said: 'Best go back to your tasks,' and they began unwillingly to disperse. I led the rest of us into the little parlour.

It was normally such a pleasant place; well lit, its settles padded with bright-hued cushions, its rugs made of glossy furs, and since the day, though it was now sunny, was still not warm, there was a fire in its hearth. Now its cheerful air seemed unsuitable, out of tune. The room also seemed congested, with so many of us in it. We stood looking at each other and then Wilder rounded on Gladys.

'I said it; the mistress said it. You create trouble, yes, out of thin air! Can you not hold your poisonous tongue? There was nothing to see that wasn't natural enough but what you've said will get round; it will turn into gossip. Too many of us heard it and if we all swore to hold our tongues, I wouldn't trust you to keep your word! I know you! Madam . . .' he turned to me '. . . I am sorry. You have so much on your mind just now. But we must deal with this. There will be gossip and it must be scotched. There will have to be an enquiry.'

'Quite right,' said Brockley with energy. 'I am sure that madam will agree. We're all ashamed of you, Gladys. Was there ever a bigger nuisance than you, on this earth?'

'I'm not clear what Gladys here was talking *about*,' said the count. 'Gladys, were you suggesting that I or Lestrange seized hold of this unfortunate maidservant and thrust her down the stairs because she had overheard us talking about my wardrobe – in a language she couldn't understand anyway?'

'She might not understand much of what you were jabbering

about,' Gladys told him, 'but there might be a word or two she got right and maybe it weren't about the latest fashion in doublets! What I said, and what I think about what I showed you, I stand by.'

Her dark eyes, which were still bright despite her age, were flashing, and her back, usually somewhat bent, had straightened. 'And yes, there did ought to be an enquiry, look you! That's what I wanted, what I spoke up for. If old Gladys has made you stop pretending and *find out* what happened, then old Gladys is proud of it and you can keep your snooty reprimands to yourself!'

'No one is pretending anything,' I said furiously. 'Accidents are accidents. It never occurred to any of us that this was anything else until you thrust your crazed ideas at us!'

Ben, scarlet with embarrassment, said: 'I don't know if what Master Wilder thinks is right or not. Joan and me are . . . were . . . affectionate and one can't always remember . . .'

'This is all absurd!' Renard was angry. 'Of course this can be nothing but a most grievous mischance! Mistress Stannard has enough on her mind already, and should not be made anxious by these wild imaginings.'

'Indeed, such talk is unhealthy and improper.' Father Ignatius had been quiet up to now but suddenly spoke with authority.

Brockley, ignoring him, said: 'I consider, as Master Wilder obviously does, that there should be an inquest.'

'So do I,' I said.

Yes of course there should. Gladys had realized what I had not. In a house where confidential matters of state have been discussed, a servant is caught listening at a door and next day, has a most unlikely accident! Questions must certainly be asked. And with that, a huge wave of pure exhaustion broke over me, worse than the weakness that had attacked me in the courtyard. I could no longer cope. To the demands of the queen and the simple fact of Joan's death had now been added this lurid possibility. I didn't know what to do with it. I did know, however, that I must do something. I must do several somethings. I must . . . yes . . . organize an inquest and a funeral, comfort Ben and then – God help me – arrange my own wedding. Yes, it was all beyond me. Miles and miles beyond me.

I sank on to a settle, leant back and closed my eyes, for dark specks were swimming before them. I heard Sybil and Dale exclaim, and then they were beside me, and so was Ambrosia, and the three of them were helping me to my feet, steadying me back upstairs. Vaguely, I recall being undressed and got into bed. I heard Brockley's voice outside the door, saying to someone that madam had had enough. Then I slept.

I woke next morning with a savage migraine, worse than either of the attacks I had had when Captain Yarrow was in the house.

I was abed with this one for two days and when it had passed, I developed a fever which lasted for two more. Meanwhile Brockley and Wilder between them arranged the inquest. In Hugh's day, Hugh himself had been the local coroner when necessary; now, the task had fallen to Dr Fletcher, the Hawkswood vicar, but the business was still, as always, held in an upstairs room in the Hawkswood tavern, the White Falcon. My fever was down when Joan's inquest took place but I still felt too weak to attend. Brockley, however, told me about it.

It was a brief and formal affair, he said. There was a jury drawn from respectable Hawkswood families plus two men from Woking, our nearest small town, and they unanimously brought in a verdict of accidental death.

'Dr Fletcher said that sadly, snooping servants were a commonplace,' Brockley told me. 'Then he said that they rarely got themselves murdered on that account, and the stairs were obviously known to be hazardous because they were deliberately not polished. Master Wilder's theory about the marks on Joan's neck occasioned some laughter.'

'I daresay. Did anyone mention Master Spelton?' I asked.

'No, madam. Should they have? He was only a courier from the court, gone from the house before Joan's death.'

'I suppose you all know that I accused Joan of eavesdropping on me and Master Spelton,' I said flaccidly. 'She may have overheard him speaking to me of some confidential matters. Just as I fell ill, I was wondering if that was relevant

somehow but . . .' I had had time to think and doubt had
grown. Whatever Joan had heard Spelton say, I couldn't
connect it with the count. It was all a muddle. 'I think my
idea was wrong,' I said. 'And Spelton wouldn't have liked his
business to be mentioned in public. I am glad it didn't arise
at the hearing.'

Joan was buried the next day. I felt better by then, and managed
to be present, riding slowly to the church with Brockley watch-
fully beside me, and leaning on Sybil's arm during the service.

On the following day, a Thursday, the count once more
requested my answer to his proposal. Unable to see any way
out, I told him (though getting the words out nearly strangled
me and sent a menacing bolt of pain through my left eyebrow)
that I had accepted his suit. He bowed, expressing pleasure,
but so formally that I wondered whether he was any more
enthusiastic about the prospect than I was. We exchanged a
kiss. That too was formal.

'So when is the wedding to be?' Sybil asked me that evening.
Everyone else had retired but shaky though I still was, I had
asked Sybil and the Brockleys to join me round the fire in the
little parlour to talk for a while before bed. My betrothal had
given me no joy. I felt very lonely and longed for the comfort
of good and trusted friends. I hadn't wanted to talk about the
wedding, but it was on their minds as much as it was on mine.

'Saturday week,' I said. 'I told Count Renard that I needed
to regain my strength properly. I would have waited longer,
out of respect for Ben Flood, but the count thinks the death
of a mere servant doesn't warrant any more delay.' I added,
rather grimly, 'The count brought a licence with him.'

'That man,' said Brockley, 'is heartless and presumes too
much. I am sorry to speak out of turn, madam. But I wish
you would not do this. Why can't you just say no? I say this
man has no heart and *your* heart surely isn't in it.'

'I am marrying for policy,' I said. 'The queen's policy.
Hearts are irrelevant.'

'It may be all right,' said Sybil. 'He spoke very well at the
inquest. He made a good impression on the jury and on Dr
Fletcher.'

'He was persuasive, right enough,' said Brockley. 'But he

is also the brother of a foreign king and the jury was afraid
of him. I could tell. He tried to talk us out of holding the
inquest at all, you know!'

'He only asked us whether it was really necessary,' said
Sybil moderately. 'He didn't really protest much, just seemed
surprised that so much to-do should follow an unlucky accident
to a servant. Ambrosia protested more than he did! She said
it would be so embarrassing for him, poor man, if there were
any suggestion that he had anything to do with Joan's death.'

'He has enough sense to know that if he objected too much,
that would look suspicious in itself,' retorted Brockley.

'We did right to hold the inquest,' I said. 'Gossip assuredly
would have got round. Too many people knew Joan had been
caught listening at the count's door the day before she died.
That kind of talk would be embarrassing, all right.'

Brockley shrugged. 'It came out that the count and Lestrange
and Father Ignatius were all seen out in the garden at the time
the accident happened. Everyone's content with the verdict,
except Gladys, of course, but we all know how awkward and
opinionated *she* is!'

'And you agree with her!' said Sybil.

'Let us say, I have doubts,' said Brockley sombrely.

I was holding my peace about them, but so had I. Years
ago, when gossip had been rife concerning the queen's relationship with Dudley, his wife had died by falling down a
flight of stairs and the scandal had rocked the nation. The
inquest then had brought in a verdict of accident. I was one
of the few people who knew that the verdict was wrong.
Perhaps that was why I now, unwillingly, shared Brockley's
uncertainties. I said: 'Pushing someone down a staircase isn't
a very sensible way to go about killing them. It's too chancy.
Joan might have landed at the bottom with nothing more than
a few bruises!'

'Bah!' said Brockley inelegantly. 'What about the bruises she
did have? They're why I'm wondering now. Once when I was
in France, on campaign with King Henry, I had to kill an enemy
sentry. I broke his neck by putting an arm round his throat – it's
not difficult if one is strong enough. As I did it, my fingers dug
into him just where those marks were on Joan's neck.'

'Did you say that at the inquest? You haven't mentioned it before!' I said sharply.

'No,' said Brockley. 'I wish I had but I've only just remembered it. It was so long ago. But I tell you this, the count has surely had martial training. Probably Lestrange has, too. They would know how to grab her and break her neck for her and *then* thrust her down the stairs. There'd be nothing uncertain about that.'

'Dear God!' said Sybil and Dale, both together. I stared into the fire, questioning myself. Was I really preparing to marry the man who might – just might – have been responsible for the death of Joan?

Yes, I was. For Elizabeth's sake and for the safety of the realm. The inquest verdict was perfectly reasonable and might well be the truth. I could not back out now because of my suspicions. They were so shadowy. Little bruises, Brockley's wartime memories of killing a sentry . . . And Count Renard was half-brother to the King of France! To accuse him now would start a monstrous scandal. Joan was at peace for ever in Hawkswood churchyard and there I must let her rest.

It was too late to do anything else. I had not enough strength to face trying and I assuredly did have much on my mind. Such as my wedding.

EIGHT
Wedding Morning

I went towards my wedding with feet that dragged. I settled with Gilbert, whose Christian name I was now dutifully using, that it should take place in Hawkswood village church. I found that my bridegroom had no wish for any kind of state affair, and when I had sent word to Cecil and Walsingham to tell them that the nuptials were to go ahead, but that we wished for a quiet ceremony, they replied that this was in accordance with the queen's wishes, too.

After all, their joint letter pointed out, this was not a union of heads of state, or even – please would I forgive them for saying this – even of their official relatives. If it took place quietly, its significance to the two royal houses concerned would not be diminished but the delicacies of protocol would be preserved. There would be a proclamation about it, naturally, after it had taken place, and once Dr Fletcher had informed the court that this had happened, the treaty that the marriage was to strengthen would be signed.

So we would wed in Hawkswood. Brockley would give me away and Dr Fletcher would marry us. It would of course be a Protestant ceremony but Gilbert said he did not mind. It would ensure that our union was lawful in England, and after all, we could have a Catholic ceremony once we reached his chateau in France. I in turn accepted that.

Time seemed to speed up, as the days no doubt do for those facing execution. Meanwhile, I did my best to create the right atmosphere. I walked and rode and talked with Gilbert, determined to get to know him and encourage myself into affection for this man in whose company I had agreed to spend my life. Oddly enough, I had a feeling that he was doing much the same thing. He told me of his first marriage and his grief at the death of his wife. 'It was a fever that would not abate

whatever the physicians could do.' He held out his right hand, where the great square-cut ruby flashed. 'This was her wedding gift to me. I used to wear it on my left hand but I changed it to the right when I decided that I would marry again. One can't mourn for ever. All the same, will you mind if I go on wearing it?'

I assured him that I would not, and said that I too would like still to wear Hugh's wedding ring – on my right hand. Gilbert went on to tell me more of his home in France, of the amusements that it would provide for me and the interesting guests we would entertain there, and he reiterated the promise that we would spend a few months of each year in England, visiting Hawkswood and Withysham and perhaps the court.

'I understand that you are attached to your houses and I would not deny them to you. I love my home, too. It was a terrible grief to me when I was exiled and cast out of it. And since you are sister to the queen, it is natural that you should attend on her now and then.'

In response, I told him of my past, the tasks I had undertaken for the queen and Cecil; my three marriages; even my one affair, which I had been forced into. I think I had a slight hope that hearing of that would discourage my suitor, but it didn't. He had apparently been told about most of my past before he started out for Hawkswood. He accepted it without any sign of disapproval.

An uncertain friendship did burgeon between us, but there was no real warmth in it. We exchanged kisses sometimes but there was no passion in them and he never attempted to go further. Knowing that he was well-read and liked poetry, I sometimes talked to him about that and such conversations were interesting, but he often discussed literature with Ambrosia as well, usually over dinner, and I noticed that he seemed to enjoy that more than he enjoyed such discussions with me. I knew I should mind but I didn't. Indeed, I was grateful that the count had agreed that Sybil and Ambrosia could both come to France as my attendants. Unlike Captain Yarrow, Gilbert was quite happy to leave my choice of companions to me and didn't even cavil at the prospect of Gladys.

I paid attention, of course, to choosing a gown to be married in. Dale and Sybil helped me and we spent much time over it, yet the merriment and deep interest which should accompany such a task was lacking. It was a duty, nothing more.

On the wedding eve I arranged a feast but unlike the dinner which graced Renard's arrival, it was not a success. Even Hawthorn's cooking was flawed: the soup lukewarm, the roast overdone and the conversation stiff. I retired early. The deep pink dress with silver trimmings that I had finally chosen for the morrow had been hung on the handle of the clothes press. I lay in bed for a long time looking at it by the light of my candles. Then I snuffed them and tried to sleep, and for hours could not. It was nearly dawn when I finally fell into a heavy doze, and half-light when I woke again, to see grey skies beyond my window and to feel a matching greyness in my mind.

And then I knew.

I couldn't do it.

My reasons paraded themselves relentlessly round inside my head. I had been so sure that Joan, because she had eaves-dropped on the count, must also have been the one who did the same thing to Master Spelton and me. Yet, recalling her denials now, they had the ring of truth. I still didn't believe that anyone else in my household would have done such a thing, but *someone* had; I was sure of it. I *had* heard sounds like someone pressing against the door. Not brushing it in passing, but pressing close to it. So who else was there?

Count Renard and his companions, that was who. However improbable it might seem, I really had had two eavesdroppers under my roof. And Joan had said she had seen Lestrange coming out of my room. *He* said he had just opened the door and looked in. That wasn't the same thing. Whatever had induced Joan to put her ear to the count's door had surely been something more than just seeing Lestrange open a door and look inside. She said she had seen him coming *out* of my room. And next day, she had fallen down a straight flight of unpolished stairs and broken her neck.

It made a pattern, a chain of events. A shaky chain, a thin chain, but a chain. Gladys had been right. She had glimpsed it and so had I.

And in any case . . .

Even if he were utterly innocent of Joan's death, I still did not want to marry Gilbert Renard. I didn't like him enough. I didn't like him at all! He had no attraction for me, physical or otherwise. I didn't want him. I didn't want him in my bed, my life, my world. I certainly didn't want him inside *me*. I could not, *not*, walk to an altar on Brockley's arm and say *I will* to Gilbert. The vicious curb that Brockley had shown me still haunted my imagination, as did the count's heavy-handedness with my own horses. I didn't want to be married to a man who treated his horses as he did.

I couldn't, wouldn't, marry Count Renard, not even for Elizabeth, not even for England. The queen must find another substitute. If Hugh had lived, she would have had to, anyway. I was her sister, yes. I was her subject, yes. But I was not her slave. I remembered Billington saying so, standing there among the trees of Hugh's woodland and looking at me with those steady blue eyes. Even Robert Dudley, Earl of Leicester had said it. He had himself defied the queen's orders about marriage – and survived it. Even Cecil had wanted me to understand fully what I was doing. Cecil surely had doubts too.

I sat up, feeling my sleepless hours like a weight between my eyes. In decency, I must tell Gilbert first, and do so at once. I had slept with my bed curtains partly open, as I usually did. Now, I pushed them wider, thrust my feet out of the bed and opened my mouth to call for Dale to help me rise, but before I had uttered a word, Dale herself came into the room, accompanied by Sybil. Sybil was crying. Dale on the other hand looked like a cat licking stolen cream off its whiskers. I stared at them in astonishment.

Dale said: 'Ma'am, there can be no wedding today. I'm so sorry.' She didn't sound sorry. 'Your bridegroom has . . .' and now she did hesitate, evidently feeling that she had been too bald-spoken. But she drew a fresh breath and continued, almost in a gabble. 'Your bridegroom has run away.'

'In the night,' said Sybil tearfully. 'And not alone! Ambrosia has gone with him! They left letters! On the big table in the hall. One for me, from Ambrosia; one for you, from the count. Ambrosia's says that she is sorry to grieve me, her mother,

but she and Gilbert – *Gilbert*! So familiar! – want to be together.
She says he has promised to get her sons back for her. For
the meantime, they are going to France and Father Ignatius
will marry them when they reach his chateau of the birds,
because Count Renard wants to share the celebration with his
tenants.'

She paused, overcome by her tears. But she shook them off
and looked at me wretchedly. 'You hardly knew her, Ursula,'
she said. Only in moments of stress did Sybil use my Christian
name, but this was one of those moments. 'You only saw her
when you met her at the pie shop in Cambridge, and then she
was distracted and being bullied by her father. But there are
two sides to her. One is kind and practical: a good girl, helping
in the pie shop; a girl who made a good wife and a loving
mother. She cares so much for her sons! But also, there's this
other side, a romantic side . . . as a young maid, she was in
love with love, wanting to be in love, to be carried away by
it. I think that because marrying John was a convenient thing
to do and everyone approved, she persuaded herself that he
was her shining knight, though he was really a rather dull
man. And now this! She thinks she's in love but I think she
just wants to be, and he can offer her such a glamorous life
. . . I . . . Can you understand? And forgive her?'

Forgive her! Except that Ambrosia had hurt my much-loved
Sybil, I could have fallen at her feet in gratitude, had she been
there to receive gestures of thanks.

I gave Sybil the assurance she wanted, while my mind
absorbed the wonderful change to my world. The sky was still
grey but for me, the sun was shining. There would be no
wedding and I would not be the one to call it off. Brockley
appeared, a paper in his hand. 'Madam, has the news been
broken to you? Yes, I see that it has. Here is the note Count
Renard left for you. You left it behind, Mistress Jester.'

'I meant to bring it but I forgot. Reading Ambrosia's letter
overset me!' Sybil was still tearful.

'No matter.' Brockley handed the count's note to me.

It was a brief letter, in educated French: I could hear Gilbert's
voice in my head as I read it. He was sorry to leave me in
such a fashion, but he had fallen in love with Ambrosia and

she with him and sometimes these things happened. Perhaps
it was as well, for now that he had learned to know me better,
he did not think we would ever be truly happy together. The
difference in our religions troubled him. He had never been
truly at ease with the idea of being married by the Anglican
rite. He did not wish to persecute Protestants but he could
never become one himself. He wished me well with all his
heart and begged me to wish the same for himself and
Ambrosia. He intended to marry her honourably, in his own
home, and would leave her untouched until their union was
made lawful. He would take care of her and do all he could
to reunite her with her children. Please would I and her mother
believe him. And so, my dear Mistress Stannard, farewell.

I folded the missive up and said: 'Have they all gone – the
grooms, Pierre Lestrange, Father Ignatius? Their horses?
Ambrosia's pony?'

'Yes,' said Brockley shortly. 'And how they got them out
without being heard, I can hardly imagine. Simon and Netta
have the room above the stable block where their horses and
mules were kept.'

'They probably wrapped the animals' hooves in sacking,' I
said. 'There are plenty of old sacks in that block – they're
piled in that empty end stall. Anyway, Simon and Netta these
days are either up in the night looking after their baby, or else
fast asleep. Netta says they wake when the baby cries, but
otherwise the broken nights make them sleep like the dead.'

This theory was confirmed very soon, when Dale had got
me dressed and we had all adjourned to the great hall because
after all life must go on and everyone needed breakfast, all
the more because of the upheaval. Arthur Watts came to say
that a pile of cut-up pieces of sacking had been found a short
way along the track leading to our gatehouse. Gilbert and his
companions had silenced their mounts' hooves and made their
getaway unheard in the depths of the night. They were heaven
alone knew how far away by now.

'We must go after them!' Sybil was distraught. 'We must
get Ambrosia back!'

'She may not agree to come,' I said. 'She is a widow, not
a young girl, and she can dispose of herself as she wishes.'

'He may cheat her! Who is to say he will really marry her? And besides, she will have to live as a Catholic!'

'So would I have done,' I said tiredly. 'Though as the count does sympathize with the rights of Protestants, to the point that he got himself thrown into exile for it, I probably wouldn't have been obliged to do more than attend Mass now and then. Neither will Ambrosia. And Sybil, I for one am thankful that the count has gone. I don't want to see him again.'

'Nor any of us. Good riddance, I say,' said Gladys, expressing, as so often, the opinion that others were too polite to put so roundly.

'You mean we are *not* to pursue them? Oh no, I can't believe this of you! I can't believe you would deny me! Why can't we give chase?' cried Sybil, and burst into wild weeping, there in the great hall, just as Adam Wilder was putting out fresh bread and cold lamb chops on the sideboard.

'Sybil, don't,' I pleaded. 'Let me *think*! And let us all eat.'

Over the meal, at which Sybil just picked miserably, I pointed out that even if we did give chase, and caught the count and his party up, we could do nothing to force Ambrosia – or any of them – to come back to Hawkswood. No crime had been committed, at least not as far as we knew. 'What about Joan Flood?' Sybil screamed, and was echoed by Ben Flood, who was in the hall as well, helping Adam.

'The inquest verdict was accidental death,' I said. 'Would I have agreed to marry the count if there were any lingering doubts?'

Brockley gave me a shrewd look but held his peace, whereupon Gladys helpfully expressed his thoughts for him. 'To please the queen, you might, indeed you might. Reckon you did.'

I glowered at her. 'Hold your tongue, Gladys!'

But she had spoken the truth, of course and every single person in my house probably knew it as well. We finished the meal in a difficult silence. At the end, I told Wilder to send Phoebe and Margery upstairs to clear out the abandoned guest rooms, and told Netta to see if the count's two grooms, who had been in a stable loft next to the one where she and Simon slept, had left anything behind. I then retired to the little parlour, to be alone, and savour the fact that I was not going to be married to Gilbert Renard or anyone else, today or ever, if I could help it.

Before withdrawing, I told the household, including Sybil, that I was not to be disturbed unless the house actually caught fire. She went away still weeping and I felt guilty but I still wanted, thirsted for, a little solitude. I would comfort her presently, I told myself. I would go up to the nursery later, and collect Harry and Tessie for a walk in the grounds. Sybil might come with us; it would help to calm her and put things in perspective for her. But just for a little while, I must have stillness. I must have peace.

I had it for just ten minutes, before Phoebe was in the room. She had a dustpan in her hand and Margery was behind her, peering excitedly over her shoulder.

'Phoebe,' I said. 'I told everyone that I wanted to be let alone for a while. What are you . . .?'

'Madam,' said Phoebe, deferentially but firmly, 'I think you should see this.'

NINE
Giving Chase

'This' turned out to be a sheet of crumpled paper, slightly singed. Phoebe slid it carefully from the dustpan on to the small table in the middle of the room, adding as she did so, that it might come to pieces if handled roughly.

'It was at the back of the French gentleman's fireplace, when I brushed the ash out. Likely he tossed it in when the fire was low, and it went over to the back and didn't all get burnt. I can't make out much of it but – well, I still thought you ought to see, madam. I think it's to do with Master Spelton, that stayed here one night, and then there's a word . . . I think it says Huguenots . . .'

'Thank you, Phoebe.' I went to the table and stood resting my fists on it while I read without touching the paper.

It seemed to be rough notes of something. The paper had been scorched at the top, but the first line began with *Chris*. Then came a lost portion, and then, further to the right, were the letters *elton*. That meant Christopher Spelton, surely. Phoebe, who was literate, had seen it at once. Below, a number of words had been lost where sparks had burnt the paper, but enough was legible to be interesting.

It was in French. The first line began with *Preten*. After a few burnt letters came *besog* and then something that definitely translated as *two royal houses*.

The second line began with what was surely *Confidentiel*, though a few letters were missing. Then came *encourage*, followed by a further burnt hole and then came *Huguen . . . symp*.

I stared at them. Could *Preten* be the first part of *pretendu*, meaning pretended or alleged? What about *besog*? Didn't *besogne* mean something like *task*? *Alleged task . . . Ostensible mission*? As for the next line . . . *encourage* . . . that was virtually the same in both tongues. Yes, Phoebe was right; it was surely to do with encouraging Huguenot sympathizers, which was one of Spelton's purposes in France. I stared and stared and the missing words seemed to appear within my brain, bridging the gaps.

Ostensible mission is to encourage friendship between two royal houses

Secret mission, to encourage Huguenots and their sympathizers.

These notes, in fact, reflected precisely what Spelton had told me in what should have been complete confidence – except that I had reason to believe that somebody had listened at the door.

And I didn't now believe it was Joan. The whole odious pattern shook itself and took on a new shape in my head. Joan had not been the eavesdropper when Spelton talked to me. She had said she thought it was Lestrange and that made sense. But she *had* eavesdropped on Gilbert Renard and she had made out something, although I wouldn't let her tell me what it was. My quarrel with her had been conducted in shouts and, indeed, was known to everyone in the house. If I had wanted to inform Gilbert that Joan had been eavesdropping on a private conversation of his, I could hardly have organized things better. And if Joan had been listening to a conversation about the things that Christopher Spelton had said to me, might that have put her in danger? It was plain enough now that Gilbert knew about Spelton's missions in France.

He had no business to know about them and couldn't have done so unless either he or Lestrange had had an ear to the door when Christopher was talking to me. He knew Spelton already and could well have known that he was an agent and wondered what had brought him here. And tried to find out.

And I, by losing my temper and shouting at Joan, had obligingly told him that he too had been spied upon.

And now, Joan was dead.

Ben had not been harmed, but I had ordered Joan not to repeat, even to him, anything that she had heard, and my angry voice had probably told Gilbert that too. Besides, if he wished to get away with her murder, he would stand a better chance if he didn't strew the landscape with multiple bodies.

Gilbert and his companions were said to have been in the garden at the crucial time but what of it? Any of them – even the elderly and cheerful Father Ignatius – could have slipped briefly back into the house by one of the rear entrances. Lestrange was the most likely. The count would probably prefer to give orders rather than carry out such tasks himself and Father Ignatius, because of his calling and his age, seemed an improbable candidate.

I found myself working it out. Had Lestrange been waiting his chance? Drifting in and out of the house? Caught her alone and persuaded her somehow to go to the upper floor on some errand, and then seized his opportunity when she was about to come down?

Yes. It was clarifying now. It was quite possible that Gilbert's property had only been restored to him on condition that he did some spying on behalf of the French royal family. Especially on behalf of the queen mother, I thought. She had a devious reputation. When the deputation came to me at Withysham, to propose the marriage, they had mentioned the danger that an unknown spy at court posed to England. It now seemed, ironically, that Gilbert Renard might be that spy.

Gilbert had been oh, so willing, to say that when we were married, we would spend a good deal of time in England. And might visit the court.

I looked round at Phoebe and at the excited Margery. 'I want everyone in the great hall, the entire household, as soon as possible,' I said. 'Go and tell Adam Wilder. The grooms are to be there as well – Netta can tell Simon and get him to bring the others. Quickly, now!'

When I had them all assembled, I told them briefly what I believed I had discovered.

'As you must all realize, there will be no marriage today,' I declared. 'Count Renard ran off in the night, taking all his own people with him and also my guest Mistress Ambrosia Wilde, and not only that. We have found some notes in the count's room – he had meant to burn them but probably it was at the last minute, with the fire burning low, and they didn't catch alight properly. The count and his companions are bound for France and it seems that he has been spying for

France, and is taking with him information which the French should certainly not have. It will put an honest man, a servant of her majesty, in grave danger.'

I paused, suddenly overcome by alarm, not for myself but for Spelton. I remembered his trustworthy air and his pleasant brown eyes. I remembered too, the feeling I had had that here was a friend. If harm came to him because of treachery in my house, I would feel responsible for evermore. I also reminded myself that I must be careful what I said. No one else must guess at the nature of Spelton's purpose in France. One never knew.

I resumed. 'Poor Joan Flood, we know, listened at the count's door and he and whoever he was talking to would have heard me accost her, heard us quarrelling. I forbade her, loudly, to tell me what if anything, she had learned, but if it was very secret, he may have feared that she might still do so. It looks as though poor Joan may have died, if not at Count Renard's hands, then on his orders . . .'

'I knew it, I knew it! That count killed my Joan or told that man of his, that Lestrange, to kill her and when I get my hands on them . . .!' Ben shouted, shaking his fists in the air, and was then overtaken by Sybil crying out that we had *got* to get Ambrosia back; she had to be rescued from the hands of a murderer, 'She must, must, *must!*'

'We certainly have to give chase,' I said, when I had managed to wave them both to silence. 'Tell me, do any of you have the least idea of the direction they could be taking? From here, there are a good many possible routes. The count may choose not to make for Dover or any of the Thames' ports, simply because they might well be his likeliest choice and pursuers would know that.'

They all looked puzzled. I said: 'Did any of you ever hear, from him or any of his party, including his grooms, anything that might give us a clue? Did you ever hear mention of, say, friends living in such and such a place between here and Dover or London or the south coast? Or any reference at all to the Thames, or the name of any port? Anything that might help us decide which way to go?'

I waited for a moment but most of them just looked

bewildered. A few whispered to each other, but all the whispers seemed to be accompanied by shaking heads.

'Please,' I said, 'think hard and speak up at once if anything occurs to you. We have to set out quickly. The count has had many hours' start. I shall go, and Mistress Jester, and we shall take the Brockleys with us, and Joseph . . .'

'And me!' Ben Flood burst out. 'You can't leave me behind! If they Frenchies killed my Joan, then I want to get at them!'

'You can't ride, Ben,' I said. I looked at him gravely. 'I'm sorry,' I said, 'but even if you could, you had better not come with us. If we catch up with them I don't want you attacking anyone physically and I suspect that you might. We want to retrieve Mistress Wilde and stop the count and Lestrange from leaving England. They must not get away to France.'

'But if it was them hurt my Joan . . .!'

'*No*, Ben! That's enough! I'm sorry but I mean it.' Ben subsided, with tears in his eyes. 'Joseph, you and Arthur can help by saddling horses in readiness. We'll carry essentials in saddlebags; we won't need pack animals, they'd only slow us up. Go out to the stable now – that is, if you have nothing to tell me. Did the count's grooms never say anything useful?'

'They never said much at all,' Arthur Watts informed me. 'Surly pair, they were. Efficient in their way, but not as patient with their horses as I like a groom to be. I wouldn't have had either of them in my stables.'

'I agree with that,' said Brockley.

'Most of you should stay here and talk for a while,' I said. 'Something may occur to one of you. Hush, Ben. Try to be calm. I shall be in the little parlour for a short time, alone – in case for some reason one of you wants to see me privately. Some of you must start the preparations to leave, though, as well as Arthur and Joseph. Dale, go upstairs and pack, for me and you and Brockley. You know what to take for a hurried journey. Sybil, you must pack too. Simon, fetch the saddlebags up to them, if you please.'

I left them. I had taken them by surprise and if they had time to think and remember, something useful might emerge. Time was not something we could afford to waste and the sooner we were on the road, the better, but although sitting there in the little parlour with folded hands felt like wasting it, it was not. If we could possibly establish the right direction for our pursuit, it would be worth a short wait.

So I sat solitary, looking out at the garden without seeing it, going over in my head the final things I must do before leaving, instructions I must give to Adam Wilder about the household, and to Tessie about the care of little Harry, and of course I must say farewell to Harry, who must be reassured because he always cried if I went away. I did not expect anyone to come to me, but I hoped for it just the same. And then came a tap on the door and in answer to my call to come in, Ben Flood appeared.

His eyes were still wet and he was as white as a corpse or a ghost, even including his bald head. He closed the door behind him and came forward nervously, an incongruous figure in his stained leather apron and hose and his patched working shirt. Joan must have done those patches, I thought distractedly. Who would do them now? I said: 'Ben? Have you something to tell me? If you want me to change my mind, I have to say that I can't. You *can't* ride, and we shall have to ride fast and that alone would be enough. I am truly sorry but . . .'

'No, Mistress Stannard.' He stood uneasily before me, his brown eyes resembling those of an embarrassed spaniel. 'I know I couldn't manage on a horse. I knew it all the time, really, only . . . but, Mistress, there's something else I know. I couldn't speak up among all those others; they'd be angry, and besides, I'd promised Master Lestrange to hold my tongue, only now it seems that maybe he killed her and well, I don't think I need keep my word now, and besides, there's Mistress Wilde gone off as well, very likely with the man who gave Lestrange his orders . . .'

He stopped for breath. 'Gently, Ben,' I said. 'Just tell me, what do you know? Is it to do with the direction the count and his people have taken?'

'It was something that that man Lestrange, asked me. It was before Joan . . . died . . .' He choked but then went on. 'He came to me when I was alone, out in the garden, looking to see how the herbs were coming up. Master Hawthorn, he likes fresh herbs, he don't like using the dried ones as he has to in winter . . .'

'Don't ramble, Ben. Get on with it. I can see that you're still troubled about breaking some promise or other but I think you've got to. What did Master Lestrange say to you?'

'He said I was a good Catholic. I'd been to two Masses said by Father Ignatius, you see. He said he thought he could trust me not to repeat this talk we were having, but he'd soon have a confidential errand for his master and he wanted to know if I knew of any Catholic houses near London – places he'd naturally come to if he set out from here by the straightest way, and where he might be welcome to stay while he made further travel arrangements. A private house, not an inn where anyone enquiring after him might be told he'd been there. He said he and the count didn't know enough about English houses. The errand had nothing wrong about it, he told me, but it was secret, though he could say that it was to do with something that would benefit Catholics, and that anything done to uphold the faith couldn't be wrong. I believe that too, Mistress Stannard . . .'

His voice trailed away, probably because of my expression. 'Ben,' I said, 'we're about the same age, so you must remember, as I do, the things that happened when the queen's Catholic sister Queen Mary was on the throne. The people who were so horribly executed because they didn't share her faith and wouldn't lie about it! She did that to uphold her religion, let me remind you. And it was wrong.'

'But she did it to save the souls of heretics, madam! I have often worried about your soul, Mistress Stannard, and Master Stannard's soul too, wondering what fate will befall you both after you die . . .'

'If what you believe is true then God is a monster and not worth worshipping. Now . . .'

'Madam!' Ben was scandalized.

I swallowed my exasperation. There were more important and practical matters to deal with just now and I had no time for theological debates. 'Never mind all that, Ben. What did you say to Lestrange? I take it you told him of a place where he might find hospitality, close to London? What house and precisely where is it?'

'Just outside London, madam. It's called Stag-Leys because there are deer around there – not that there's a deer park or anything like that; the place is a smallholding; they raise pigs and vegetables or did when we knew it. The Sterling family live there – Joan and I once worked for them. They are good honest Catholics though law-abiding. They go to Anglican services at times, to keep out of trouble, but one of their servants is a priest and he says Mass for them now and then. He doesn't seek converts, mistress, I know he doesn't. It's not against the law to say Mass, only to try to convert people, and the Sterlings keep the law. Oh, dear heaven, now I've said too much; I'm in such a state, I can't think properly. If that Lestrange creature or that count hurt my Joan . . . Mistress Stannard, you won't . . .?'

Ben's face and voice looked desperate. I filled in the gap for him. 'Sometimes the authorities assume that anyone who is a priest and says Mass *must* also be looking for converts. Yes, I know. But I shan't pretend to be a Catholic, so the household will be careful what they say to me, and I won't ask awkward questions. Their priest is in no more danger from me than Father Ignatius was. Go on.'

In a shaking voice, Ben said: 'I told Lestrange that he could probably stay with the Sterlings if he needed somewhere. I suppose he was asking for his master and all the others, really.'

'I wouldn't think so. I doubt if the count was already planning to elope with Mistress Wilde even before Joan's death. But they could now be using your advice to Lestrange, and if so, they mean to take a ship from a Thames port. Thank you, Ben. By the way' – a thought had occurred to me – 'did you mention your talk with Lestrange to Joan?'

'Yes, madam. She is . . . was . . . my wife, after all. I trusted her.'

Perhaps that was another reason why Joan had taken to listening at doors. That, as well as seeing Lestrange come out of my room, had made her so suspicious that she tried to learn more about Lestrange's secret errand. She had perhaps thought that Lestrange had searched my room for anything that a spy might find useful. Correspondence with Cecil, for instance. He wouldn't have found anything, for my private papers were locked up in a deed box which in turn was locked in a cupboard in the study. But Joan had recognized the danger signs and tried to act on them, out of loyalty to me. If only she had come to me first! As it was, I had stopped her mouth when I should have let her speak. And now . . .

Ashamed, I spoke very gently as I asked him: 'Did Joan tell you anything of what she heard when she tried to eavesdrop on the count and whoever was with him – Lestrange or Father Ignatius, I expect?' I asked. 'I told her not to, but did she?'

'Yes, she did!' Probably emboldened by my soft tone, Ben said, quite aggressively: 'We were man and wife! We didn't have secrets. She didn't hear much because they talked French together – the count and Lestrange – but she did hear the count mention Spelton and then laugh and she didn't like the sound of that. She didn't like the laugh, if you understand me. Mistress Stannard . . .' Once more, he stopped for breath.

'You and Joan thought that the count might wish ill to Master Spelton?'

'Yes, Mistress Stannard.'

'I agree.' Guilt made me feel sick. Joan had tried to warn me, I wouldn't listen and by now Spelton was presumably in France, all unaware of the danger on his heels. But I knew I must now resume a tone of authority. 'Ben, you are not to speak of this to anyone. I mean it. There's to be no chatting to your fellow servants about anything we have said in this room. Do you understand?'

He nodded. 'Yes, madam.'

'Good.' I then realized that he wanted to say something more. His eyes were frightened. 'What is it, Ben?'

'I . . . do I just go back to my work, madam? I mean . . .'

'Am I going to turn you off? No, Ben. You've just buried your wife. I wouldn't be so cruel. But in future, please remember that you are employed by me, not by any of my guests, least of all those I never invited in the first place. Joan had more loyalty than you. Go back to the kitchen. I must see to a few last things and then I and those who go with me must be off, and at speed. But before you go, *exactly* where is Stag-Leys? How do we find it?'

TEN

Misdirection

Once we were on our way, my spirits began to rise. They usually did, when I set out on an adventure. It was because of this odd quirk in me that I had for so long worked as a secret agent for the queen and Cecil. I could have stopped. I could at some point have said, 'No, I have had enough, this is the end.' But somehow, whenever I was called upon, I responded. Reluctant and protesting as often as not and yet, the moment I started out, my reluctance always faded.

Even when I was longing for the peace and quiet of my home, I had never simply abandoned my assignment and gone home. I could have made excuses. I would have made myself unpopular with my royal sister and some of her Council, but I would have pleased others. Sir Francis Walsingham didn't approve of employing women on secret missions. But when I was on an assignment, it never occurred to me just to drop it and go home.

A friend of mine had once said that I had something in common with wild geese. I had only to hear the call of adventure, and I would respond like a goose that hears the cry of its kin. There was truth in that.

And whenever I set out on any mission that could be called adventurous, I always wore the open-fronted gowns with the hidden pouches inside, containing extra money, picklocks and a little dagger. I did so this time. Brockley also prepared himself, 'For anything that might happen,' as he put it, having had long experience of adventuring with me. On this occasion, he carried a sword and a few things that he called 'useful oddments', which he put in a shoulder bag because they were too awkward for a saddlebag. They included a tinderbox, four lanterns and a bundle of candles for them.

It occurred to me just after we had set out that in all the
haste and distress I had omitted to send word to Walsingham
or Burghley to tell them what had happened. I should have
done. Indeed, they might have sent help of some kind. I must
see to it as soon as possible.

The weather was cold and dull but it was dry and the roads
weren't bad, for late February. It was a little over twenty miles
to our destination, and we covered it easily enough in five
hours, allowing for halts for refreshment and limitations on
our speed, because although we didn't have any pack animals,
we did have Sybil and Dale.

Neither was much of a horsewoman; in fact, they were both
capable of falling off a horse while it was standing still, but
we were trying to rescue Ambrosia and I could not deny Sybil
the right to come with us. As for Dale, she didn't like Brockley
to go off with me and leave her behind. She knew that we
had once been closer than we should have been. She also knew
that I was not a danger to her, but she was still jealous at heart
and I didn't blame her.

She and Sybil would slow us down a little, but not as much
as they would have done if they were travelling pillion. So I
put Sybil on the reliable Bronze and Dale on Magpie, who
was placid as well as massive, and hoped for the best. I was
riding my beautiful black mare Jewel, while Brockley had his
cob Mealy and I mounted Joseph on the long-legged chestnut,
Redstart.

'You get to Stag-Leys a couple of miles before London
Bridge,' Ben had told me. 'Go past Stag-Leys and you'd soon
come to the George Inn and that ought to be the natural place
to stay for anyone wanting to arrange a passage to France,
only Lestrange insisted that he didn't want an inn where he
might be remembered if anyone enquired after him. It would
be even easier to remember a party! I recommended Stag-Leys.
You can't miss it; the house is right beside the road. It's like
a cottage – a sort of overgrown one.'

He was right. Stag-Leys was easy to recognize; indeed, I
had half-recognized Ben's description. I had seen the place
any number of times on journeys to and from London. It was,
as he had said, an oversized cottage, attached to a smallholding.

We could glimpse vegetable plots and timber outbuildings behind it. Its plastered walls were painted cream and it was thatched, with a small flower garden at one side, where snowdrops and crocuses were out, harbingers of spring. It was a welcoming place. One felt almost embarrassed at the idea of disturbing its charm.

There was a fence along the roadside. We dismounted and tethered the horses to it. Then I said: 'Before we announce ourselves, you should all remember that though Ben Flood says this is a law-abiding household, it is also Catholic. We had better not speak of the information that Count Renard is almost certainly carrying to France. As far as the Sterling family are concerned, he is suspected of murder – we need not go into too many details – and Mistress Wilde, unaware of that, has run off with him and we hope to fetch her back to safety. All right?' Everyone nodded agreement. 'So, in we go,' I said.

We left Joseph to watch over the horses and I led the others through the front gate. We walked up the short path to the front door, a solid oak affair with a shiny brass knocker. I applied the knocker and the door was answered at once, by a slightly dishevelled young woman with a cap that was not quite straight, a somewhat grimy apron, and a duster in one hand. She looked at us enquiringly, out of ingenuous blue eyes.

'Mistress Sterling?' I asked, cautiously, because as we rode, it had occurred to me that if Ben and Joan had left the place some time ago, it might have changed hands. Ben might have sent Lestrange into a hotbed of Protestants by mistake.

However, he had not. 'The mistress be in the kitchen. I do be a maid here,' said the young woman, smiling. She was clearly a country girl, from somewhere much further from London. 'I'll get her for thee. Who do I say wants her?'

'Mistress Stannard,' I said. 'I am actually trying to find a group of people who may have sought shelter here. A Frenchman and his servants.'

The maid shook her head. 'There's been no one like that here. But here's the mistress herself; you'd best ask her.'

She stepped back to make way for a woman who had

emerged from somewhere in the back regions and presumably from the kitchen since a smell of baking bread and frying onions came with her and a waft of warm air, as from a lively cooking fire. She hastened towards us along a passageway, or perhaps surged towards us would describe it better, for she was a large lady. She was even more untidy than her maid-servant, with coppery hair escaping from a cap as hopelessly askew as the maid's, a much-creased brown dress, its sleeves rolled up to the elbow, and an open neck. Despite the chill of the day, her face and her double chins were shiny with sweat. 'What is it, Deborah?'

I saved Deborah the trouble of answering by saying: 'I am Mistress Stannard; I take it that you are Mistress Sterling?' and on receiving a nod, repeated my enquiry, this time adding a couple of names. 'The Frenchman is Count Renard, and he has – he is escorting – a lady, a Mistress Wilde, and he has a manservant called Lestrange, and a chaplain and two grooms.'

'All those folk, putting up here as if we was an inn, and the George not that much further on?' Mistress Sterling threw back her head and uttered a hearty laugh. 'Not that we haven't room, not now that most of my chicks are grown and gone; two sons gone to sea, I have, and three daughters wed, and only the eldest lad still here, since this place'll be his when Stephen's gone . . . no, we've no guests here, only our good selves, and haven't had, since my brother and his family came at Christmas.' But the laughter and the loquaciousness were hiding something. I had seen it flicker in her big pale grey eyes and so had Brockley, for he moved closer to me as he said: 'You are sure, madam? Did such a party of people perhaps seek directions here, even if they didn't stay?'

Mistress Sterling shook her head and at the same moment started to close the door. Just as, behind her, a door on the left opened and Pierre Lestrange stepped into the passage.

He shot one glance towards the open front door and retreated instantly but not soon enough. '*That's* Lestrange!' Brockley barked and without more ado, he sprang forward, thrusting the front door wide open again, and attempted to push past the mistress of the house. She exclaimed angrily and got in his way but Brockley shouted: 'It's a matter of murder, madam;

do you want to be a party to that?' and shoved harder and more successfully. The indignant Mistress Sterling staggered back and Brockley made purposefully for the room into which Lestrange had so hurriedly withdrawn. Sybil and I rushed after him, with Dale on our heels. Sybil was calling Ambrosia's name at the top of her voice.

I expected a response to that, but Ambrosia neither appeared nor called in answer and when we flung open the door on the left we found only Lestrange, standing in the middle of what was clearly a parlour, since its plastered walls were adorned with a couple of pretty hangings and the floor was strewn with fresh rushes, and the place was furnished with cushioned settles and a pair of polished cupboards, and two small tables, one with a vase of snowdrops on it and the other with an unlit lamp and a sewing basket, open. There was a small hearth, laid ready for lighting. Lestrange, standing in an aggressive attitude and grasping a drawn sword, was an incongruous sight.

I had never really taken his appearance in before; I think he cultivated unobtrusiveness. I knew nothing about him beyond the fact that he spoke good English and could play the lute. His voice was as quiet as his footsteps; he was of middle height and had one of those nondescript, forgettable faces. It was less forgettable just now, because he was scowling angrily. He half-raised the sword.

'Put that down!' Brockley snarled. 'Do you want more blood on your hands? Where are the rest of you?'

Lestrange didn't sheathe his weapon. 'What are you talking about? There isn't any rest of us. I'm here on my own. I've an errand to France for my master and it's no business of yours. And what's all this about more blood on my hands?'

'Joan Flood, one of Mistress Stannard's servants,' said Brockley, 'mysteriously fell downstairs – or do you and your master murder people so often that you forget them five minutes later?'

'Murder? What *is* all this?' said Lestrange, and was echoed from the hallway by Mistress Sterling, wildly shrieking: *'Murder! Do you say this man has murdered?'*

'It seems very likely, madam,' said Brockley without turning round. 'We have reason to suspect it. Now then, Lestrange.

Where are the rest of you? Your master, Mistress Wilde, Father
Ignatius . . .'

'I've never heard of them!' cried Mistress Sterling, now
thrusting her bulk through the door behind us. 'This man came
here alone, wanting to stay while he sought a passage to France
or some such thing. Honest Catholic business he said he was
on and that's not against the law, not yet, though that man
Walsingham'll make it so one of these days, I don't doubt.
There's been no talk of murder nor of this French Count
Whatsit . . .'

She ran out of breath. At the same moment, Lestrange raised
his sword and leapt forward, aiming the blade straight for
Brockley's heart though not I think with really lethal intentions, but as a ploy to sweep Brockley out of his way for he
gave Brockley time to sidestep, which Brockley duly did, very
neatly, towards the table with the lamp and the open sewing
basket. Inside the basket were colourful silks wound on
bobbins, a needle case and a small pair of shears. Brockley
had had no chance to draw his own blade but he grabbed the
shears and struck like an adder at Lestrange's sword hand.
Lestrange let out a yell and dropped the sword, whereupon I
stooped and caught it up. It was astoundingly heavy and I
only just managed not to drop it again as I backed quickly to
the door and out into the passage.

Deborah, Sybil and Dale were standing there, mouths open
in either horror or excitement or conceivably both, for in the
parlour, mayhem had now broken loose. Lestrange, scattering
blood from his injured hand, had closed with Brockley, while
Mistress Sterling, screaming imprecations, seemed to be trying
to pummel both of them. The tables had been overturned and
the rushes underfoot were littered and tangled with crushed
snowdrops and the shards of what had been an earthenware
lamp and the flower vase and also the sewing basket and its
contents. The basket had been kicked in the melee and now
lay upside down in a corner.

I stood there staring and then, to my alarm, saw that Brockley
was getting the worst of it, because although he had been a
soldier and knew something about fighting, he was years older
than Lestrange, who was also the more powerfully built of the

two. In his manservant's black doublet and hose, moving about in his unobtrusive fashion, his muscular development hadn't been noticeable but it was all too obvious now. Despite his injury, Lestrange had got hold of Brockley round the chest and was crushing the breath out of him, undeterred by Mistress Sterling's fists pounding on his back.

I rushed forward again, clutching the sword with both hands and started to whack whatever bits of Lestrange I could reach with the flat of it. It was useless. 'Stop it!' I shrieked. 'Stop it, stop it, *let Brockley go . . .!*'

I sounded like a petulant child and for all the effect I was having, I might as well have been one. But in the passage, Sybil, Dale and Deborah were all shouting for help and help was coming. A man's voice suddenly bellowed: *'What in the name of heaven is going on here?'* and I heard Dale cry out something in reply and then two men burst into the room.

I and my sword were brushed aside as though we were dust motes. I stumbled backwards over one of the fallen tables and fell. Dale and Sybil ran in to help me and by the time they had got me to my feet, bruised and gasping but otherwise unharmed, the adversaries had been dragged apart and were being held respectively by a big middle-aged man and a wiry young one, both in the dun-coloured shirt and hose, the sleeveless jerkin and leather leggings and mud-stained boots of farmers. Mistress Sterling, in tears, had collapsed on to a settle and between sobs was wailing thanks to heaven that Stephen had come.

Stephen had to be her husband; she had mentioned him before. The younger man was presumably their eldest son; indeed, they looked like father and son since they had the same light-coloured hair falling over their foreheads in the same way, and identical grey eyes.

'Are you all wood wild?' Stephen was shouting. 'We could hear you from the other end of the cabbage field! What's going on in here and who are these people – these women and this man? And why is *that* woman' – he jabbed a thumb towards me – 'holding that great big sword? It's as tall as she is!'

'If you will let me speak . . .' gasped Brockley.

'It's all right, Brockley.' I had got my breath back by now.

'I will explain. We are sorry for the disturbance, sir. I am Mistress Stannard, Brockley there is my manservant and these two ladies are his wife Frances, who is my tirewoman, and Mistress Sybil Jester who is my companion. Until last night *that* man, whose name is Pierre Lestrange, was staying at my house in Surrey, with his master, a French count named Gilbert Renard, and a priest called Father Ignatius, and two grooms . . .'

'What *is* all this rigmarole?' Stephen Sterling had a rustic accent but an educated vocabulary. He also had considerable presence. He had brought an air of authority into the room and with it the hope of restoring order.

'They sound quite crazed to me, Father,' his son said angrily, but was waved to silence and into the gap, I said: 'Please let me finish. You can't understand unless you do that. There had been talk of a marriage between the count and myself but mysterious things began to happen including the death of one of my servants, Joan Flood. It looked like an accident but I now have reason to believe that she was murdered and possibly by Lestrange or his master. I don't wish to discuss the reason for our suspicions but believe me, it is real. Last night, the count and all his companions left my home secretly, taking with them another guest of mine, the daughter of Mistress Jester there, a Mistress Ambrosia Wilde. They left letters saying that she, not I, is going to marry the count and . . .'

'I can't let my daughter go off and marry a man who might have done murder, or ordered it!' Sybil broke in.

Lestrange tried to interrupt as well but the son had a hand over his mouth. He flailed unavailingly and sent blood spatters from his damaged hand flying into the young man's face, causing him to swear in disgust. I overrode them both. 'I won't let people who may well have caused the death of my servant Joan Flood get away with it!' I declared, as forcefully as I could. 'We believe that the party are bound for France and will seek passage from a Thames port and may have stopped here on their way.'

Lestrange succeeded in freeing his mouth. 'It's all rubbish! This Joan Flood, she just slipped and fell down a flight of stairs! I am on a lawful errand for my master, as I told you this morning, an errand likely to do good to Catholics every-where. My master and the rest, as far as I know, are still at this woman's house, Hawkswood.'

'They are most certainly not!' I retorted. 'They left in the night, as you did and presumably *with* you – which means they're somewhere here!'

'They're not here, they're not! There's only this man Lestrange!' bawled Mistress Sterling from her settle.

'No, they're not!' said Stephen Sterling, glaring at me. 'They may have left your house, madam, but they didn't come here. You can search this house, but you won't find your missing count or any of the folk you say are with him. Search where you will! They travelled on horseback, I suppose? Well, you're free to search my stable – search every outhouse on my land if you like, and look in my piece of pasture. You won't find them or their horses.'

His wife wailed in protest but he snapped: 'Hold your noise, Margaret!' over his shoulder and she fell silent. He turned back to me. 'I've heard of you, Mistress Stannard, at least I think I have, so I'll pay you the courtesy of supposing that you really think you are tracking down someone who has harmed one of your people. But you won't find anyone here other than this man Lestrange. You've been the victim of misdirection, I think.'

ELEVEN
Asking the Way

S tephen Sterling, very much the master of the house and the man in charge, now gave orders. He called Deborah in, told her to find another maid to help her and get the parlour cleared up and then announced that we would withdraw elsewhere to continue with what he described as *unravelling this muddled tale*. 'And Tom,' he added, addressing his son, 'get a napkin out of that cupboard there and wrap it round this fellow Lestrange's hand; he's smearing blood all over everything.'

When this was done, he led the way out, maintaining his grip on Brockley, while Tom kept hold of Lestrange.

Deborah, pop-eyed with excitement, was shooed away but, with Sybil and Dale, I followed the men along the passage and in at another door, where we found ourselves in a dining room. It was well proportioned and well lit, since it had several leaded casement windows with views over the smallholding and a glimpse of woodland beyond, but it had a dusty, disused look. The family probably ate in the kitchen as a rule. The central table had benches along each side and we all sat down, looking oddly formal, as though we were an official meeting.

The Sterling menfolk each sat beside his captive. Both Lestrange and Brockley were seething but Lestrange now seemed intimidated. Brockley did not, but I didn't want him to disrupt the gathering. It would do no good. I managed to catch his eye and he kept quiet.

'And now,' said Master Sterling grimly, 'I would like to hear this extraordinary story all over again. Mistress Stannard, maybe you'd kindly explain how all this started. How came you to be courted by a French aristocrat? And why would you think he's murdered a servant of yours?'

I obliged, though with a degree of caution. That I was the

queen's sister was not actually a state secret but nor was it freely bruited about. I merely said that I had once been a lady of the queen's household and that friends at court had had the idea that I should remarry, and had arranged for Gilbert Renard to visit me so that we might get to know each other.

'Only, as it happened, Mistress Jester's widowed daughter Ambrosia Wilde was staying at my house just then, and she and Renard took a fancy to each other. And then . . .'

This was difficult. I did not want to talk about Christopher Spelton's secret mission, not under this Catholic roof. Indeed, I had no business to speak of it anywhere. There was something about Sterling that made me inclined to trust him but not with that kind of secret. I hesitated for a long moment, which made Master Sterling scowl alarmingly, and then admitted Spelton's existence but said that he had a private purpose, a duty he had to carry out for her majesty Queen Elizabeth and that although I knew that this was so, because he had told me ('I am trusted in court circles,' I said), I did not know what it was.

But, I explained, I had reason to think that he had been overheard when he was telling me the little he did, and soon after that, I caught my servant Joan Flood attempting to overhear a conversation between Renard and Lestrange.

'There was a great to-do. I was angry with Joan and shouted at her, but she told me that she had seen Lestrange coming out of my room, as if he had been snooping there.'

'I was looking for you, madam! I *told* you that!' Lestrange burst out. 'My master wanted to speak with you and I couldn't find you downstairs, so I tapped on your door and when there was no answer I just ventured to look inside!'

'Did you, indeed?' I said disbelievingly. 'Well, I also know that Joan's husband, who is also in my household, told her of a conversation he had had with you, about places to stay near London for someone bound for France on a mission so private that he didn't want to use an inn. Ben Flood recommended Stag-Leys, which is why we're here now. Then, between one thing and another, Joan took to spying on you and your master and she heard the name of Christopher Spelton spoken. And then she fell downstairs and died.'

'There was an inquest! The verdict was accidental death!' shouted Lestrange.

'Some of us didn't trust that verdict,' snapped Brockley. He and Lestrange glowered at each other.

'Last night,' I said, 'the count and his people *and* Mistress Wilde disappeared in the night. We're afraid that Mistress Wilde has fallen in love, and run off with, a killer and perhaps a spy, interested in whatever Master Spelton was about. We set out in pursuit.'

'I see,' said Sterling, still grimly. 'Nothing certain, all suspicion, but the sort of suspicion we don't want anywhere near us. Who knows what'll come of us when the law starts poking its nose into all this? Catholic we are and proud of it but we keep the law of the land and we don't want trouble.'

'There would be no trouble,' I said. 'We just want to take Lestrange away, and persuade him to tell us the right road for finding the count and his party. He must surely know. Once we've got him away, you can forget him, and us.'

'Of course he knows!' Brockley exploded. 'If they're not here and didn't come with him last night, then I'd wager anything he knows where they *did* go. Isn't that so?' He twisted in his seat and glared at Lestrange. '*Isn't that so?*'

'No!' said Lestrange. 'As far as I know, they were all asleep in bed when I left. I had no notion they were going to leave as well.'

The sheer improbability of this took my breath away for a moment. And everyone else's too, I think, for there was a silence all round. Then I recovered myself.

'But why did you leave in the middle of the night, then, if you were going alone?' I asked. 'You could have left on an errand for your master at any time. Who would question it?'

'I did as I was bid. I left at night because he told me to.'

'Why?' demanded Brockley, and received a wordless shrug in answer.

'This is getting nowhere,' said Sterling.

Margaret Sterling had been fidgeting. Throughout all this, she had apparently retained a grip on reality, and on the duties of a hostess, even a reluctant one. Suddenly she broke in: 'Didn't these people arrive on horses? Where are their horses? Did you leave a groom with them, mistress?'

'Yes, I did.' I dragged my mind back to Joseph, waiting patiently in the road while our horses nibbled the verge. They must all be tired, hungry and thirsty. 'The horses are tethered to your fence and a young groom is with them. Our belongings are there too, in saddlebags. Could they all be looked after? I don't know how long we'll be here.' I shot Lestrange an unfriendly look and then gave Sterling an enquiring one.

'Quite,' he said. 'Tom, Jimmy should be in the stables at this hour. Go and tell him to bring in Mistress Stannard's animals and her man; he'll find them in the road. Tell him to look after them, and to unload the saddlebags and bring them into the passage. I fancy our visitors will be staying the night.' His tone was not precisely hospitable. 'I feel,' he said, 'that we have much to talk about and it's getting near to suppertime already. Tom, when you've seen Jimmy, come back here and be quick about it. We may need you.'

I started to demur about staying and to say something about the George Inn but Sterling waved this away. Tom rose obediently to his feet, but said: 'What d'you need me for?' as he did so.

'I said before – I've heard of Mistress Stannard there. I reckon her tale can be believed. So we may need to get a little more sense out of Master Lestrange.'

Whereupon Master Lestrange swung his feet over the bench he had been sitting on, kicking Tom's thigh on the way, sprang up and lunged for the door. Mistress Sterling and Dale both shrieked, Sybil half-rose, clutching at the table, while Tom and Brockley simultaneously got up and hurled themselves after Lestrange. They wrestled him to the floor just as he was jerking at the door handle.

'Oh no, you don't!' Brockley gasped. 'You know where your master and the rest are now and before God, you'll tell us!'

'I don't know anything – let me go! – you're going to knock me about to make me tell you things I can't tell you because I don't know . . .'

'Oh yes, you do!' Sterling dragged him up. 'Tom, you and Master Brockley bring him back to the bench where he was and hold him a moment. I'll put him under guard.'

Leaving the two of them to drag a swearing and resisting
Lestrange back to the table, Sterling made for the largest casement window, flung it open, leant out and whistled, a penetrating
sound that carried. It was answered by a distant barking, the
deep bark of a big dog. Then, apparently, from nowhere, a tawny
hound appeared at a gallop. Sterling drew back and the hound
leapt through the window and straight into the room, to stand,
tongue lolling, in front of his owner.

Sterling pointed to Lestrange, who had now been forced to
sit on the bench, though this time with his back to the table.
'Guard him, Wolf!!' The dog at once lay down on his front,
facing Lestrange, and it was clear that he was well named,
for he did look remarkably like a wolf. He fixed Lestrange
with a predatory gaze and growled softly.

'All right,' said Master Sterling with an air of relief. 'Tom,
find Jimmy as I said, give him my orders and then come back.'

Tom, rubbing his thigh, gave Lestrange a menacing glance
and departed. I stared at Lestrange's back with dislike and
said: 'Master Sterling, I am sorry to have made you treat a
guest in such a way, but I am also grateful to you for believing
me. It is vital that we find these people. Only . . .'

'I tell you I don't *know* where they are!' Lestrange shouted,
causing Wolf to half-rise, bristling.

'Better sit down. Good teeth, Wolf has,' said Sterling.

'I too regret the position we've placed you in,' said Sybil
miserably, seating herself again. 'But my daughter . . . to think
she may have run off with a murderer . . . I can't bear it!'

'You won't have to,' Brockley assured her. 'Once I get to
work on our friend here, he'll spill everything he knows and
be glad to.' He and Master Sterling exchanged glances and I
realized that the situation had altered. Sterling and Brockley
were now allies, of each other and of myself.

I had been about to say that I didn't want the truth beaten
out of Lestrange; I just wanted him questioned. Now, however,
I thought better of saying so in his hearing. Let him feel
threatened. However, I once more caught Brockley's eye, stared
at him hard and gave him a tiny headshake and a tiny wink.
In response, he half-closed one eye. He had understood. I
relaxed, and observed with relief that Dale hadn't noticed

anything. Brockley and I still had our rapport and it could be very useful but it must be hidden from Dale.

I noticed, though, that the unspoken exchange hadn't escaped Sterling. He in turn looked at me and he too let one eyelid droop. I gave him a smile and a little nod, which Lestrange saw but unlike Brockley did not interpret correctly. He had already gone very pale. Now he began to mumble something. Prayers, by the sound of it.

'I don't believe,' I said, addressing Sterling and Brockley together, 'that the count would have sent him off without telling him where to rejoin the party, and to do that he'd have to know that the others were leaving soon and where they were going. That's obvious.'

'I was to go to his chateau when my task was done, of course! He'd meet me there!' shouted Lestrange.

'So you did know he was planning to leave us,' said Brockley. 'By which route would he travel if he was setting out for France? Surely you know that much!'

'Yes, what's the good of pretending you've no idea which way he'd go?' Dale screeched. 'You think we'll believe that!'

I said: 'I was told he had been back to France twice since he came to live in England, so I suppose he *has* a usual route. Though I realize that this time he may have chosen a different one – to fool pursuit. He didn't confide in you at all, you, his confidential servant, Master Lestrange? Never told you he was taking Mistress Wilde with him to France and never mentioned from which port they meant to sail?'

Sybil burst out: 'He could have made for Dover, or the south coast or even Norwich! He might well take an unusual road, wicked creature as he was, and eloping with my daughter too! We need to know! We *must* know! We must catch up with him before he can marry Ambrosia. Master Lestrange, we can't believe that you can't tell us, so *please* tell us! *Please!*'

'No, I won't! I can't!' Lestrange's voice was shaking, but he was looking all round him as though in search of an escape route and his voice had a desperate undertone that made Wolf get up again, snarling. Trembling, Lestrange said: 'I keep my master's counsel; I'm loyal to him.' He tried to straighten his back. 'I wouldn't tell you even if I knew,' he said hastily.

'Too late,' Brockley told him. 'You've as good as admitted that you do know. Well, we'll soon have it out of you. Ah. Here's Tom.'

'Three to one. We'll go to one of the outhouses,' said Sterling. 'No need to upset the womenfolk.'

'We'll only need to pummel him a bit, or maybe you could set Wolf on him. Or we could heat a poker in a brazier,' Brockley agreed in a bright voice. 'He'll speak in no time.'

The threat sounded all too genuine. I looked at them in alarm but Brockley sketched me another wink and Master Sterling gave me a glint of a smile.

'Let us go,' said Sterling. 'Rest, Wolf!' The dog got up on his haunches, shook his shaggy coat and gazed at his master, tongue lolling. Sterling started to drag Lestrange to his feet. And Lestrange disintegrated.

It was horrible to watch. I saw the sweat spring out on his temples and the violent tremor that overtook his whole body. He struggled against Sterling, gobbling out the word *No!* over and over. Tom went to help his father and between them they hauled him upright and held him there, since his knees were clearly unable to support him. Sterling said: 'Right. That disused tool shed will do. There's an old brazier in there.'

'*No! No!*' Lestrange shrieked. 'I'll tell you!'

TWELVE
Calling for Help

'Whitefields. The count always stops at a house called Whitefields just outside Dover when he arranges passages to Calais. That's what he did when he went back to France to talk to the king about getting his lands restored. He did that twice, like Mistress Stannard says. The Fergusons at Whitefields are friends of his. He met the family years and years ago when he visited England as a young man and travelled about. They were new to England too; they came from Scotland. A pair of grandparents, their married son and his wife, and then the grandchildren, a son and two daughters, grown up now though none of them's wedded yet.'

He paused for breath, looking from one face to another, as though anxious to know whether he was telling us what we wanted to hear. We waited, and he resumed.

'The Fergusons came south because the grandmother was ailing and they thought the Scottish climate was too harsh for her, that south England might be kinder. The place is a small manor with a home farm and two more that they rent out. It's called Whitefields because of the chalky soil. I didn't travel that way because the count told me not to. He said we had important news to deliver to France and it had got to get there and if we went separately, that would give it the best chance . . .'

'That important news might be what he overheard Master Spelton say to Mistress Stannard,' said Brockley. 'Together with other things too, if he's a genuine spy. Have you and he been spying for France?' he shouted. Lestrange gobbled, looking terrified and Sterling shook him violently. 'Well, have you? *Have you?*'

'We're honest Frenchmen, honest Catholics!' bleated Lestrange.

'Oh, let him be,' I said. 'Let him go on with what he was saying.'

Master Sterling growled but relaxed his grip. Lestrange swallowed and said: 'My master meant to go by way of Whitefields this time too. He said as much to me. You can find it by . . .'

It poured out of him in a stream. It was painful to watch though I was relieved there had been no need to use force. I knew in my heart that if he had proved obstinate, Sterling would have wanted to proceed to force and it was possible that Brockley would have agreed with him. Even Sybil might. She was anything but ruthless but she was desperate for Ambrosia's sake.

At the end of Lestrange's account, Sterling demanded to know precisely what the important news was that was to be reported to France. He did so in such a menacing way that Lestrange, trapped between fear for himself and a powerful reluctance to break his master's confidence, started to gibber. I rose hurriedly to my feet. 'Stop!'

Everyone turned to me enquiringly. 'Whatever Lestrange here intends to report in France may well be very private indeed. It must not be blurted out here!' I told them. I was thinking rapidly. I adopted a pacific tone of voice. 'Master Sterling, this is your house, and we have descended on you without warning. But we are all tired. You said we could stay here tonight. If so, we would be grateful.'

'Surely, Mistress Stannard! I wouldn't think,' said Sterling drily, 'of letting you go off at this hour or in these circumstances! But what of *him*?' He pointed to Lestrange. 'And are we really not to know what news – or information – he is carrying?'

'Better not,' I said.

Brockley said: 'It's possible that he is carrying state secrets. No one has the right to know those without the consent of the Royal Council.'

While Sterling mulled this over, I said: 'Have you any secure place where Lestrange can be kept for a night and a day? It probably wouldn't be longer.'

'Yes, yes, I've a fine sound cellar. He wouldn't get out of that in a hurry, but . . .'

'Tomorrow,' I said, 'we must ride for Dover. We dare not delay and I need both Brockley and my groom to be with me. Somehow, we have to catch up with the count and his companions and prevent them from carrying any reports to France themselves. Master Sterling, could you, tomorrow, send a sensible messenger – Tom, perhaps? – to Hampton Court, where the royal court now is, to deliver a letter addressed to Sir Francis Walsingham. He should be there, with the court. I can tell Tom at exactly which entrance he should present himself and what to say to the gate-guard. A letter bearing the seal of Mistress Stannard will be respected; so would a request for a reply that the messenger can bring back.'

I thought I could rely on that, at least. To become the queen's representative in a political marriage game amounted to quite an elevation in the world of the royal court.

I said: 'The result should be that Walsingham will send men to collect Lestrange from you. This is a matter of espionage as well as possible murder. It needs to be dealt with at a higher level than that of the local constable and fortunately, Hampton Court can be reached quite quickly. Once this man is in Walsingham's hands, you need concern yourself with him, and us, no longer.'

'*Walsingham?*' Lestrange's eyes had bulged with fright at the first mention of Walsingham's name and he began to plead and protest. Master Sterling looked at Brockley and Tom. 'Help me get him down to the cellar. Then, Tom, find one of the farmhands and stand him outside the door as a guard. Someone will have to be on guard all night. We'll do it now.'

It was done. Lestrange, white with fright, struggled so hard that before he could be taken out of the dining room, Master Sterling had to fetch a length of rope so that his hands could be tied. Then, as the three of them dragged him out of the room, he started to cry. He was right to be afraid, for Walsingham's questioners were notorious. Not for the first time, I hated the way of life that fate had decreed for me, and wished with all my heart that I were not Elizabeth's kin.

Only, I was. I was at once her sister and her subject, and I owed her a loyalty that must not fail.

Master Sterling came back presently, rubbing a bruised

cheekbone. 'That's done. Your man Brockley is trying to calm the fellow down and offering to fetch clean clothes from his room for him. He's wet himself, poor devil. Brockley seems to be a decent Christian man and he's keeping to that, even though Lestrange did manage to punch him in the eye. He says we shouldn't leave him all night with his hands tied, and we've given him a pallet to sleep on. You will want to write a letter, I take it, Mistress Stannard. I have a study you can use.'

He showed me to the study, not much bigger than a broom cupboard but no doubt adequate for the needs of Stag-Leys. A battered stool was placed at a scratched table, on which was a pile of paper and a writing set with quills, ink and sander. On a shelf behind the table were some old-fashioned tallies, no doubt recording bushels of cabbages and apples and numbers of calves or piglets. It also held a couple of glass tumblers, and an earthenware cider jar on the floor in the corner was presumably there for anyone – Master Sterling or his unidentified priest – who found account keeping too much of a strain without alcoholic lubrication.

I settled myself on the stool and set about preparing the letter which Tom must carry to Walsingham.

It took a long time, as I had a long story to tell and I wasn't satisfied with my first draft, which meant starting again. But by the time I was finished, I had fully explained why my wedding had been cancelled, and all that had happened since. I had asked for Lestrange to be collected as a matter of urgency and I had also asked for men to be sent to Dover at speed to support us. My little party might catch the count up but we might need help if we were to stop him from sailing.

We ate supper in the kitchen with the family and a crowd of farmhands. Master Sterling said beforehand: 'The farmhands will know much of what has gone on, of course, since I've been arranging for them to act as his guards. They know that we have a French spy in the cellar. Deborah would have told them anyway! But I have spoken to them myself. They will ask you no questions. This is a Catholic household but an honest one. Treason finds no friends here.'

He was right. The hands greeted us civilly, paid no attention to the bruise on their employer's cheekbone and Brockley's incipient black eye, and then talked about a new onion patch that was promising well and argued amiably over the best treatment for a cow with a cut on one of her legs, while they did justice to the supper with the good appetites of outdoor men. Only one didn't quite match that description, and that was a quiet, grey-headed individual who, I gathered from the conversation, did no heavy work but kept a general eye on things and reported on anything that required attention. And kept the accounts in order and said Mass, I reckoned.

The Sterlings made us comfortable that night. Sybil and I shared a smoothly sheeted bed in one chamber, and were able to undress by a warm fire, while the Brockleys had the adjacent room, also provided with a fire, and Joseph was settled in a room over the stable, along with other grooms and farmhands.

Sybil and I, however, slept uneasily and I woke at once when there was a light tap on the door. I sat up, nudging Sybil and reaching for the candle on the table by my side of the bed. The tap came again and I said *come in* in a low voice, while I slid out of the bed and lit the candle from the embers of the dying fire. Brockley stepped into the room, also carrying a candle and what looked like a small scroll of paper.

'Madam? I am sorry to disturb you, but I had to bring this to you as soon as possible. I had no chance earlier; you were never out of the company of our host.'

'Bring what? What is it, Brockley?' I sat down on the edge of the bed and set my own candle on the table. Sybil, behind me, was pulling a pillow into place to support her head and saying: 'What's that in your hand, Brockley?'

'When we took Lestrange to the cellar, madam,' Brockley said, 'he looked such a mess – doublet torn, and not just that . . .'

Brockley much disliked mentioning anything at all coarse in the presence of ladies. Master Sterling had thought otherwise. 'It's all right, Brockley, Master Sterling told us. You offered to fetch clean clothes for him, didn't you?'

'Yes. We were going to untie his hands before we left him, so he'd be able to change. Well, seeing him in such a state gave me an idea. He told me where to find things in his room and I just went and got them. Only,' said Brockley, 'his saddlebags were there too and I searched them. I found this. It was sealed and addressed to some French name I didn't know. I took the liberty of breaking the seal. It's all in French but I can read that. Here you are, madam. It tells us all we need to know.'

I took the scroll, which unrolled itself in my hands. Brockley put his candle beside mine and in their double light, I read the letter. I said: '*My God!*'

The letter detailed the information that Lestrange was carrying. The warning about Spelton's double mission was there, but there was much more. There were details of a new plan to build warships at speed, explaining where the shipyards were and how the business was to be financed. In less than a year, England would have the one hundred and seventy ships that earlier, she had only pretended to have.

There were also details of a plan, under discussion by the queen and her council, to send a very secret mission to Spain, with a view to resuming diplomatic relations and possibly offering trade advantages in exchange for an undertaking not to support any attempt made by Mary of Scotland to foment a rising in her favour in England. There were other things, as well, of a minor nature. But these . . .

We all looked at each other in the candlelight. The flames flickered, dancing over the sloping ceiling and the beams that crossed it and curved down the roughly plastered walls; the small hearth with its glowing embers, a woven wool mat in red and blue on the plank floor in front of it. This house was full of warmth and security, part of the safe everyday world in which I longed to stay but could not, for Sybil's sake and for Spelton's.

I said, wearily: 'We have to give chase even into France if it comes to it. We have to do our utmost, whatever the outcome. If the count gets his copy of this to its destination, it could endanger England as well as Christopher Spelton! I can only pray that Walsingham sends some men hotfoot to Dover to back us up. My letter asks him for help. And now we'd better try to get to sleep.'

THIRTEEN
Whitefields

We made an early start. It was a Sunday and normally I wouldn't have chosen to travel on the Sabbath, but there was no time to spare and Mr Sterling, when I apologetically mentioned the matter, agreed with me. We must make the best speed we could, though some of us were very tired and unfit. Brockley was tough considering his age, but the hair that had once been brown was now mostly grey and fighting with Lestrange had taken much strength out of him. His black eye was truly spectacular. Dale looked exhausted.

Tom left early on his errand to Hampton Court with my letter. Before he set off, I asked for it back since I wished to add something extra concerning the paper found in Lestrange's room. But he was still on his way before dawn, and we set out soon after. Daylight was still not quite complete when we mounted. The sky was overcast, which worried me. I hoped the weather would stay dry for our journey.

It did, but by the time we reached Dover on the evening of the second day, Dale was telling me that she couldn't abide another half-hour in the saddle because her back ached and her behind was too sore and Sybil was in much the same state as I could tell from the strain in her face, although she said nothing, or not about that. Instead, she said that if this was Dover, where was Whitefields? Had we passed it? We must, *must* get there. She had got to find Ambrosia. To Sybil, finding Ambrosia meant far more than catching up with the count.

We had pulled up at the roadside to talk it over. 'It's nearly dark,' I said. 'I'm too weary to go any further myself – nearly as bad as you, Dale. We should find an inn.'

'I agree, madam,' Brockley said. 'Fran must rest. That inn

we've used before, the Safe Harbour, is just along the road from here. I think we should go there for the night, if they've room.'

Sybil started to protest but then did what I had half-expected her to do ever since we left Hawkswood, which was to fall off her horse while it was standing still. 'That settles it,' I said, while Brockley and Joseph were dismounting to help her up. She had gone down in a slow slither and was not hurt. Once on her feet, she started to apologize. But I looked at her drawn face and said: 'No, Sybil, you're worn out too, and it's too late to descend on these Fergusons and create a disturbance, which we certainly would if we found our quarry there. We'll try the inn.'

'But we're here in Dover; we can't be too far away from this house Whitefields!' Her voice was shrill. 'What if Ambrosia is there now but we miss her by delaying till tomorrow?'

'Don't *argue*, Sybil!' I snapped. 'We go to the inn.'

At the Safe Harbour, the ostler and the landlord were still the same, and remembered us. The landlord, a broad-built, smiling fellow called Ralph Harrison, welcomed me and the Brockleys by name, expressed himself pleased to meet Mistress Sybil Jester, and introduced us to his twenty-year-old daughter, who had come to help him run the inn. 'Left her with my sister after her mother died, but we all have to work in this world, and best she should work beside me, her father, till she's married. Ain't that so, Bessie?'

Bessie agreed that it was. She was a buxom girl, with a mass of brown hair that kept escaping from its cap, and she was as full of smiles as her father. They promised to see that we were comfortable.

They kept their word and that night, when Sybil and I were once more sharing a bedchamber and a bed, she admitted that I had been right. She, as much as Dale, had needed rest and food. 'And it was good food, too,' she said. 'But if we just miss Ambrosia . . .' she added unhappily.

'We'll give chase,' I told her. 'We'll follow the count and his companions no matter where they lead us. If necessary, we'll trail them all the way to France and the Château d'Oiseaux. But Walsingham's men may catch us all up and if they're in time, the count will never embark, and you'll have Ambrosia safely back.'

'I hope so. Oh, dear God, how I hope so.' Sybil tried to smile. 'Dale hates the sea,' she said.

'Let us hope she won't have to face it,' I replied. I paused, my head on one side and then added: 'If they haven't sailed yet, they won't for a while, I fancy. Listen. There's a wind getting up.'

In the morning, when we set out to find Whitefields, we did so in a gale. It wasn't raining, but the wind was howling like a hound pack and ragged black clouds were racing eastward across a cold, pale sky. As we rode out of Dover, Joseph, pulling his cloak hood further over his ears, looked up at the sky and for once broke his habitual silence.

'Reckon the Wild Hunt's abroad,' he remarked, loudly on account of the wind.

'The what?' I asked him, also in a shout.

'Oh, just a tale my mother tells of a night, when it's dark and windy and she's got us all gathered round the fire.' Joseph came from a large family in Hawkswood village, and went back there now and then for an evening off. 'She says in weather like this, after dark, the devil goes hunting with the souls of the damned as his hounds, and the screech of the wind is them baying!'

His voice rose to a positive bellow during the last sentence, as the gale rose to new levels of noisiness. He then relapsed into silence again but Dale took advantage of a brief lull and said: 'Hunting what? Doesn't sound very Christian to me. More like something a pagan would believe.'

'It's a story from before Christianity,' said Brockley unexpectedly. 'I think it was one of the old Norse gods that did the hunting then. But I never did get clear what they were chasing. What does your mother say about that, Joseph?'

'Nothing. Just that the devil was running his hounds, like,' said Joseph, looking embarrassed at being obliged to go on talking.

'Hunting for more wicked souls to put in his pack, I expect,' said Sybil. 'Which is much what we're doing ourselves, this moment!'

Her voice had to rise to a shout once more, because the wind
had again broken into a howl. Overhead, a couple of gulls went
past, wings outspread, flying like leaves on the wind.

I thought how pleasant it was for Joseph, that he still had
a mother to tell old tales round the fire. My own mother died
when I was sixteen, and we were both living in Sussex with
my Uncle Herbert and Aunt Tabitha. I always thought that she
had let go of life because she was unhappy and certainly my
aunt and uncle had never been very kind to either of us. Perhaps
they would have been kinder if she had ever told them who
fathered me. Maybe if they had known I was the daughter of
King Henry, they wouldn't have been so harsh.

Though it was true that they had at least sheltered us and
I had had an education. If we went back to Withysham this
summer, I would visit them. They had been angry with me
over the arrival of Harry, out of wedlock, but they were growing
old and might be reconciled if they actually saw him, I thought
hopefully.

When we went back. I only hoped it wouldn't be too long.
That the question might be *if* more than *when* had not yet
occurred to me.

Whitefields, when we got there, was nothing at all like
Stag-Leys. It had a lodge, where two enormous mastiffs
bounded out, baying, to announce us, followed by a brawny
lodge-keeper, who demanded our names, looked dubious when
I leant down to shout into his ear that our business was private,
but finally summoned someone called Sam to run to the house
ahead of us. Sam proved to be a lad of about fourteen, already
showing his father's hefty build. He trotted off and we followed
him uphill along a winding path between fields and paddocks,
until we reached the house itself.

It was not all that large, but it was still manor-house size
and seemed to be a small imitation of Hampton Court, since
it was built of rosy brick with grey brick as a decorative border
round doors and windows. The roof did not have crenellations
but it had ornamental chimneys, several of which were emit-
ting smoke into the wild sky. Standing outside was Sam, along
with three other men.

'Joseph,' I said, 'I think two of those men are grooms.

They'll take our horses. You go with them and see that all's well. Brockley, I want you to stay with us, as our escort.'

'As you wish, madam.' Brockley was a stickler for seeing that our horses were always properly cared for, but Joseph was reliable and Brockley well understood the seriousness of our purpose.

I was right about the grooms. Along with Joseph, they were taking our bridles and helping the ladies out of our saddles almost as soon as we reined in. The third man was a butler, black clad and equipped with a gold chain of office and a gold ring on his right hand. Like the lodge-keeper he wanted to know our business but I said it was both confidential and urgent and we would be glad if the master of the house – 'Master Ferguson, is it not?' – could spare us a little of his time. I tried to be calm and dignified though it was difficult because the screech of the wind still obliged me to shout.

'I will enquire of Mr Ferguson,' said the butler, using the modern Mr instead of Master. One day, I thought, everyone would use it. It was the coming thing. 'Please come this way,' he added.

Joseph went off with the grooms and the horses, while the rest of us were led inside, relieved of our cloaks, and shown to a parlour, a somewhat dark place as it was on the north side of the house and was panelled in dark oak. It was chilly, for though a fire was laid, it wasn't lit. The wind howled, shaking the square-leaded windows. We sat down on the settles and stools and there, for a time, we stayed.

Because, I fancied, Mr Ferguson was otherwise engaged. There was a sense of disturbance in the house and not just on account of the gale. This was a human disturbance. Somewhere, not far away, there were raised voices. A man was shouting angrily, a woman trying now and then to protest, and what sounded like a younger man's voice was also trying to make itself heard. Brockley rose from his stool, went quietly to the door, which the butler had closed after him, and opened it a crack. The distant argument began to separate into words.

'. . . how many times must I say it? She may be a pattern of virtue and a flawless cook, which my daughter-in-law doesn't need to be, and she may be as pretty as an angel but

she's a tavern-keeper's daughter and you're not bringing her
here as your wife and that's . . .'

The younger man's voice interrupted but the woman spoke
at the same time and I couldn't make out what either of them
were saying. Then the older man overcame them, command-
ingly. '. . . my last word, Duncan! With you it's first one thing,
then another! As if you haven't caused trouble enough already!
I'll hear no more of this. It's time you were married but not
to Bessie from the Safe Harbour . . .'

Brockley closed the door. 'Well, well. We've walked into a
family dispute. So it's pretty Bessie from our inn that the son
of the house fancies. He's got good taste, if you ask me. But
the heir to a manor house and a wench from the inn . . . a bit
of a misfit by most standards and she won't have a fine dowry
to sweeten it, I daresay.'

'It's none of our business,' I said.

A door slammed. Someone had walked out on the alterca-
tion. The wrangling voices ceased. There was a pause during
which I thought I heard a quieter exchange and thought that
the butler was announcing our arrival. Then brisk footsteps
approached the parlour. The door was flung open and in
came a tall, ginger-haired man, elegantly clad in a turquoise-
coloured doublet and hose, but with a frown on his brows
and no very friendly look in his green-hazel eyes. He walked
masterfully in, leaving the door open behind him, and stopped
in mid-floor.

'Good morning. I am Mr Hamish Ferguson.' He had a slight
but definite Scottish accent. 'My man Morley said we had
unexpected guests. I apologize for keeping you waiting. I have
a romantic, impulsive son who believes himself in love with
a nice but quite unsuitable young woman. Children ought to
be a joy but often enough they're more trouble than they're
worth. I've two grown daughters as well. The elder says no
to every match she's offered and I won't put young Sheila on
the marriage market until Katherine is settled. I like things
done in an orderly manner. Now, I understand from Morley
that you' – he looked at me – 'are a Mrs Stannard, and that
these are your women and your manservant, who seems to
have had an argument with someone recently.' He was looking

at Brockley's black eye. 'You say you have business with me. How can I help you?'

I introduced my companions and started to explain our errand but I didn't get very far before he interrupted me. 'Yes, yes, Count Renard and his party have been here, but they left yesterday and sailed from Dover towards evening. They were lucky and found a skipper willing to transport their horses. I hope they got across to Calais before this gale set in, though they would have the wind behind them, at least. I wouldn't like the worry of travelling with horses in bad weather. I am sorry, since you obviously need to catch up with them – a daughter of Mrs Jester here has eloped with the count, you say?'

'My daughter Ambrosia,' said Sybil.

'Well, you've missed them,' said Mr Ferguson flatly. 'They only spent one night here.'

The butler reappeared in the doorway and coughed. Mr Ferguson turned round. 'What is it, Morley?'

'The visitors' groom wants to speak to Mr Brockley there. Something about one of their horses, apparently.'

'Go on, Brockley,' I said. He hurried out and I watched his departure anxiously, wondering what the trouble was. Mr Ferguson began to suggest that we might like some refreshments, but we had hardly said yes before Brockley was back, looking concerned. I looked at him questioningly.

'Joseph says your mare Jewel has some heat in one foreleg, madam. She may have strained something on that long ride we've had from Hawkswood. Mr Ferguson,' he addressed our host directly. 'May we ask a favour? Could we take shelter here at least until the gale has passed? It would give the mare a little while to recover. She really shouldn't go any further today – and we would rather not have to go out and seek shelter elsewhere in this weather. The landlord of the Safe Harbour said that he wouldn't have room for us a second night.'

Ralph Harrison had said no such thing. But Brockley gave me a warning glance and I merely said, 'I don't want Jewel to go lame. Would it be a great trouble if we asked you to let us rest here till tomorrow?'

Most owners of big houses accommodate benighted travellers on occasion. Mr Ferguson did look put out but he knew his duty as a host.

'You will be welcome.' He didn't sound particularly welcoming but at least he was saying the right words. 'We have spare rooms enough,' he said. 'Morley, my compliments to my wife and please tell her that we have guests for the night. Tell the cooks that these people will be dining with us and request Mrs Morley to get two bedchambers prepared, and see that the groom has a bed as well. Meanwhile, perhaps we could have some wine and pasties. Our guests have been on the road for some days.'

Under cover of Mr Ferguson's orders to Morley, I muttered to Brockley: 'Is the trouble really with Jewel?'

'No, madam,' Brockley muttered back. 'But Mistress Ambrosia's pony is in the stable. It's distinctive, dapple grey at its front end and smooth iron grey at the rear. Joseph says he knew it at once. Our good host says their horses sailed with them so why didn't they take this one? According to Joseph, it can't have been left behind because it was lame or ill – he says it's standing four square in its stall and has its nose in its manger, eating heartily. He is quite sure it's Mistress Wilde's pony. Seems odd to me.'

To me, too.

FOURTEEN
Ruby by Moonlight

The refreshments were duly brought and a maidservant lit the fire. The gale continued to roar and rattle the windows. We made conversation with our host. Presently, a small bustling woman dressed in black, with stout black shoes and a stout girdle from which dangled a huge bunch of keys that clinked as she walked, came to collect us and was presented to us as the housekeeper Mrs Morley and was presumably the butler's wife.

Businesslike shoes briskly tapping, she led us up a winding staircase and on to a wide gallery overlooking two sides of a great hall. As we followed her, Brockley, speaking into my ear because of the gale, said: 'Walsingham's men could have got here ahead of us and caught the count before he sailed but they obviously didn't. Only, why not?'

'I know,' I said, in turn speaking into Brockley's ear. 'I've been wondering too. I hoped they'd overtake us on the road.'

I was very disappointed that they had not, and I was puzzled too. Had something gone wrong? Had Tom's errand somehow failed? Had a stupid guard, perhaps new to his post, treated the letter carelessly and not had it sent straight in to Walsingham's office? Should we have alerted the local constable and sent him with Tom to give him official standing? Was Lestrange still in the Sterling cellar? Stephen Sterling wouldn't like that at all. I could think of no way to find out.

I shook my head despairingly at Brockley. We were walking along a short side of the gallery first of all and I thought it probably doubled as a minstrels' gallery on occasion. It gave a good view of the hall, which was not unlike the one at Hawkswood except that it was bigger, and decorated, as the Hawkswood hall was not, with weaponry hung to make patterns on the darkly panelled walls.

There was a long central table with a white cloth on it, benches along each side, and carved armchairs at each end. There was also a fire with a ginger-headed young man sitting disconsolately beside it. The passionate and impulsive Duncan, presumably. A dark-haired girl in a yellow gown was sitting beside him and talking to him, and seemed to be urging him to something. She didn't appear to be getting much response. I wondered if this was the difficult Katherine, encouraging rebellion.

There were doors off the gallery, all shaking in the wind and I could feel the gallery itself vibrating beneath my feet. The wind suddenly redoubled its efforts, its howl rising to a new level of noise and the door that we were just passing shook violently and then burst open. It promptly slammed again but not before I had glimpsed what was inside. Brockley, who was beside me, was looking at me and noticed nothing, while the others had passed it already. I kept on walking, trying to take in what I had seen. It was hard to believe, yet I knew I had made no mistake.

I held my peace while we were led round the corner to the gallery on the long side of the hall, and been shown into our allotted rooms. They were not big but both were provided with four-poster beds, clothes presses, washstands and fur rugs, and each had a small prie-dieu. Mrs Morley did not comment but it was clear that this was a Catholic household. Quite possibly, she supposed that we were all Catholic as well. I hadn't said anything to the contrary. The rooms had hearths and the maidservant who had lit the fire in the parlour had also got one going in the bigger room of the two, and was now laying the fire in the other, which had been allocated to the Brockleys.

Our saddlebags had been brought up and there were jugs of washing water ready. Mrs Morley chivvied the maid into making haste with the Brockleys' fire and then shooed her downstairs. After that, she looked round to make sure we had all we needed, bobbed a curtsey and left us. We heard her brisk footsteps and the jingle of her keys retreat along the gallery. Listening intently, I thought I heard her stop and exclaim about something but I couldn't make out more than that. The tapping of her feet resumed and was lost in the racket of the wind. I shut the door, which reduced the noise considerably. Dale and Sybil were unpacking saddlebags in the room I was to share with Sybil and Brockley was similarly occupied next door. 'Dale,' I said. 'Fetch Roger. I have something to tell you.'

'Are you *sure*?' Brockley asked when I told them what I had seen. 'Just one glimpse . . . I mean . . . you're not imagining things because it's so odd that Mistress Wilde's pony seems to be still here?'

'You should know me better than that,' I said. 'I'm sure. But of course we should confirm it. We need a proper look.'

Sybil went nervously to the door, peered out of it and then crossed the gallery to look down into the hall. Coming back, she said: 'No one's about. The hall's empty. Those two young people have gone. We could do it now.'

'Not all of us,' said Brockley. 'It wouldn't do if we were *all* seen, crowding round a door where we have no business. Madam, it had best be you and me.'

'It's back round the corner,' I said. 'It's the second door we'll come to.'

'Let us be quick,' said Brockley.

We were certainly quick, more so than we intended, for although the door was still shaking, it showed no sign now of bursting open and when I tried it, it was locked. It had probably come open again and Mrs Morley had noticed. Well, I had heard her exclaim about something. No doubt she had secured it, taking the key away with her. Very likely, it now hung on the massive bunch at her belt.

'Madam,' said Brockley urgently, 'did you bring your picklocks with you?'

'Yes, but I can't use them here and now in broad daylight. Someone might come up here, or into the hall, at any moment and see me. It can take several minutes to open a lock, as you know. We'll have to leave it until tonight.'

'Unless the bedchamber keys are all the same,' said Brockley hopefully. 'They might be.' He fumbled in his belt pouch. 'Here's the key to our room. Let's see.'

He tried the key. It didn't work.

'After dark,' I said tersely. 'Now, we have to behave like innocent guests, and prepare to dine with our hosts.'

Before dinner, Brockley and I went down to the stable to see for ourselves whether the grey pony was Ambrosia's Irons. There was little doubt of it. Not one horse or pony in a thousand could have the same curious colouring as Ambrosia's pony, and as Brockley said, if the animal now in the stall beside Jewel was not Irons, well, it was true there was such a thing as coincidence, but he didn't believe this was an example. 'Not if you're right about what you saw, madam, anyway. It can't be.'

'As a daughter, you're frankly a disappointment, Kate. You must learn to be more womanly. So take that sulky look off your face and get your grandfather's food on the table and get ready to feed him. It's your turn. Do it at once!'

'Sheila doesn't mind feeding him and I hate it. I can't eat my dinner properly if I have to feed him his at the same time and he doesn't *like* me feeding him anyway. I do the least thing wrong, fumble or something, and he hits out at me. He doesn't do that to Sheila! Let Sheila do it, or Peters. Why does he have an attendant if not to do things like feeding him? Or we've got footmen and scullions who could . . .!'

'Sheila is not as clumsy and careless as you are. Naturally he likes her better. If you were more careful he would like you too. Try harder! Peters has enough to do, looking after him the rest of the time and it's not a footman's task, nor a scullion's! Do as you're bid! Here he is now!'

The wind was dropping at last. We had all returned to our rooms to make ourselves tidy for dinner, which was announced by a gong. When we stepped out on to the gallery, the harsh voice of an angry female came clearly up to us. There was the sound of a slap and a cry. We all stopped to look over the balustrade and saw that the central table was laid for the meal, and that a very aged man was being brought in by a manservant, on whose arm he was leaning.

The dark girl we had caught sight of earlier was waiting to receive him. Her small, pretty face was reddened on one side and her expression was one of tight-lipped fury. Under the grim gaze of a tall, angular woman with a heavy shawl round her bony shoulders, hard dark eyes and an uncompromising mouth, she helped the manservant to seat his charge and tied a napkin round the old man's neck. She did this quite gently and yet somehow conveyed that she longed to strangle him with it. Morley came in with a steaming bowl of something and gave it to her. She set it on the table, just as her father and a younger girl, dressed in yellow like her presumed sister, came in and sat down.

There was a pause, during which the old man picked up a spoon and banged it on the table and shouted something incomprehensible from a toothless mouth. The angular woman gave the dark girl a nod, and the girl took the spoon away from her grandfather, and began to feed him from the bowl.

'What an enchanting household,' growled Brockley.

'Our places are set. Come along,' I said. 'Before they see us gawping.'

We hurried on down, pretending that we had noticed nothing. Once in the hall, we were introduced to those we hadn't met. The angular woman was Mrs Ferguson. She greeted us civilly but gave a strong impression of controlled anger, presumably with the dark-haired girl who, as we had surmised, was Katherine, and also, I thought, with the ginger-headed young man, who was indeed Duncan, the son of the house.

Katherine herself greeted us politely but briefly, over her shoulder, while continuing to feed the old man, who spluttered and dribbled and certainly didn't seem to like being fed by her much more than she liked the task of feeding him. Once he knocked her hand away just as she was bringing a spoonful to his mouth, so that the contents of the spoon went all over the table, whereupon he cackled with geriatric laughter.

The younger girl was Sheila, the Sheila, no doubt, who wasn't to be allowed to marry until her parents had managed to get rid of Katherine. She was like Katherine in feature but was less defined, her hair brown and her eyes hazel instead of being dark like her sister's hair and eyes. She was the only one who gave us a genuinely friendly smile, and it was she who made most effort to talk to us. We on our side told a carefully restricted version of our errand. Mistress Sybil's

widowed daughter had run off with the count, and there had
been a strange event back at Hawkswood, involving the death
of one of our cooks under odd circumstances. The count could
have been concerned in this, in which case, Mistress Wilde
might have run off with a murderer. Everyone exclaimed in
horror.

The polite greetings over, Mr Ferguson pronounced a brief
grace – the grandfather, clearly, hadn't wished to wait for
it – and at last the rest of us could begin the meal. It was
an uncomfortable one. The food was good but the air seethed
with family friction and with something more than that; a
sense of unease that had no obvious connection with their
private squabbles. Hamish Ferguson and his wife kept
exchanging glances for no apparent reason, and Duncan was
entirely silent. On our side, we were all concentrating so
hard on not saying anything unwise that our efforts at conversation grew more and more stilted. We were thankful to
leave the hall and return to our rooms, saying that we needed
rest.

Without discussing it, we all went at once into my
bedchamber, shut the door after us and stood looking at each
other.

'Something's badly wrong for sure and they all know it,'
Brockley said.

'Yes. They're on edge; I could feel it,' I said.

'If you're right about what you saw, it's hardly surprising.
Well, first of all, we have to make sure. But, madam, once we
have, then what do we do next?'

I shook my head. I had been worrying about the same thing.
'At the moment,' I said, 'I haven't the slightest idea. What
can we do? Ask Mr Ferguson to explain?'

There was a silence while we all tried to imagine this and
failed. Then Sybil said: 'First things first. We make sure.
Frankly,' she added, 'I'd be relieved to know you're right,
Mistress Stannard. Only, in that case, where is Ambrosia?'

No one had an answer to that.

Dale said: 'Well, at least that wind has gone. I'm tired out
with all this travelling but I'll be glad to get away from here
and we don't need bad weather hampering us as well when

we go. I can't abide this feeling of being frightened all the time.'

We kept to ourselves for the rest of the day. Brockley went out to the stables before supper to tell Joseph all that had happened. 'In case we have to get away in the middle of the night. He needs to be ready. You never know,' he said to me when we all met to go down to supper.

Supper was eaten in the same unease as dinner, except that this time Sheila fed the old man and we were spared Katherine's scowls and his visible dislike of her. After supper there was an attempt at entertainment. The table was cleared, the old grandfather's attendant, Peters, produced a guitar and played for us. We did our best to seem appreciative, but retired as soon as we could.

'Midnight,' I said to Brockley as we were parting to go to our rooms. 'Just us two, I think. With luck, we'll only be a few minutes. We only need to open that door and just look. Meanwhile, we should keep alert, just in case they try to move – it.'

'With us up here,' said Brockley, 'I doubt it.'

By midnight, not only had the wind completely ceased, but after one brief rainstorm, the sky had cleared. A full moon shone in at the tall windows of the hall, casting white light and black shadows over table and balustrade, except for the dull red embers of the fire.

Sybil and I waited, fully dressed, until we heard Brockley's soft tap on the door. He and Dale were both there and I let them in, pleased to see that Brockley had brought one of his lanterns. I braced myself. 'Let's get this over.'

Despite Brockley's presence, I was tense and nervous. The task before us was not one that sat well with the silence of the sleeping house, the darkness and the cold moonlight. I felt in my hidden pouch to make sure my picklocks were safely there, which they were, and noticed that my hand was trembling. 'We must be very quiet,' I said.

'Don't be long,' said Dale tremulously. Sybil said: 'Good luck,' as though we were setting forth on a perilous voyage to Cathay.

Stealthily, Brockley and I made our way back along the gallery and round the corner to the short side, Brockley holding the lantern on his right, the side away from the balustrade. The gallery creaked a little under our feet, no matter how careful we were. 'I wish we knew where everyone else sleeps,' he whispered to me. 'I'd like to think they were well away from here.'

'Me too,' I whispered back. I came to a halt. 'This is the room.'

'I hope you really are sure. This moonlight distorts things. I just hope we're not about to walk into the marital bedchamber.'

'I doubt it,' I muttered. 'If I'm right, they wouldn't want *that* in the room next door.'

I tried the door first, in case it was no longer locked, but it was. I got out my picklocks. My hands were certainly shaking and I fumbled as I chose one of my slender steel aids to prying into other folks' business, and slid it into the keyhole. It was the wrong choice and I had to try again with another one. Brockley stood behind me, directing the lantern-light on to the lock, his eyes and ears alert for any movement in the house. The lock yielded at last and I pushed the door gently open. It made no sound. I pushed it wider and slipped inside, Brockley behind me.

A moonbeam from a window on the far side of the hall came in with us, casting a long white shaft of light across a bare plank floor and on to the canopied bed. The canopy only sheltered the bedhead; there were no curtains to hide the sheeted shape that lay there, or the dangling hand and arm that had slipped from under the covering. The moonlight showed the shape and size of the hand, a man's right hand for sure, and gleamed coldly on the great ring on the fourth finger. It leached all colour from the square-cut stone but Brockley brought the lantern nearer and the flame brought out the deep rich red of a ruby.

'That's what I saw,' I said. 'A shape, a dangling hand, and that great square ring. Brockley . . .'

He stepped closer and pulled back the sheet.

I had made no mistake. Count Renard lay on the bed, stone dead. He was reverently laid, with his left hand still resting on his breast, and beneath it, a little crucifix. The body was dressed, but there was no doublet on its upper half, just a loose shirt of white silk. At least, it had been white. I looked, and gagged.

Brockley said: 'Chrrrist!'

The front of the shirt was one huge stain of blood, black in the moonlight but hideous all the same. The count's left hand and the crucifix lay on top of it. Brockley, gingerly, moved the head and then we saw that it had been half-severed.

'So now we know,' Brockley said.

'Yes.' I was trembling violently, seized by an irrational fear of the horror on the bed, as though at any moment it might open its eyes, might move, might suddenly stand up, but it would not be the count who would arise, only his body, possessed by some passing spirit or demon, wandering in the darkness of night and the mystery of the moon.

'Yes. We know. Now let's get away,' I said.

'Oh my God,' said a voice from behind us. 'The count told us things about you, Mrs Stannard. He said you made him nervous, you were such a strange woman. He said you were known at court. That you had a reputation.'

FIFTEEN
Scotland Versus France

We all swung round but we knew the voice before we saw his face, white and frightened in the moonlight. Duncan Ferguson, the young ginger-headed son of the house, who was being crossed in love by his father.

'I sleep on this side of the house. I'm the only one that does,' he said. 'My parents and the wenches are on the other side. I like my room because it looks to the north and I can see the Pole Star from my window on clear nights. I don't close the shutters at night because I like to see the sky but moonlight can send you mad, they say, so I don't care for south-facing rooms.' He seemed to realize that he was rambling and pulled himself up. 'I heard a noise,' he said. 'Footsteps, and I thought it came from this direction. So you've found him. But how?'

'Earlier, the wind blew this door open just as I was passing it,' I said shortly. 'I saw a hand dangling from under the sheet, and I recognized the ring on it.' I tried to speak plainly, and was fighting my shivers and my irrational fears. I recalled that I was the sister of a queen and the daughter of King Henry the Eighth. It was not my business to cower in fear, even from a situation like this.

'This man,' I said, 'was until lately a guest in my house. I now know that he was not a guest I would wish to harbour, but that doesn't mean I wanted him murdered. I was told, by your father, that Count Renard had been here but had travelled on to France, with his companions. Now I find him laid in a room in this house, with his head half off. How did this come about? And where *are* his companions? Answer me!'

Brockley remarked calmly: 'This is an uncomfortable place to hold a discussion. Shall we go back to Mistress Stannard's room? Her women are there and they too should hear the answer to madam's questions.'

Back in my room, Sybil and Dale were waiting nervously in the candlelight, sitting side by side on the bed. They looked horrified when we came in with Duncan, who whispered: 'Sorry, sorry,' to them, as Brockley pushed him on to a stool, before lighting some extra candles.

I closed the door quietly. I was trembling in spite of myself. I sat down on the bed next to Sybil. 'We found what we expected,' I said. 'It's the count and he's dead.'

'Very dead,' said Brockley grimly. 'Almost beheaded, in fact. Now then, young Duncan, just what happened? How does a guest, who no doubt believed himself to be among friends, come to be lying murdered in a disused bedchamber in your house? Who killed him?'

There was a long, aching silence. Duncan began to say something and then stopped, his mouth quivering. 'Well?' barked Brockley.

More silence. And then: 'I did,' said Duncan abjectly.

We all stared. 'It wasn't murder,' he said. 'He left this house, making for the port and the ship where he'd got passages for all his party. But I went after him and challenged him to a duel. I won,' he added with a touch of pride.

'A *duel*!' I exclaimed. 'But – why?'

'Duels aren't murder!' Duncan insisted.

'Duelling has never been legal for untitled gentlemen,' Brockley told him, 'and as it happens, the queen does not approve of it for anyone and she has now made it illegal for all, though juries are tolerant in cases of severe provocation. That could save you, perhaps, despite your lack of a title. But it would have to be very severe provocation indeed. What was it?'

'Titled men? I didn't know that. But I was provoked, right enough. Oh, yes, indeed, I was certainly that. He was very open that he was carrying news to France, about things he'd learned at your home, and earlier, at court. He said that he had to warn the French royal family that a spy called Christopher Spelton had been sent to work in France, and he had other news, too. He didn't tell us what the news was or what this Mr Spelton had gone to France to do, but he was quite frank that he'd been spying. He thought we'd approve, as we're Catholic too, and anyway because we're – we were – his friends. But he was wrong; we're loyal subjects of the queen and what he was doing was . . . wrong, so wrong.'

He stopped for a moment, as if unsure how to continue. Brockley said: 'Go on.'

'All right. My father can remember the days of the Catholic Queen Mary and he said he pitied her victims that she executed for heresy. Father saw a burning once, when he was a boy. He still has nightmares about it. We don't want those days back, he said. He said it to Count Renard! But the count said that Mary of Scotland, who to his mind should be queen here, is a gentle soul and no one need fear her. He said that she wouldn't persecute anyone for having a faith different from hers; he himself did not believe in that, and had even been exiled from France for speaking up for the Huguenots. But Father said Mary could never get the throne without help from abroad and that would mean Philip of Spain and *that* would mean the Inquisition.'

'It assuredly would!' I snapped. I had steadied myself.

'Yes. Father told the count that England is safe and quiet now and we like it that way. We didn't want to help the count at all but he *was* an old friend and had trusted us because of that. As I said, he didn't tell us what the information was that he was carrying and Father said we didn't want to know. Father said we wouldn't report him, but he must get on his way to France and never come back here. It should have ended there. Only,' said Duncan, rubbing his forehead, 'he still couldn't seem to understand how much we were shocked by his spying. He tried to recruit me.'

'Recruit *you*? How?' I demanded.

'He took me aside and told me he could write to friends in Queen Elizabeth's court and get me a place there, and once I'd settled down, I could take over his spying duties. He wouldn't be in England much in the future, he said, and he wanted a replacement. He was grateful for our promise of silence and wanted to do something for us in return. He said that a sharp young man even in quite a modest position would have chances to find things out, and I would have a salary from France as well as my court salary – for whatever post I was in – and I'd be working for the Catholic faith and the kingdom of God! I was so angry!' His voice rose, and I said: 'Hush.'

'I was insulted, I tell you!' said Duncan, though he lowered his tone. 'It *was* an insult to think I'd agree to anything like that. I said so. He smiled and said, well, think it over. You know where my home is, if you want to get in touch. He left a couple of hours later and I saw him go, but I was seething, *seething*. How could he expect me to consent to such a thing? How could he? I was growing angrier and angrier and in the end I couldn't leave it there.'

He was speaking faster and faster, as the memories overcame him. 'I went after him,' he said, 'and caught up with him and challenged him. It was against my honour not to. His companions told him to ignore me but he was one of those men who won't refuse a challenge.

'He was brave, I suppose,' said Duncan unwillingly. 'And he had a sense of honour too, I think. It wouldn't let him refuse a challenge, even from someone as unimportant as me. Anyway, we fought, with swords. It was under those trees that overhang the track just a little way from our lodge gates. It was queer. There were birds in the trees and they flew away in fright when the swords began to clash. I'll always remember that. He was a good swordsman but so am I and I'm younger and faster. I made a lucky swipe and took his head half off.'

He paused and then said in a hushed voice: 'There was so much blood. I never saw so much blood. The grass was scarlet, all round him. It was horrible! I never thought it would be like that. It smelt . . . awful.'

He fell silent and in that silence, we heard movement just outside the door. We all tensed, looking at each other in alarm. Then the door quietly opened and for one horrible second, I wondered if the count had indeed risen from his bed of death and was walking in the moonlight. From the gasp that Dale gave, I knew that she had shared the same nasty fantasy. Then it dissolved, as Hamish Ferguson walked into the light.

'I haven't been sleeping,' he said. 'I've been prowling. I heard voices and tried to discover who was speaking. Then I recognized my son's voice and took the liberty of listening

to what it was saying. When I heard him mention clashing
swords and blood, I knew it was time to intervene.'

'I told you to hush, Duncan,' I said. 'My life just now seems
to be haunted by eavesdroppers. Master . . . Mr Ferguson, this
room happens to be a ladies' bedchamber.'

'If my son had been misbehaving in a more obvious fashion,'
said his father coldly, 'I would be annoyed, but if you had no
objection, well, I wouldn't interfere. However, it was clear
from what I heard, that matters were far otherwise. Just what
are you doing here, Duncan?'

'They know. I heard noises and I went to see and I found
them in that room – where the count is,' said Duncan miserably. 'They know all about it.'

'And you filled in the gaps, I suppose. With you it's first
one thing, then another! As if you haven't caused trouble
enough already!'

In my mind I heard the echo of the words we had all heard
when we first entered the house and listened to Mr Ferguson
shouting at his son in another room.

'He hasn't told us all,' said Brockley. 'What happened to
the count's companions – his chaplain and his grooms and
Mistress Wilde? Where are they?'

'Well, answer him,' said Ferguson, as Duncan hesitated.

'Gone,' said Duncan. 'They just fled when I killed him,
afraid they'd be blamed or arrested as spies if the authorities
were called and the whole story was told. Both, I think. That
chaplain – Father Ignatius – kept telling them that they'd all
end in a dungeon if they didn't get away. The grooms were
terrified. The priest said to them that they had passages on a
ship and had best use them; that the count had had messages
to deliver . . .'

'He certainly had,' I said with feeling. 'And a man,
Christopher Spelton, who is a servant of the queen as well as
our friend may be put in danger if those messages reach the
court of France! The situation doesn't just concern the death
of the count!'

'Indeed? Well, the priest said he must deliver the count's
messages for him and then they just went! They'd found a
ship that would take their horses.'

'They didn't take Mistress Wilde's pony,' said Brockley. 'It's in the stable here.'

'Yes, where is Mistress Wilde?' demanded Sybil. 'We came to find her, that most of all!'

'She went with them,' said Duncan, but he only said it after a brief hesitation. It was very brief but that was enough.

'She did *not* go with them,' I said. 'Now then! *Where is she?*'

There was another pause, a longer one. Then Master Ferguson said: 'She was hysterical. She refused to go with the others, and they said they wouldn't take her anyway. Duncan here caught the count only a short way from the gates and the lodge-keeper had heard and seen everything. He helped to get Mrs Wilde back here. She was shouting and frantic and swearing she'd report it all to the Constable in Dover Castle, and if she had, well, my romantic, impetuous nitwit of a son would probably be a prisoner in the castle now. Yes, Duncan, you *are* a nitwit, and don't call it being chivalrous and honourable and all the rest of it. *Sensible* is a better virtue. Count Renard didn't have it, either.'

'That sounds right,' I said thoughtfully, and Ferguson nodded. Addressing me directly, he said: 'He was one of those men who just don't know right from wrong. They don't think things out. They muddle through life. He didn't treat his horse well' – Brockley at this point growled in agreement – 'but he wasn't really cruel; it just never occurred to him to try a different way of controlling it, or simply try another horse! Anyway, we did what we could for Mistress Wilde. We gave her a soothing draught that quietened her down a little. It's made of poppy juice, I think. Not English poppies; this comes from the Mediterranean and we know a ship that imports it, the *Lucille* . . .' For a moment, he seemed to lose the thread of what he was saying. His face looked tired and worried.

Duncan, taking up the story, said: 'We got Mrs Wilde away, anyhow. There was a coastal trader in port, about to set sail for Scotland.'

'We paid the skipper the earth to take Mrs Wilde along,' Master Ferguson said, recovering himself. 'My wife sent her own maid with her and the lodge-keeper's elder son went too,

as their escort. We didn't want to harm her! But we couldn't
have her here, getting Duncan into trouble. She'll be all right.
She's going to Edinburgh, where I have kinfolk, and one of
them is looking for a wife. He's in good circumstances and
about her age and if she can be brought to agree, she'll have
a good match there. If she won't agree, well, my kin will look
after her. They'll find her a place in their household. They
won't turn her out into the street but they'll make sure she
doesn't communicate with England. I sent instructions with
her – the maid Annie has them in her charge. They won't want
a member of the family arrested and tried for unlawful killing,
any more than I do.'

'You've sent my daughter to Scotland and told your kinfolk
there to push her into a marriage with one of them? You're trying
to bundle her, a grown woman over whom you have no authority
whatsoever, a woman with a right to dispose of her own person,
into marriage with a complete stranger? Treating her as though
she were your property?' Sybil's voice shook with rage.

'She can refuse the match if she likes,' said Ferguson. 'I
said, she won't be turned out into the street. There are thousands of couples who married while they were still strangers,
and thousands of people who are ready to push grown women
into marriages for purposes of convenience. I gather that Mrs
Wilde's erstwhile in-laws have been trying to do that to her.
It's common enough.'

'But Mistress Wilde is not a member of your family! You
had no right—' Sybil burst out, only to be interrupted at once.

'I may have done her a favour,' said Ferguson. 'I believe
her in-laws are trying to force her to marry their chosen suitor,
by keeping her children from her. A decent husband – and my
kinsfolk *are* decent – would be a protection from them and
perhaps will help her to regain her sons, just as competently
as any foreign count could do.'

Sybil, unimpressed, said fiercely: 'We'll go after her, believe
me, we will. We'll fetch her back. Maybe Mistress Stannard
here won't report your son – you won't, will you, Ursula?'
Her eyes pleaded with me. *Don't make trouble for us or
Ambrosia. Don't make things worse.* 'What good would it do
and what use was the count to anyone anyway?'

'What were you going to do with the count's body?' I broke in.

'Bury it, tonight. My butler Morley is an ordained Catholic priest and would have given the count true burial rites, somewhere in my grounds. Your presence here made that impossible for tonight.'

'I see,' I said.

Sybil said persistently: 'Never mind all that – burials and messages, they're not the point! We have to find Ambrosia!'

'How?' I asked her. 'Do we have to search the whole of Edinburgh for her? I doubt if Mr Ferguson here will tell us where to look.'

'No, I shan't,' said Ferguson frankly. 'I will help you get to France, but not to Scotland. I will see that you don't go to Scotland, even if I have to have you put aboard a French-bound vessel in fetters.'

'They might go to Scotland later, Father,' said Duncan miserably.

'By then, you will be safely away,' said Ferguson. 'I have friends who live in Italy; you can go to them for the time being. I am buying time. Even Mistress Wilde can't be kept quiet for ever, but she can be kept quiet for long enough – and perhaps she will be more reasonable after a while.'

'For the moment,' I said, 'there's no question of going to Scotland. We have to go to France. The news the count was taking there, that Father Ignatius is now taking for him, will put Christopher Spelton in danger and . . .'

'Surely not! They'll just order him out of France!' Sybil protested. 'They've been trying to create an alliance with England; they won't put him in prison; they'll just send him home.'

'They might do anything,' said Dale ominously, reminding me once more of how she had once, in France, come near to being executed for heresy.

But she had made a good point. 'We can't be sure what they'll do,' I said. 'The French king and the queen mother are reportedly the sort that don't let their right hand know what the left hand is about.'

'But we can't do anything about these secret messages now!'

Sybil shouted it. 'They're on their way to France and that's
that! That man Father Ignatius will deliver them and we
couldn't stop him, not in his own country, even if we did catch
up with him. All we'd be going there for is to warn Spelton
but we'd be too late anyway and I can't believe he's really in
danger and *what about Ambrosia*?'

'Mrs Jester, the decision doesn't rest with Mrs Stannard, it
rests with me,' said Ferguson. 'I want you on your way to
France as fast as possible. After that, the future must take care
of itself, but your lost Ambrosia will not come to harm, either,
I assure you. I urge you to let her go.'

'I will *not* let her go!' Sybil wailed, bursting into tears.

'I said, the choice is not yours,' said Ferguson coldly. 'The
fact that the count was apparently a spy might be a strong
defence for Duncan and so might the fact that he apparently
tried to recruit my son into his own deplorable trade. I hope,
Duncan, that I can clear your name or get you pardoned in
due course but all that will take time. Meanwhile, the rest of
you are bound for France as soon as possible, and that's the
end of it.'

Duncan said: 'The *Lucille* is in port. This afternoon, I
escorted Kate into Dover because she wanted to shop, and we
met Mrs Briars and her daughters. We'd gone into the Safe
Harbour . . .'

'I'll wager you did,' said his father exasperatedly. 'And had
a nice snuggly kiss from pretty Bessie, no doubt. What with
you wanting to marry an unsuitable girl like Bessie and Kate
refusing to marry anyone at all . . . children! Oh well, better
you sow your wild oats with Bessie than with the Briars girls.
I don't like the Briars family,' he added to me. 'Mrs Briars is
a shrew and rumour has it that her daughters are no better
than they ought to be. But somehow, Kate and Duncan have
made the family's acquaintance and Kate seems to like the
girls. It worries me but perhaps it can be useful now. All right,
Duncan. Go on. I take it you found the Briars women in the
Safe Harbour and they told you the *Lucille* was in port. Captain
Garnett is Mrs Briars' cousin, I believe.'

'Yes. And Mrs Briars and her daughters were having ale
and chicken pasties in the inn,' said Duncan, 'and Mrs Briars

told us that the ship was in and her cousin was finding himself a cargo for her next trip. He goes anywhere; he doesn't make regular runs,' he explained, for our benefit.

'He'd take us to France?' I asked.

'Scotland!' protested Sybil.

'He'd take you to Cathay or Ultima Thule as long as he was adequately paid,' said Ferguson. 'I wouldn't be surprised if he did a bit of piracy as a sideline, myself. I don't like Captain Garnett any more than I like the rest of his family. But yes, he'd carry you across to France, though not your horses. He doesn't carry livestock. You can leave your animals here and collect them on your way home, if you wish. We'll look after them.'

'Well, we can't leave Joseph to look after them,' I said. 'We'll need him in France, when we hire mounts. But I can leave you some money for their keep.'

'I'm agreeable to that.'

We had money with us, of course. We each carried a good sum in case we should get separated, and we each had plenty of it in high-value coinage, to reduce the weight. 'I'll pay you as soon as our passages are fixed,' I said. 'I'll see this Captain Garnett tomorrow.'

'No, I will,' Ferguson told me. 'I want to be quite sure where Garnett is asked to take you. You are *not* going to Scotland and I shall make that clear to him. You will travel on his ship to the destination that I arrange with him. I am sorry to make threats but if I have to lock you all up and have you taken to the *Lucille* under guard – I have plenty of menservants – then I will. One thing about Garnett, I fancy, is that if his passengers come on board under duress, he won't blink an eyelid. You may take that as final. But you have little to complain about. You will at least have a chance to help this man, Spelton, about whom you are clearly worried and, meanwhile, I will get Duncan here to safety. Frankly, at least for the time being, I want you to be somewhere else, like Mistress Wilde.'

'We know too much,' I said. 'Yes, I see.'

SIXTEEN
Tired of Trouble

I t was some time before we finally went to bed and when
we did, I doubt if any of us slept much. I didn't sleep at
all. Hardly were Sybil and I alone before we were quarrelling, the worst – indeed as far as I could recall, the only
– real quarrel we had ever had.

'Ursula, we have to go after Ambrosia. We must. These
people she's been sent to; how do we know how they'll treat
her? She's out in the world all alone and it's not much better
than if she'd married that . . . *count!*' She made the word
count sound as though it were a vicious epithet.

She stopped to draw breath and I said patiently: 'And how
would we find her, in Edinburgh? We have no idea where in
the city to look for her, or even the names of the people she's
gone to. It may not be Ferguson. And meanwhile, Christopher
Spelton may have gone to his death, unless we can warn him
in time.'

'He won't be in danger, I don't believe it, I keep saying so!
But Ambrosia! Ursula, we must make arrangements of our
own, find a ship to take us north. In the morning . . .'

'Master Ferguson won't let us do anything of the kind. You
heard him!'

'We must escape! We could do it now, before dawn, the
way the count left Hawkswood! Ursula . . .'

'We're going to France, Sybil. Ambrosia is not in danger
of her life as far as we know, but Spelton may well be . . .'

'He *won't!* He'll just be expelled from France!'

'You say that because you want to believe it but there's no
certainty. There is no sense in trying to reach Scotland and
every reason to chase Father Ignatius to France. Now let us
get into bed and try to sleep. In the morning . . .'

'In the morning, we've got to try to get away and find a

ship going north, we've got to, I can't believe you could be
so heartless, Ursula. Never in all these years . . .'

'Sybil, don't you understand? This situation isn't of my
making! We don't actually have any choice. We're bound for
France whether we like it or not.'

'I will *not* go to France! I'll go to Scotland alone if I must
and . . .'

'Master Ferguson won't let you and nor will I. Sybil, be
reasonable. I'm so tired of trouble . . .'

'I won't be reasonable, I won't, won't, won't! If you are
cruel enough to see me go alone, then I pity the trouble you'll
have with your conscience, but I *will* go alone and . . .'

'You will not.'

'You are wicked and cruel!' shouted Sybil, in a voice that
I feared might wake the entire house, and then, to my horror
and astonishment, she sprang at me and tried to claw my face.
I seized her wrists, holding her with all the strength I had until
she suddenly softened and began to cry, while I stood gasping
and shaking. I had never seen Sybil, calm, sensible Sybil,
behave in such a way. It was as though I had been harbouring
a live volcano in my house all these years.

'Sybil, please,' I said feebly.

But the storm was over. She had collapsed on to the bed,
sobbing wildly and crying out that she was sorry, she was
sorry, but Ambrosia, her daughter was out there all alone . . .

'When we return from France we will go to Scotland,' I
promised. 'Ferguson won't be able to stop us then. I don't
know how we'll find her but perhaps we will. We'll try, and
with luck, we'll rescue her then. Now, for the love of heaven,
let us go to bed.'

In the morning we were all jaded and unrested and came late
to breakfast, to find that Ferguson had had his early and gone
out immediately afterwards. Sybil and I were silent and
awkward with each other and from the uneasy glances that
the Brockleys kept giving us, we knew they had heard the
quarrel. As soon as we had all eaten, the four of us went out
into the grounds – and were at once aware that we were being
watched, not to say stalked, by a couple of strapping footmen,

who were sauntering about outside the house. They never came close to us but they were never too far away, either. In addition, three burly gardeners were working between us and the gate.

'Master Ferguson meant what he said, I think,' Brockley remarked. 'If we try to leave the grounds, those tactful guards would stop us.'

'I want to try,' said Sybil, though half under her breath, and more to herself than to us.

'I don't,' said Brockley. 'It would be five men – six if the lodge-keeper joins in – plus two mastiffs, against me, Joseph, and three women. And if we did escape, we wouldn't have our horses.'

Sybil said no more. We wandered about for a little, looking at the flowerbeds in the formal gardens behind the house, not that there was much to see though no doubt they were pretty when they were in bloom. The day was dull and cold. After a while, we went back indoors and withdrew to our rooms, where Sybil and I – and probably the Brockleys as well – lay down and tried to make up for lost sleep.

From the moment we rose that morning, I had set about trying to mend the rift, and Sybil had been trying, as well. We had to make the best of things. The Brockleys, without saying so, seemed to concur. We were all in this together, after all. We were all gentle with Sybil and though for the most part, she was silent, when she did speak to anyone, including myself, she was polite. We made ourselves ready for dinner and went down to the hall in good time, to find, however, that Ferguson was there ahead of us. Before we were even seated, he told us, with an air of great thankfulness, that Captain Nathaniel Garnett would be ready to sail for France the next day, and had said if the wind held as it was now, we'd have a smooth crossing to Calais. 'And thank heaven for that,' said Ferguson. 'Something's going right, at least. I'm tired of trouble.'

I could sympathize with that.

Dinner was served. Apparently it was once more Kate's turn to feed her grandfather and although this time she didn't actually try to refuse, her face was sullen and her father kept giving her angry glances. The sweet course consisted of omelettes filled with hot jam, and Kate, sullen or not, dutifully performed her task, until a drop of jam fell on her grandfather's hand, whereupon he let out a cry, struck the spoonful she was offering him aside and then swore at her. His attendant, Peters, left his seat and came to the rescue, signalling Kate to hand over to him. Ferguson's mouth tightened and when the meal finished, he told Peters to help Ferguson senior away. Peters did as he was bid. And then Hamish Ferguson exploded.

'I have had enough! Trouble all the time and now there's to be an end to it. It's bad enough having a corpse in the house and finding out that when he was alive I was entertaining a spy. I feel I'm practically a traitor myself, now! On top of all that, I have a son who challenges a French count to a duel and says he wants to marry a tavern wench!'

He shot a glare at Duncan, who was just getting up to leave the table and now left it all the faster. His father promptly turned his ire on to Kate. 'But you!' He pointed a furious finger at her. 'Sulky and difficult, you don't like helping in the house or even helping to take care of your grandfather. You ought to be married with a household of your own! Well, I'm putting a stop to *your* nonsense, at least. You've a good dowry; I can get you married within three months and maybe sooner and I'm going to and this time you won't say no, because if you do, I'll do what I have never done, and beat you till you consent!'

'Please behave yourself better, Kate,' said Mrs Ferguson, sitting stiffly at her end of the table. 'How often have I begged you to? You are impossible. You mix with unsuitable people – worse even than Duncan's choice of company! The tavern girl at least has an honest reputation!'

'You've asked about her?' said Ferguson, looking startled.

'I wanted to know,' said his wife. 'If my son wants to marry, I want to look at the wench. There's nothing against her except that her father keeps an inn while we farm and invite the Constable of Dover Castle to dinner.'

Mistress Ferguson, it seemed, for all her stiff manners, had some human attributes. Duncan, it seemed, might have an ally in his mother.

And so might the younger girl, Sheila, who had been listening in a bright-eyed silence, which contrasted strongly with Kate's glowering one.

'Does this mean I can marry soon, as well?' she now asked. Kate turned her scowl on her sister but Sheila ignored it.

'As soon as your sister reaches the altar,' said her father reassuringly. 'We might have a double wedding! Now, that would be fine. Wouldn't it, Kate?' There was a touch of pleading in his voice.

'No, it wouldn't,' said Kate, and with that, threw herself out of her seat and followed her brother out of the hall.

Mistress Ferguson looked at her husband, who passed a hand across his brow and then said: 'I must do it now. Don't plead for her! I don't want to escort a bride to the altar who has stripes on her. I shall show her I mean what I say and that I won't tolerate any more resistance.'

'We could lock her in her room for a few days on bread and water,' said Mrs Ferguson.

'We've done that in the past but she turns sickly. Better the short, sharp option.' Ferguson rose to his feet and left the hall with determination in his step. His wife said nothing more, but sat biting her lip. The servants were coming in to clear away. I glanced round at the others and we left as well, returning to our rooms, where, on my recommendation, we distracted ourselves by once more collecting our cloaks and going out into the wintry garden.

I encouraged us to hurry, reminding the others that on our earlier expedition outside, we had found a side door that opened straight into the formal garden. But we didn't move quite quickly enough. As we made our way towards the back of the house and passed the foot of the main staircase, we heard, upstairs, the sound of an ominous swishing and Kate's voice, crying out in pain.

'Might do her good,' said Brockley. 'She's not what I call a dutiful daughter. Though I can see why she doesn't enjoy feeding that disagreeable old man!'

'So can I,' I said. 'And I'm sorry for her.' The aunt and uncle in whose house I had grown up had been free with the birch, and for all her wilfulness and sulky airs, I couldn't dislike Kate. I had probably resembled her when I was young. I had been unhappy and I thought Kate too was in some way discontented with her lot, though by most people's standards, her parents were responsible and patient. But that distressing sound made me pity her.

'I know what it feels like,' I said.

SEVENTEEN
An Act of Betrayal

Throughout all this time, I think we had all been alert for the sound of hoofbeats, for the arrival of an armed authority from Walsingham, which would take the situation in hand. But there was still no sign of any reinforcements when we left Whitefields the next day to go aboard the *Lucille*.

We started out through a sea-mist that shrouded Dover and muffled our voices, but before we reached the harbour it had lifted and the sun came out. We rode as far as the quay, escorted by Ferguson and a couple of grooms who had come with us to lead our horses back. The Brockleys and I were travelled enough to know something about shipping and saw at once that the *Lucille* was a sturdy brig, although she looked as though she could do with a fresh coat of paint.

'She's a bit weathered. I hope she's comfortable,' Brockley remarked as he and Joseph and the grooms heaved our saddle-bags off our horses. We were carrying our belongings that way, for we would hire horses for travelling in France.

We said our farewells, took our baggage and made for the gangplank. Our approach had been observed and at the top we found a tall man waiting to greet us. He had a drooping moustache and eyes so deep set that they were surely forever in shadow. His smile was broad, revealing splendid teeth, which sounds attractive but was not. He introduced himself as Captain Garnett, and for once I found myself agreeing with Mr Ferguson, in that I took an instant dislike to him.

This redoubled when, as he led the way along the deck, he was bumped into by a ship's boy who had suddenly emerged from a companionway. Captain Garnett grabbed the unfortunate youth by the scruff of his neck, shouted at him for carelessness and then spun him round and literally kicked him back down the stairs, shouting: 'Now you'll have to come up again and this time look what you're about or it'll be the cat for you!'

A sailor who was coming along the deck just then exclaimed in protest that the boy was his nephew and there was no need for that, Cap'n.

'He gets no special treatment for being the first mate's nephew, Bones,' Garnett barked at him.

'Nor should he. He just needs *fair* treatment,' said Mr Bones. I noticed that his body stiffened as he spoke, and that his voice had a pleading note in it. He was a lean man of around forty, with untidy dust-coloured hair and a thin face with a sharp chin. He looked mature and not timid but I sensed that he feared the captain, and that only concern for his nephew had made him speak.

Garnett, however, merely growled: 'You talk too much, Bones, as I've told you often enough!' and brushed past him, followed by me and my companions still clutching our baggage and glancing at each other with raised eyebrows.

We had to wait to get down the companionway, as another sailor came up it just then. This one was stocky and swarthy with a black beard and black hair tied back in a queue. 'Standing up for your nevvy again, Bones?' he called, addressing the retreating back of the first mate.

'Well, he *is* my nephew,' shouted Bones, over his shoulder, and strode on.

The lad in question emerged from the companionway again at that point, gave Captain Garnett a scared glance and carefully dodged round him before following his uncle back along the deck. As we at last began to descend the stairs, Brockley muttered into my ear that this didn't strike him as a happy ship and it wouldn't surprise him if Captain Garnett used those lovely teeth of his for eating people who had annoyed him.

'I know,' I muttered back. 'I'm glad it isn't a long voyage to Calais!'

We were shown to our quarters by Captain Garnett. 'I carry passengers from time to time and I've had cabins fitted out for them,' he said. 'There was no room to make them spacious but I did my best since I knew I'd be carrying ladies now and then. Here we are.'

The accommodation certainly wasn't luxurious. A single door led into a kind of suite, consisting of three cabins leading into one another. They were poorly lit, though each had a narrow, sealed window high up, near the ceiling. Two of the cabins were small, with a couple of bunks not made up except for thin mattresses, and one was larger but had no bunks, just a pile of straw pallets. It also contained some barrels and a pile of pinewood planks, roped together. It looked as if the cargo had overflowed from the hold.

When the captain left us, I said: 'Since we won't be aboard long, I think we can all camp in here.' Instinctively, I wanted to keep us all together. If I had been challenged to explain myself, I couldn't have done so. That I had witnessed the captain bullying a ship's boy, considered that his teeth made him look like a cannibal and disliked the manner of just one of his crew, hardly accounted for this sudden unease, but as soon as we had been left for ourselves, I learned that I wasn't alone in it.

'I don't take to that captain,' Dale said. 'I can't abide seeing a harmless lad treated like that and I didn't take to that fellow with the black pigtail either. I'm glad we're all staying together.'

'I agree,' said Brockley in sombre tones. 'I'll be glad to step ashore at Calais. I wish we could see out.'

'So do I,' said Dale in heartfelt tones. 'One of the things I can't abide about sea travel is the way one can't see out.'

'It won't be for long,' said Brockley comfortingly. 'I think we'll have a good wind for it.'

'I wish it were longer, and going north,' said Sybil, half under her breath. No one answered her.

Joseph hadn't been listening. Instead he was examining the pallets and now remarked that they seemed comfortable enough, and he'd found a cupboard with blankets in it.

'But no sheets or pillows?' said Dale.

'Seemingly, no,' said Joseph. 'But I expect the captain has them on *his* bed.' Dale and Sybil looked depressed but Joseph, unperturbed, remarked: 'Well, the blankets are good. The thing is to keep warm,' and I remembered that it had never occurred to me to provide the Hawkswood grooms with sheets. Perhaps I should have done. When we got home . . .

And when would we get home? I didn't want to be here, didn't want to go to France. I wanted to be back at Hawkswood. What was Harry doing now? His nurse Tessie would take good care of him but was he missing me as I was missing him? I wished I could be alone to cry.

But I was not alone and home was far away. Elsewhere in the ship, there were sounds that I recognized: orders being barked out, hurrying feet. The ship stirred and we began to hear the sound of the wind in the rigging. The wooden walls of our cabin started to creak. Our journey to France had begun.

We all began to fret because we couldn't see out, and after we had been under way for a while Brockley said we ought to go out on deck. 'We can breathe the fresh air and watch the white cliffs dropping astern.'

'I wouldn't call that a treat,' Dale said. 'I never see the white cliffs disappearing without wondering when I'll see them again. But I'd like some air and something to look at.'

'So would I,' I said, and with that I went to the door and lifted the latch.

Without result, as the door appeared to be stuck.

Brockley came to my assistance but the door would not yield even to his added strength and he stopped, saying: 'I was afraid of this.'

I had stepped back too. 'What do you mean?' I asked.

'When our good captain left us here,' said Brockley grimly, 'I *thought* I heard a bolt being quietly shot. I hoped I was imagining it but I wasn't. We've been locked in.'

The words went through me like a crossbow bolt, rousing up the uneasy feeling that had made me want to keep us together. I looked at the others. Joseph's eyes were wide; Sybil was biting her lip and Dale was wiping away a tear. I said: 'It could have been a mistake of some kind. We could hammer on the door and shout.'

'I don't think it was a mistake,' Brockley said. 'And I don't think pounding on the door will bring anyone to release us, with apologies. Someone might bring us food, presently . . .' For the sake of the others, I didn't say, *What if they don't?* '. . . and then we may learn more. Anyway, we'll soon be in

Calais and they'll have to release us then. Let's not make a disturbance just yet. We don't know what all this is about.'

'Some crafty scheme by Ferguson, I've no doubt,' sniffed Dale. 'He said he didn't care for Captain Garnett, didn't he? But maybe he's using him.'

'For what?' I asked. 'It can't be to keep us from going to Scotland! What does he suppose we might do? Jump overboard and start swimming up the North Sea? This doesn't make sense.'

'No, it doesn't. Master Ferguson didn't strike me as a very likeable fellow,' said Brockley, 'but he did strike me as honest. I think we had better be wary. We don't know what we're dealing with. For the moment, let them think we haven't realized.'

Dale said: 'I'm frightened.' Nobody answered, which meant of course that we all were.

We each pulled out a pallet, set them on the floor and sat on them, since there was nothing else to sit on, and then we followed Brockley's advice for what seemed like a century while the rectangular patches of sunlight from the little high windows moved gradually across the floor, their shapes slanting over the floor and walls and narrowing until they had almost vanished. Brockley, who was watching them, suddenly stiffened. 'What is it?' I asked.

'It's the light.' Brockley got up. 'Joseph, help me move one of those barrels under that window there.'

Joseph obliged. The barrel was clearly heavy, for they had to heave and strain, but when it was done, Brockley clambered up on top of it and was able to peer out, turning his head this way and that, as though trying to see fore and aft.

'What is it?' I said again.

'This is a starboard side,' said Brockley.

Sybil said: 'Starboard?' in puzzled tones.

He said tersely: 'I mean they're on the right-hand side of the ship. The left-hand side's called port.' He twisted his neck again. 'This is all wrong,' he said grimly.

'What is?' said Dale anxiously.

'Our course,' said Brockley. 'It's about noon. If we were sailing to Calais, at this time of day the sunlight ought to be coming from this side, at least mostly. Well, it isn't. It's ahead of us and even tending to the port side. I can see the ship's shadow on the water. I'd estimate that we're sailing more or less south-west. I think we're off course.'

'But – then where are we going?' cried Sybil.

'No one knows,' said Brockley ominously.

I drew a sharp breath. I was remembering the day that Sir Francis Walsingham, Sir Robert Dudley and Sir William Cecil arrived at my Sussex home of Withysham to propose the marriage between me and Renard. I had recalled the conversation at the dining table that evening.

I said: 'Brockley, if we're no longer making towards Calais and have turned south-west, then either we're making for somewhere else in France, or we're going to turn west and go zig-zagging against the wind in the English Channel. In that case . . .'

Brockley's eyes met mine. Dale said plaintively: 'I don't understand.'

'Nor do I,' said Sybil. Joseph seemed bemused.

Brockley said: 'I'm guessing. I could be wrong.'

Shortly after that, we at last heard feet approaching our door, and heard the sound of bolts being slid back. Captain Garnett came in, smiling, followed by two other men, the one with the pigtail and the other by contrast small and wiry, with red hair (a much brighter shade than the ginger hair of the Ferguson men). His eyes were unusual, being almost amber in colour, and the effect was oddly unpleasant, though more because of their expression than their yellowness.

When I was at court as a lady of the bedchamber, one of the other ladies had had eyes like that, but she was a charming and sweet-natured woman, and her eyes were beautiful, like sparkling topazes. This man's eyes were feline. I shrank from all three of them but was then distracted by a fourth member of the party, because it was Katherine Ferguson.

I opened my mouth to exclaim but had no chance. Captain Garnett spoke first. 'Here you are, dear Kate. Here are your friends. I've done my best for them but this ship isn't luxurious, I fear.'

Katherine was looking at us nervously. 'I've run away from
home,' she said. 'You know what my father did to me yesterday.
Captain Garnett and I –' she gave him a quick, adoring glance
– 'have been in love for months but I know my father would
never agree because he doesn't like the family. I'd have run
away to Nathaniel long ago but he put every penny he had
into buying this ship and fitting it out the way he wanted to,
and he hasn't saved enough yet to give me a proper home.
But yesterday I couldn't bear it any more, so I've run away
to him.'

'She's a resourceful wench,' the captain observed. 'Last
night, she put some dresses and things in a hamper and hid
them in the grounds of her home.'

'My maid Amy looks after Sheila as well, and Mother too,
now that she's sent her maid away with Mrs Wilde,' Katherine
said, 'so it was easy to hide the things without Amy knowing.
She has so much to do! Then I slipped away at dawn and
came to the *Lucille* and I said I'd live on board with Nat until
he could provide a home on shore for me. Lots of captains
take their wives to sea with them . . .'

Her voice faded away, I think because of the complete lack
of response from the rest of us. My companions and I were
probably looking shocked while Garnett and his two crewmen
were smiling in a most disquieting way.

'I'm sorry that your quarters aren't as nice as mine,' said
Katherine. 'I shall share Nat's cabin, of course. We'll marry
in Calais. We must be nearly there by now. How long will it
be, Nat?'

'Well,' said Garnett, 'as to that . . .'

The other two laughed.

Evil, genuine evil, is a rare phenomenon. I had met it before
but not often. Most of the people who had been a danger to
me had been so because they had beliefs that made them
enemies to my country and the queen I served. They were
usually convinced that they were honest servants of God.
Others had been criminals in a commonplace way; wicked,
but not yet over that undefined but very real boundary into
the land of souls irretrievably lost.

Only once or twice had I encountered the real thing but I

had met it, and because of that, I could recognize it. I had recognized it now, in triplicate. It emanated like dark smoke from the tall person of Captain Garnett, from the pigtailed, square-built man on his right hand, and from the feline little redhead on his left.

Who were now formally introduced to us.

'Let me present my companions to you,' Garnett said. His voice was even and quite educated, I noticed. 'You may as well know the names of the people who will help at times in bringing your food to you, because with this wind it will take a good few days to reach our destination. This . . .' with a thick hand, adorned by a massive gold ring, he pointed at the dark man '. . . is Reg Myers, second mate, and this . . .' he indicated yellow-eyes, '. . . is Robbie Brown, one of my sailors, only no one ever uses his real name. He's known as Leo, because he has the eyes of a lion. And the temperament, too. He's not a man to annoy. These two are the finest of my crew, though Alfred Bones, who you met when you first came aboard, is the best navigator aboard and very experienced, which is why I made him first mate. Bones will also visit you on occasion to make sure all is well with you. With you all.'

He smiled at Katherine, a curiously horrid smile, which caused her to stare back at him in bewilderment. 'You won't be sharing my cabin, my love. I might be tempted and fall, like Adam when Eve offered him an apple. I shall take pains, on the contrary, to preserve your virginity, because it will add so much to your value.'

'I knew it. *Lundy!*' muttered Brockley.

'My *value!*' Katherine's voice shook. The truth was breaking in on her, but slowly, fighting against the trustful love that evil was destroying before our eyes.

'It was lucky that your arrival coincided with theirs,' said Garnett, nodding at the rest of us. 'All together you amount to a reasonable consignment, a gift from the gods, as it were. Quite a rare piece of luck for me. If you want to know where you're going, you will be sold to some – er – businessmen based in the Bristol Channel. They will deliver you eventually to the North African coast and sell you for a sound profit. I have done quite well from supplying them. Young virgins are especially valuable in their eyes. I have no fear that you will lose your virtue among your friends here, so I will leave you with them and they can comfort you.'

'But . . . but . . .' Katherine's face was a mask of horror and incomprehension. She clutched at his arm. He detached her.

'Your friends,' he remarked, 'aren't as valuable as you but they're by no means worthless. Two able-bodied men, one young . . .'

'Here! You just stop that! Me and Mr Brockley ain't horses for sale!' Joseph burst out. He was promptly grabbed by Myers, who spun him round and wrenched Joseph's right arm up his back so that he shouted out in anguish. Myers, who seemed to have the strength of a bull, then tossed him to the floor, where he lay gasping and clutching at his right elbow.

'Don't damage them, Myers,' said Garnett. 'I've told you about that before. I like to sell sound stock. As I was saying, two able-bodied men and four women, one a virgin, and three mature ladies, one of them at least quite likely still able to bear children . . .' He grinned at me and I stifled an angry gasp. 'Not bad, not bad. Many older men like mature ladies in their household. Such ladies are less demanding and exhausting than young ones. And women are always needed to cook and clean. Oh, yes, there are markets for all of you in the Mediterranean world.' Myers and Leo laughed sycophantically.

Choking, I gulped out: 'Did Master Ferguson arrange this with you? Does he know what you intend to do with us?'

Captain Garnett appeared scandalized. 'Of course not. He is not such a man as would do a thing like that – even though he was unaware that his daughter was going to run off with me. I think he has vague suspicions about me but he knows nothing and I doubt if he has ever dreamed what my secret trade really is. He would have the Constable of Dover Castle boarding my ship and marching me off in chains before I had time to turn round. No, no. Kate assures me that though she left a note, she didn't say where she was going. Is that not so, my love?'

He smiled toothily on Katherine, who seemed to have been

struck with paralysis. Now the paralysis broke into a scream. 'I came to you because I loved you and you said you loved me!' She turned to flee from our cabin, only to be seized by Myers, who caught her in passing, as it were, almost lazily, by stretching out an arm and closing a hairy hand round her shoulder. He jerked her back from the doorway.

'Now, now, there's no use in you having the vapours, my wench,' he remarked in would-be soothing tones. 'You can't get off the ship while we're at sea, anyhow. What's all the fuss? I am letting you and your friends stay in the comparative comfort of our passenger quarters and you're bound for a new life in a warm climate; what's so awful about that?'

'*Nat!*' shrieked Katherine. 'You can't do this, you can't betray me like this! I trusted you, I loved you, I can't believe . . .!'

She tore herself free of Myers and leapt towards the captain, attempting to cast herself into his arms. He threw her off. She at once sprang at him again, shrieking and trying to pummel him. Leo pulled her away and slapped her, which made her shriek still more loudly. Brockley tried to wrench her out of Leo's grasp but a blow from Myers's fist sent him reeling. Leo threw her on to a pallet, where she lay face down, sobbing wildly. Sybil and I went to her, but she kicked out at us as if we too were her enemies and we drew back, not wanting to make the scene worse.

'It's always better for young wenches not to use their own judgement in matters of trust,' said Garnett smugly. 'Dear Kate, you should have stayed safe at home and done as your dad told you. I don't raid on the east coast; you'd have been safe enough then. I'd have given you a few good times and that would have been the end of it. I do my raiding along the Devon and Cornish coasts,' he added to the rest of us in conversational tones. 'It's handier for delivery to my customers.' He paused and then remarked: 'I hope none of you will give any trouble. For the moment, and out of consideration to my dear Kate there, I am leaving you here in reasonable comfort, but I have real slave quarters down below and you wouldn't like those at all. But they're where you will go, in irons, if you're intransigent.'

Brockley was sitting on the floor with his back to a wall,

nursing his bruised jaw. '*Are* we going to Lundy Island?' he asked indistinctly.

Garnett looked at him. 'So you know where my customers have settled themselves?'

'Yes.' Dale had gone to help her husband, and with her assistance Brockley now got to his feet. 'We learned it from senior members of her majesty Queen Elizabeth's court,' said Brockley. 'Mistress Stannard happens to be a sister of her majesty.'

'A sister? You jest, my friend. The queen only had one sister, who is now dead, or her majesty would still be just a princess.'

'King Henry had – liaisons,' I said. 'My mother served Queen Anne Boleyn until she was sent home in disgrace, with child. I was the child. But our relationship is known to her majesty. There will be a great hue and cry if I disappear.'

'I landed you safely at Calais,' said Garnett, not in the least disconcerted, while his henchmen listened admiringly. 'You vanished in France. No one will imagine that I had anything to do with that. But in the eyes of my customers, if you truly are the queen's sister, that will enhance *your* value greatly, and my profits with it. We will leave you now to settle down and accustom yourselves. Behave and we'll treat you kindly enough. A meal will be brought to you soon.'

'I shan't eat it. I shall starve myself to death rather than be a slave!' shouted Katherine, turning over to make her voice heard.

'Oh, you'll eat,' said her faithless lover. 'You ran away to me because your father beat you. When you find out what I can do in that line, you will do everything I tell you, including eat your meals. I don't want to sell half-starved goods to my friends on Lundy.'

He turned away, making a *let's leave them* gesture to his companions, and then they were gone. We heard the bolts outside the door slam home, noisily this time, whereas before it had been done softly, no doubt to keep us quiet for as long as possible. The ship lurched and there was a change in the motion.

'We're altering course,' said Brockley. 'We're turning west – I'm sure of it.'

'Oh God, oh God!' Katherine wept and this time did not resist when Sybil sat down beside her and put an arm round her.

I sat down on her other side. I was shaking. Slavery. In a far country where there was no chance of help. I would never see Hawkswood again; never see England . . . never see Harry again! At that, such a fury and grief rose up in me that I thought my heart was going to tear itself, raging, from my body; thought I might burst and disintegrate all over the cabin. I looked at Sybil with contrition.

I was still worried about Christopher Spelton but he was small and distant compared to my longing for Harry. If it came to the choice, I would abandon a thousand Christopher Speltons to their fate sooner than miss even the faintest chance of being again with my little son. I understood far better now why Sybil had attacked me.

I tried to take hold of myself, clenching my teeth, attempting to *think*. I would have liked to roll on the floor and pound it with my fists and be hysterical but that wouldn't help anyone. I said: 'It will take a long time to get through the English Channel with an unfavourable wind, and then round the toe of Cornwall to reach the Bristol Channel. There's time to plan something. We must! We have simply got to escape!'

EIGHTEEN
The Power of Fear

Brockley said: 'Katherine, how much do you know about this ship? Have you been aboard her before? Did Captain Garnett talk to you about her very much, and if so, what did he say?'

'People mostly call me Kate,' Katherine said miserably. 'Even my parents when they're not cross with me, only they so often are. Will you call me Kate as well? I can't help much, I've never been on the ship before.' She sat up on her pallet. Tears ran down her face. 'Oh, what a fool I've been!'

'Love does that to people,' I said. She had behaved very badly but at her age, I probably wouldn't have realized that. At the age of twenty, I had crawled out of my bedroom window at the house of my uncle and aunt, slithered down a sloping roof, dropped into the arms of Gerald Blanchard, who was officially betrothed to my cousin Mary, and run away with him.

But Uncle Herbert and Aunt Tabitha, though they had sheltered me, had not been very kind, all the same, and Gerald was an honest man. I had possibly had better judgement than Kate. But I had been just as wild.

Had Gerald lived, I might well have remained peacefully with him for good. My life of adventure had arisen by chance – and a need for money when I was widowed. Yet, as I knew at heart, my unlikely career would not have persisted as it had without that wildness, that urge for excitement. I thought Kate had it too.

'The past is the past,' I said to her. I spoke gently. 'But Garnett surely spoke to you about his ship, even if he didn't show you round her. Please tell us all you know. How did you meet him?'

'I met him at Mrs Briars' house – the woman Duncan and

I got to know in Dover. We met her daughters first, when there was a fair. I was there with Sheila and we came across the Briars girls when we all found ourselves looking at things on a stall – gloves, I think . . .'

'Garnett,' said Dale impatiently. 'What about Garnett?'

'Father lets Sheila and me go into Dover by ourselves now and then, as long as we go together. Well, after we met Mrs Briars and her girls at the fair, we used to go to her house sometimes. One day, Nat was there. He's a cousin of Mrs Briars. We fell in love. Sheila didn't realize. Nat and I were very careful.'

Kate hesitated and then, lowering her voice, said: 'Only it wasn't *we fell in love*, it seems. It was *I* fell in love. Only, my father would never have agreed; he doesn't like Mrs Briars or her girls *or* Captain Garnett. He knows about the family, because he's acquainted with most of the captains who call regularly at Dover. He knows Captain Garnett and the *Lucille*. Sheila and I enjoyed visiting Mrs Briars, though, so we didn't tell him that we had met her and her daughters – until he met Mrs Briars and Captain Garnett one day in Dover, by chance, and Mrs Briars let out that Sheila and I were friends with her girls. When he came home, he said he didn't mind buying a few imported goods from Captain Garnett, but he didn't care for him or his relatives and that Sheila and I shouldn't mix with them too much.'

'He clearly has good judgement,' remarked Brockley acidly. 'Well, go on.'

'He didn't actually forbid me or Sheila to see Mrs Briars and her girls,' said Kate. 'He didn't know about Nat and me and – my father is often harsh but he's fair, too. He said he didn't know anything specific against the Briars girls. He even said one shouldn't pay too much heed to gossip; that Cath and Jenny were very pretty and jealous people do say things. I think he would have been more concerned if *Duncan* had been going there – he'd have thought the Briars girls were as unsuitable as Bessie at the Safe Harbour. So when the *Lucille* was in port, I still saw Nat sometimes at Mrs Briars' house. And twice, I met him alone on the cliffs. I managed to lose Sheila in Dover and slip away to join Nat. I knew she'd worry and

look for me but she'd do that for a long time, not wanting to
go home and say she'd got separated from me. She'd give up
eventually and then she would go home, and I'd be there ahead
of her, all apologies for losing her. I didn't let her get into
trouble.' She hesitated again, looking at each of our faces in
turn and then said: 'I told my parents it was my fault!'

She sounded as though she feared angry accusations from
us. But none of us spoke. 'My parents would have grown
suspicious if it kept happening so I only did it twice,' she said.
'It was so exciting. *Nat* was so exciting! Father keeps introducing me to men he thinks I might marry but they're all older
than me and so *dull*. Nothing exciting had ever happened to
me before I met Nat, and now I find out that the Nat I thought
I loved never existed and he's done this to me . . .'

'So,' said Brockley, 'getting back to where we started, what
do you know about this ship? Surely he talked to you about
it sometimes! Are the crew all devoted to their captain, do you
know?'

Kate looked puzzled but after frowning for a moment, said
doubtfully: 'Well, no . . . no, I don't think so. He said something once . . . but does it matter?'

'It might,' said Brockley. 'I'm thinking that if by any chance
the captain's unpopular with some of his crew, that could be
the crack we could put a chisel into. We've got to escape if
we can. Any kind of weakness in the way this ship is organized, any kind of trouble among her men, might be something
we could use. What was it he said?'

'It was that last time we met on the cliffs. I asked why we
couldn't run away and get married and that's when he said he
couldn't afford a home for me yet because of what the ship
had cost him, and he said he couldn't pay his men as well as
they'd like, either. And then he laughed and told me that it
didn't matter much; he had ways of keeping hold of good
sailors once he'd got them. I didn't know what he meant. I
asked but he wouldn't tell me.'

'I don't think Mr Bones likes him much,' I said. 'The first
mate. When we came on board, we saw Garnett kick a boy
down a companionway and Mr Bones saw as well. He said
the lad was his nephew and he remonstrated with Garnett.'

We stopped talking then, alerted by the sound of bolts being drawn back and by a savoury smell. The door opened and pat on the mention of his name, Bones came in, accompanied by his nephew, each of them carrying a tray. Bones' tray held earthenware beakers and jugs respectively of wine and water, while his nephew was carrying food on his; a tureen of stew, some bread, spoons and wooden platters.

Bones kicked the door shut behind him and the trays were put down on the tops of two barrels, since there were no tables. Bones ignored the rest of us but looked at Kate.

'This is a bad business, my wench. You've been cozened and led into a trap and I'm not the only one that thinks so. Nothing we can do about it, yet it's on my mind and I'll admit I think it's wrong. But you'll have to make the best of it.' His eyes now moved to take all of us in. 'Best eat your food. Vittles are good on the *Lucille*. You'll likely fetch higher prices if you look fit and your buyers'll treat you the better for it.'

'How many men are there on this ship?' Brockley asked.

'There's you two and the captain and we've seen a couple more. That's five. How many others?'

Bones looked surprised. 'Fourteen all told. Have you got some notion of escaping? Forget it. Two men and four women? You'd have no chance.'

'Captain Garnett,' said Brockley, 'apparently doesn't pay his men as well as some of you would like but still keeps you all in order by some unknown means. What is it?'

'Now how would you know that?'

'Captain Garnett told me,' said Kate, in a small defiant voice. 'He told me himself, back when . . .'

Her voice died on a sob. Bones studied her, out of thoughtful, light-coloured eyes, and once more shifted his gaze to the rest of us, as though in appraisal while his nephew began to ladle stew into bowls.

'It's true enough,' he said slowly. 'We all reckon he gets good prices from that rats' nest on Lundy – Barbary pirates they are – and he says that that side of his business is separate from his ordinary cargoes and passengers, and he don't expect us to work at it as part of earning our ordinary wages. It's special, and we get a share of the profits. It all sounds mighty convincing but there's a powerful lot of risk and it goes against the grain with some of us and there's been a lot of talk about our shares not being all they should be. Except maybe with Myers and Yellow-Eyes, otherwise known as Leo. They're a wicked pair, as bad as he is, and we reckon he keeps them sweet by paying them better from the proceeds of his slave sales than he pays us.'

'It sounds as though some of you aren't that loyal to Garnett,' observed Brockley. 'But don't you actually know what he gets for his sales to the gentlemen from Barbary?'

'We know what the captain says he gets,' said Bones. 'There are rules we all understand. Cap'n says he divides the slave proceeds into twenty shares. That's one for each man, including himself, and six over – two extra for me as first mate, and the rest for Garnett as captain. Only thing is, we're never sure what the whole sum is. Yes, he tells us, but we wonder sometimes if he tells the truth. There's a man aboard who says he's sure he doesn't – a fellow called Magnus Clay who's been a slave in his time, but escaped and got home to England. He knows something about the rates for slave sales. Are you asking who loves Garnett and who doesn't? That's no secret but it makes no difference to you. Leo and Myers like his company and there's about four others don't mind him. The rest of us aren't so affectionate but we don't have much choice. What of it?'

'Seven or so on each side, then,' said Brockley persistently. 'Just what do you mean when you say you don't have much choice? Is that to do with whatever he meant when he told Kate that he had methods of keeping hold of his crew?'

'Yes. He's got something on all of us,' said Bones with a shrug. 'We leave him; he'll set the authorities on to us – without coming out of the shadows himself. There's two wanted ashore for highway robbery, and one for coining – that's Magnus – and Leo's wanted for murder.'

He grinned in a rueful fashion. 'I don't know exactly what he has on the rest but it's something. I got mixed up with him after I knifed someone in a brawl and I wanted to get out of the country. It was a fight over a girl,' he explained. 'They're more tolerant of things like that in France, so it's said. Only I can't speak French and I've been a seaman all my life anyway. I just took a berth on a ship, any old ship would do, I thought, as long as she was sailing straight away. The *Lucille* was ready to sail and she was going foreign. So I picked *her*.' He snorted, as if in exasperation with himself.

I exchanged a quick glance with Brockley. Here, surely, was a potential ally.

'Garnett got it out of me, why I was so eager,' Mr Bones told us. 'I always did talk too much though I reckon there's no harm in talking to you. What can you do if there's naught we can do ourselves? We start anything and lose the fight, and if he don't hang us himself, he'll see us strung up by the lawmen on shore. There's no doing much against Garnett. Which is a pity.' His nephew, who was now filling glasses and offering a choice of water or wine, muttered: 'Yes, it is!' quite passionately at this point.

Joseph, emerging from his usual silence, said: 'How did you come to be here, lad? Did you knife someone, too?'

'No, he's my brother's son and he was left an orphan before I had my brawl,' said Bones. 'I took him on, and when I ran for it, I brought him with me because I didn't want to leave him alone. He was a few years younger then, but Garnett said he could use him. And so he does; works him all day *and* half the night, if you take my meaning. Don't he, Jacky boy?'

'I hate him,' said Jacky simply.

Kate was staring at the two of them in horror. 'What . . . what do you mean? Does he . . . I mean, is he . . .?'

'He's not fussy who shares his bunk. Male or female, either'll do,' said Jacky. Kate looked sick.

'Don't upset yourself, my wench,' said Bones. 'He's all over Jacky at the moment, and when he's like that, he likely won't bother any of you ladies. You should be glad. Well, I'm weary enough of being no more than a prisoner in Garnett's hands and not even decently paid for my work, and seeing my own flesh and blood used as a catamite. But I tell you, there's too much fear on this ship – fear of the power the captain has over us, and fear of Myers and Leo as well. They're like his body-guards. Since I've been aboard, Garnett has killed two men with the cat. Deliberately. He just carried on until they died.'

I shuddered.

'Money,' said Joseph thoughtfully. 'Don't they say: money talks?'

We all looked at him and I picked up what was in his mind. 'I'd reward anyone who helped us out of this mess,' I said. 'And reward him well. And keep his secret, whatever it may be. Tell me, if you think the captain isn't paying his crew proper shares, what does he do with the money *he* gets for . . . his business?'

'He wouldn't want to leave his money ashore, though as far as I know there ain't no price on his head yetawhile, cunning fellow that he is. We mostly deliver passengers safely to where they want to go, so as yet, his reputation hasn't come to harm. A group like you is a lucky chance for him. All the same, he don't care to put his money in the hands of bankers. He keeps it in a strongbox bolted to his cabin floor,' said Bones. 'With a massive great padlock on it. We daren't tamper with that. Wish we could. If some of the men could see what they've been cheated of, well, that might annoy them. But before they'd got worked up enough to do anything about it, I fancy he'd have seen any damage to the padlock and there'd be the devil to pay.'

'Are you saying,' I asked him disbelievingly, 'that in a shipload of villains, nobody knows how to pick a lock?'

'I daresay several could,' said Bones. 'But it's too dangerous. I told you, he knows too much about some of us and . . .'

'You mean no one's ever had the guts to jump ship?' enquired Joseph.

Bones was wearing a coarse linen shirt under a sleeveless woollen jerkin. He held out his left hand and rolled up the shirtsleeve. On the back of his wrist was a brand, vivid red against the weather-browned skin. 'My initials, AB for Alfred Bones,' he said. 'Our revered captain did that when he decided that I was useful and he wanted to keep me. If I went ashore and didn't come back, he'd hire a messenger and send word anonymously to the local constable that one Alfred Bones, wanted for killing a man in a knife-fight, had been seen in the district, and there would be a description of me, including mention of this brand. Any conscientious constable would want to get his hands on me, and send me back to the authorities in the place where the killing took place. I'd be in peril for life. Garnett has a full set of brands in the shape of the alphabet. That's part of how he holds us.'

'You could tell a pretty tale yourself. About him,' Brockley pointed out.

'Who's to believe the word of a man wanted for a grave offence, with the loss of a hand, or death from a rope, awaiting him? Garnett has actually carried his threat out twice to my knowledge.'

'I still think the brand is a poor way of exerting control,' snorted Brockley. 'Sailors have all sorts of marks on them, rope burns and scars, all manner of things. When I was in the army, years ago, there was a fellow who'd been a sailor, voyaging all over the place and he had his wife's name – Mary – printed on to his right arm in some way. He'd come across some wild tribe or other that did it by cutting the skin and rubbing pigment into it. It sounded awful and he said he wouldn't do it again, but there it was, anyway.'

'Maybe,' said Bones. 'But the truth is I think Garnett likes doing it. He enjoys it best when his victims scream. I didn't but to this day I don't know how I stopped myself.'

'Ugh!' I said.

Sybil asked: 'Were the two men who did run away, actually arrested?'

'Who knows? Maybe not, but they still carry their brands and it's true enough that someday, somewhere, someone may recognize them by that, someone that knows that a man with that brand is wanted for murder or coining or what you will. No one wants to take the chance. One day, maybe, he'll go too far and the spark will explode but not yet.'

'Are we making straight for Lundy?' I asked. 'Or putting in anywhere for provisions? If so, will Garnett go ashore then?'

'We'd go straight there if the wind was right,' said Bones, 'but as it is, we'll be doing a snail crawl along the Channel. We'll put in at the Isle of Wight for fresh meat, I expect. Some of the crew will go ashore, to do that and just for the break, and Garnett will certainly step on to the Isle to find some amusement for himself. He likes a fresh playmate now and then,' said Bones disgustedly. 'One he can just leave behind after a night or two.'

'Good,' I said. 'Because I can pick a lock and I'll be only too glad to pick this one.'

But Bones would have none of it. 'Too dangerous, by half,' he said. 'The captain locks his cabin; you'd have to open that as well. What if someone came on us?'

'We'd have to pick our moment,' Brockley said. 'While the captain's ashore and everyone else is occupied in some way. But it's worth trying, surely!'

I said: 'Would anyone ever go into the captain's cabin while he was ashore?'

Bones thought not, which meant that once inside with the door closed behind us we should be safe enough, but it was still no use. 'Something goes wrong, you'd be put in irons and Garnett might have me flogged. He'd hold me responsible, as his deputy. You'd do better to make up your minds to a new life. It might not be so bad, you know. You could find yourselves in good households, in a warm climate.'

'Or horrible households in a sweltering climate,' said Brockley, but Bones was adamant.

'It's far too dangerous, even though I don't like the slave trade and no more do some of the men. Take Magnus Clay . . .'

'Magnus is a strange name,' said Sybil irrelevantly.

'Named after a Norwegian grandfather, I think,' said Bones. 'Like I said, he's wanted for coining. Things got too hot for him in England and he tried to get away to Ireland but the ship he was on was attacked by the Lundy gang and he was taken to the Mediterranean and forced to be a sailor on a cosairs' ship. He's a small man, too small to make a rower, but nippy and spry for going up the rigging. He got away one day when the ship was anchored off Naples. He saw an English ship anchored nearby. Most sailors can't swim – won't learn. They'd sooner drown quick after a disaster than swim around for hours and then drown after all. But Magnus wasn't a sailor before, and he can swim right enough. He took a split-second chance and dived off the rigging. Got to the English ship and got taken aboard and found himself, poor devil . . .'

'On the *Lucille*? A bad choice, like the one you made. I see,' said Brockley, and added: 'Does she often go foreign?'

'Yes, often enough. Depends where the cargo's going. But we don't deliver slaves direct to North Africa; not good economics since they'd have to be fed. Now, a cargo of timber or leather or ironware don't eat much. And why bother, when there's a pack of scoundrels on Lundy, ready to pay well for a good catch? When Magnus came aboard his ship, he found that Cap'n Garnett had heard of him. Knew of his past the minute Magnus told his name and out come the branding irons. Magnus hates the slave trade but he's as scared of Garnett as the rest of us. Though not so scared that he hasn't told us what he knows about the prices slaves can fetch.'

We were silent, digesting this. Bones regarded us with regret. 'Magnus and me and one or two others would slip you ashore gladly but the captain always leaves someone he trusts to guard our shoreboats and make sure no one who shouldn't sneaks down the gangplank when we're quayside. Then someone would suffer for being careless about locking your door. No, my friends. You'd best just give in to fate.'

He said no more. He and Jacky gathered up our used cups and dishes, and took them away. The bolts crashed home behind them. 'So that's that,' said Brockley glumly.

Sybil said hopelessly: 'What has happened to Ambrosia? I'll never see her again or even hear of her!'

'I'll never see my home!' said Kate.

They wept. Dale and I were lost in the silence of despair. In my mind, I saw the face of little Harry and heard him asking Tessie when his mother would come home. But his mother never would come home. We would never meet again unless, somehow . . .

'Sybil,' I said, 'if we ever do get out of this, we'll go straight in search of Ambrosia. I promise. I understand you now.'

She held out a hand to me and I took it and sat down beside her, and we stayed like that, taking what comfort we could from the warmth of our clasped palms.

And the voyage went on.

NINETEEN
Hidden Treasure

Our situation was wretched. Why, oh why hadn't Walsingham sent us help? If he had acted quickly enough, this would never have happened. I recalled, with bitterness, how both Sir Robert Dudley and Ambrose Billington had told me that I wasn't a slave. Now, it appeared that slavery was to be my doom after all. And not just mine.

There were small, embarrassing miseries on top of the obvious ones. We had no means of washing, either ourselves or our linen. 'We shall soon start to smell,' said Sybil miserably. 'And we'd better not put clean things on too often. We don't know how long we'll be imprisoned here. I thank heaven I'm not due for a course for two weeks yet, and I know Dale doesn't have them any more. I don't know about Ursula.'

'Not for over two weeks,' I said. 'We needn't worry about that for the moment, at least!'

We had buckets in which to relieve ourselves or be sick in, and seasickness did afflict Joseph for a while. With creakings and lurchings, the *Lucille* thrust her nose this way and that across the Channel, against a strengthening wind and, judging by the motion, the sea was rough.

The first bitter day drew on towards nightfall. Leo brought us our evening food, accompanied by another crewman, a most unprepossessing fellow, crude of feature. On his left cheekbone was a wen with a great tuft of dusty-coloured hair growing from it. He looked at us contemptuously and clearly saw us as nothing but animated cargo.

After they had gone, Joseph remarked: 'Even if we could get at that there strongbox and what we found started a mutiny, it wouldn't necessarily save us. Now, would it? This gang of criminals would hang their captain or shove him overboard, and then sail on to Lundy and sell us just the same.'

'They might, or they might not,' said Brockley. 'They aren't all so happy with the slave trade, it seems. If only we could get out of this cabin! If we could, then I'd say we must take the chance even if it's not a good one. We must *try*. What have we to lose? While we're anchored at the Isle of Wight and a lot of the crew go ashore as well as the captain, that would be the time to try *something*. If only we could just get out of this place! I don't know how we can stop them from bolting us in.'

Various schemes were discussed. If we could manage to overpower whoever brought us food that day, we might escape that way – except that once we were out, someone still aboard would very likely see us and raise the alarm, and we didn't know how to find Garnett's cabin, anyway. Could we take whoever brought the meal hostage in some way, or . . .?

Nothing seemed feasible. Nothing seemed remotely realistic. We argued among ourselves, growing angry because we were desperate.

The shadows deepened in the cabin. My resourceful Brockley brought out his tinderbox and a couple of lanterns and lit them. We sat about, gazing at each other's unhappy faces. The yellow light seemed to show up every line and hollow, and every pair of eyes seemed sunk into a pit. The wind wailed.

Then someone screamed.

It wasn't one of us. It came from somewhere else, further aft, I thought. It was a shrill sound and could have been either male or female. It was followed by a chorus of masculine laughter and when that died away we heard a voice we recognized, raised in a cry of *No, no, no!* And then another scream, which gradually subsided into gulping sobs. Again, there was laughter. 'That was Jacky!' I said. 'I'm sure it was! What's happening to him?'

It was a good hour later, and one of the lanterns was guttering, when the bolts were drawn back and Bones came silently in. In the bad light we could not see his face well, but it was plain that he was in a rage. It came off him like a rank smell.

'Did you hear?' he asked abruptly.

'We did,' said Brockley shortly and without troubling to say, *Hear what?* 'Was it your nephew? What happened?'

'That bugger of a captain,' said Bones, with an emphasis that made the epithet unmistakably literal, 'has branded Jacky. He has burned JB, for Jacky Bones, on to my poor lad's left wrist. He's always careful to make it the left unless his victim's left-handed. I've treated the burn and got the boy to his hammock, with a good tot of liquor inside him to get him to sleep, at least I hope so. I didn't tell you, or him, that we once lost a man through a branding. The burn went bad.'

'But – has Jacky committed any crime?' Sybil asked.

'No. But Garnett knows plenty about crimes and wanted men. Finds out all he can when he can. He can send word to any constable, naming Jacky as such and such a miscreant, some lad or other he's heard of, around Jacky's age, wanted for such and such a crime. Who's to prove Jacky's not him? Of course, the real criminal *might* have been caught already, but on the other hand, he might not. Jacky could well find himself a prisoner and in danger of his life. He's terrified now as well as in agony. Garnett finds the lad useful – "*lovable*" is the word he used while the brands were heating, said it as if he were trying to comfort the boy, and all the time Jacky was white as a ghost and pleading, and Garnett was almost licking his lips with anticipation of the pretty scene ahead. I wanted to vomit.'

Sybil drew Kate to her and put an arm round her. Dale pressed close to me and I took her hand. Bones had paused, his eyes darkening as he remembered what he had just witnessed.

Brockley said: 'Go on.'

'He called the rest of the crew to watch, of course. He always does. Garnett means to keep hold of my nephew in his usual vicious way and as far as I'm concerned he's done for himself,' said Bones furiously. 'He's gone too far. I have an affection for that boy, for my dead brother's sake as well as Jacky's. I'll take any risk, *any* risk, to deal with that swine of a man. If you mean what you say about picking locks, Mistress Stannard, when we get to the Isle of Wight I'll be asking you to demonstrate. Where did you get those lanterns, by the way? Oh, I suppose they're yours. Well, they could be useful.'

We sailed all through the night, and it was indeed a rough journey that let few of us sleep very much. The motion was easier in the morning, however, which was a relief. By dusk, we were anchoring in a sheltered position alongside the Isle of Wight. We heard someone ordering a boat to be lowered for the captain. Not long after that, Bones appeared with a meal. Jacky was not with him, but instead he came accompanied by another sailor, a small, wiry fellow with dark hair to his shoulders and a square, pugnacious face in which innocent, almost childlike blue eyes looked out of place.

They had brought trays of food and drink. They set these down and then Bones said: 'This is Magnus Clay. He's a friend of mine and no friend to the captain or to any man in the slave trade.'

'Aye, that be right enough.' Clay spoke with the accent of western England. 'And not just that. I got scars on my back as shouldn't be there. All I did was protest when Cap'n reported one of the fellows as jumped ship. I b'ain't the forgiving sort. I been awaiting my chance, like. Reckon this could be it.'

'Let us hope so,' said Bones. He turned to us. 'Eat quickly, if you will. We'll wait. Cap'n's gone ashore and taken Myers and Leo with him.'

'I loathe those two,' said Kate suddenly and violently. 'I hate those yellow eyes; they make Leo as you call him look like a hunting cat. And I've got bruises where that horrible Myers got hold of me . . .'

'I hate the captain most,' said Sybil. 'You may have fallen in love with him, Kate, but how you could, I can't imagine. How could you fall for a man with all those self-satisfied teeth . . .'

Joseph laughed.

Dale said: 'Self-satisfied teeth. That was clever!'

'Yes, a marvellous description!' I agreed.

'I admired them,' Kate said dismally. 'Then. Not now. I've changed my mind. Now I think he's just wicked!'

'Well, all three of them have gone off for a bit of a pleasure trip and likely won't be back till morning,' Bones declared. 'Two others have gone, as well, and the rest are at supper or on watch. That's five ashore out of the way. Jacky's in his hammock and me and Magnus here, we're against the captain. That just leaves six men to convince. If only we can find proof enough to swing them to our way of thinking! If we can, then with Joseph and Brockley we'll have ten men all told. That should be enough. No one's going to be about near the captain's cabin for a while and if you can get us into it, Mistress Stannard, we can work safe enough behind a closed door. I'm bringing Magnus because I want a second witness from among the crew. If we find what I hope we do, there ought to be at least two of us reporting the same thing to the final six. Two's more convincing than just one.'

The moment had come.

I didn't eat much. I was too nervous, though Bones and Clay were probably taking the greater risk. The rest of us were captives already and merchandise as well, and therefore worth preserving.

Bones said we couldn't all come crowding to the captain's quarters but Brockley insisted on coming and Dale came as well, as my attendant. Sybil and Kate stayed behind, sitting on Kate's pallet with their arms round each other, while Joseph declared himself to be their guardian. Brockley brought one of his lanterns, although Bones insisted that it must be put out while we made our way to the captain's quarters. In fact, he didn't want us to have a lantern at all but Brockley said we'd need it. 'Mistress Stannard can't pick a lock without seeing what she's doing. I'll bring my tinderbox.'

I checked that my picklocks were safely in my hidden pouch, then Bones and Clay led the way out. The Brockleys and I followed; Bones slid the bolts home after us, and then we followed their two bobbing lanterns to a flight of stairs leading upwards.

After that, I lost my bearings, but we were back on deck for a while, under a star-powdered sky. There was no moon. It would be waning by now and presumably it had not yet risen. We moved stealthily from shadow to shadow. No one was about. I remember a second set of stairs and then Bones was whispering: 'Here we are,' and we came to a halt in front of a door.

I was very nervous indeed, and so was Brockley. I heard him muttering under his breath as he struggled with his tinderbox. He got the lantern lit eventually and with shaking hands I got my picklocks out. Safety lay in speed, but with such delicate tasks the less you hurry the better, only I wanted to hurry. The picklocks rattled in my frightened grasp and Brockley noticed.

'Steady, madam. All's quiet,' he said, and held the lantern in position to help me.

I tried to breathe deeply and slowly, tried to steady my hands. The picklock I was using felt right. I had fortunately had a good deal of experience and my ingrained knowledge took over. At last came the soft, satisfying click as the lock surrendered and the door swung open. We were all inside in a trice and Brockley, the last to slip through, shut it firmly behind him. It had an inside bolt and he shot it.

One lantern wasn't enough to reveal the cabin in detail but there was an impression of luxury: a big bed with a spotted fur cover – made of leopard skins, I thought, imported and a long way from cheap – a padded settle, a floor rug also made of spotted fur, a polished table.

'There's the strongbox,' said Bones, now taking a turn at holding his lantern to show me what I needed to see. 'At the end of the bed. Fixed to the deck but the padlock's easy to get at.'

This was so. The contents of the box might well be the captain's secret, but clearly he considered that ordinary locks for door and strongbox were enough.

'Well, if he ever had to abandon ship in an emergency, he'd likely want to get at his fortune in a hurry,' said Magnus when I commented.

He was also very confident of his control over his crew, I thought. Opening the padlock was almost ludicrously easy. I lifted it off and laid it down, and then threw back the box lid. Bones held his lantern closer. We all peered.

'God Almighty!' whispered Clay.

TWENTY
Other Men's Gold

T he contents of the chest mainly consisted of little drawstring bags made of leather. They were all securely tied
except one, whose drawstring had come loose so that
some of the contents had spilled out. Clay was pointing at this.

Justifiably, because what had slipped out were gold coins,
which glowed in the light of his lantern as though they were
themselves filled with sunshine.

I picked one up and held it in the lantern-light. It was foreign
currency of some kind. It had a wreath of what looked like
laurel leaves round the edge while the centre was full of
mysterious symbols which could have included writing in an
unfamiliar alphabet. I couldn't tell. Clay, meanwhile, had
picked up another.

'Ottoman,' he said. 'From Algiers, perhaps. We were based at
Algiers when I were there. That day in Naples when I got away,
I were crossin' the deck when one of them swaggering pirates
– one of their officers as they'd be called in a Godfearing country
– dropped a purse by accident, almost at my feet. It spilt and I
helped him pick up his coins. Some of them were like this.'

He paused reminiscently and then spat on the captain's floor.
'It were a fat purse and I guess he didn't himself know just
how many coins were in it. I weren't wearing much but I had
a loincloth. Somehow or other, a couple of them coins found
their way inside it. I wouldn't quite know how.'

'Really?' said Brockley.

'I took a hell of a risk,' said Magnus. 'It would have been
all over with me if he'd realized. But I'd been scheming in
my mind for months. I could go about that ship with some
freedom, even though I were a pressed man and a slave. I
were more or less trusted because I'd pretended to adopt their
religion. I used to join them at their prayers and the like.'

'You became a Mohammedan!' said Bones, shocked. 'You never told me that before!'

'I said I *pretended*. I said the right things. Words come cheap,' said Magnus dismissively. 'But, meanwhile, I had an eye open for a chance to get away and, that day in Naples, I'd seen an English vessel – this vessel – anchored not far off. It was already giving me ideas. That dropped purse, those two snatched coins – they clinched it. I reckoned they were God's own blessing on the attempt. I reckoned any English captain 'ud take me aboard if he knew I'd escaped from *them* but it's useful, if you're casting yourself out into the world, to have a penny or two with you. I had money for my passage, if the captain proved awkward. Half an hour later, I dived off the rigging. I can swim underwater and I did, and I got to the *Lucille* and they hauled me aboard. There were the pirates on their rotten ship, shouting and shaking their fists, but the *Lucille*, she were just about to set sail, and so we did. The ship I'd dived off, she weren't ready to sail and maybe they wouldn't have bothered, just for the one slave.'

It occurred to me that though Magnus Clay didn't look like a hero, he was one, in a way.

'No decent English captain would ever have refused to take you,' Bones was saying, but Magnus was shaking his head.

'Garnett b'ain't no decent captain. He took my gold coins – grabbed them, almost. He'll do anything for money. He raids on the west coast and collects slaves for the gang on Lundy and he sells information to them, too – about other shipping, which vessels are where and carrying what. There's allus gossip in the shore taverns and he picks it up. I've heard him talking to Leo about that.'

'He does *that*?' said Brockley, horrified.

Magnus Clay shrugged. 'Easier than robbing English ships himself. That way, he gets a share without runnin' risks.'

'Are the other bags the same?' I enquired, and pulling one out at random, I undid it. This one contained English money, mostly in sovereigns. I tried another and poured a new stream of Ottoman gold into my palm. 'But . . . but . . . the value of all this . . .!'

'What's this?' Brockley had also pulled out a bag, a bulkier one, and was feeling it. 'This can't be coinage.' He pulled its drawstring loose and emptied the bag into his hand. And then gasped, as its contents overflowed his palm and tumbled to the floor. He picked it up and put it on the bed, a tangle of jewellery, sparkling like coloured fire. There were half a dozen necklaces, a whole lot of rings and bracelets strung on a gold chain, and some elaborate drop earrings, tied in their pairs. All the settings were gold or silver, with gold predominating. The stones were mostly diamonds, rubies, pearls and a few sapphires. There was also a small inner bag and when Brockley got that open, it contained uncut stones which looked like emeralds.

'So he takes payment in kind, so it seems,' said Clay. 'God knows what all this lot is worth, but it's sure enough that we never had fair shares in it.'

'He – we – have made some good hauls, raiding,' said Bones. 'There was one night we went round two hamlets on the Cornish coast, quick as lightning, gathered up every young or youngish woman we could find. We'd done some reconnoitring beforehand, naturally. Nineteen of them, we collected all told. We got into the houses, found the wenches in bed, gagged them and tied them before they could make much to-do, knocked a few husbands and so forth on the head who tried to stop us, or seized them too if they looked useful, marched the consignment to the beach and into our boats, took them out to the *Lucille*. We shoved them into the hold and then went back and did the other hamlet. It was late autumn, with pretty long nights, and it took nearly all the hours of darkness, believe me. But by dawn, we were on our way to Lundy, and when we got there, well, I fancy our hosts were mighty pleased with the merchandise we brought them and willing to pay well – though I daresay they made sure they'd still make a handsome profit back in Algiers.'

'They pay taxes there, on whatever profits they make,' Magnus put in. 'But they still do well. Go in for piracy at sea, they do – ships comin' from the new world often have gold and jewels aboard. Spanish ships, English – they corsairs as they call theirselves, they b'ain't particular. Likely enough, the pack on Lundy keep back a good bit for themselves. I daresay they cheat their own masters.'

'I've no doubt of it,' said Bones drily. 'There are luxury

goods where the pirates live, on Lundy. Carpets, silver goblets, things like that. Must be loot from ships they've seized. I've been ashore there and seen for myself. There are women on the island too. I heard women's voices.' As he spoke, he was examining another little bag. 'Ah. These are Spanish coins,' he said as he tipped them into his palm. 'More spoils of piracy, I fancy. Spain was the victim that time.'

There was a silence and then he added: 'When we raided the two villages – well, I've been on other raids too. So you can see that that knife-fight long ago ain't the only reason why I wouldn't care to set foot on English soil again. I've done worse things than quarrel over a girl. I'm an outcast for the rest of my life. Maybe if I manage to help you . . . if you do escape, you might put a word in someone's ear for me. You know a few important ears, I'll warrant, Mistress Stannard, being who you are.'

'If we escape, I'll do my best,' I promised. This was no time to be shocked by any further details of Mr Bones' past, or Magnus Clay's, either. I took Brockley's lantern from him, and shone it into the strongbox again because I thought I had seen something else in it besides the drawstring bags. A moment later, I was lifting a ledger from the bottom of the box. 'I thought so. Now, what's this?'

It didn't take long to find out. 'Got a tidy mind, seemingly, our captain,' remarked Clay.

He certainly had. The ledger was a record of his transactions, legitimate and otherwise. It was odd to see, mingled with such items as so many casks of French wine brought from France to England, or such and such a weight of pine timber from Norway to Bristol, the proceeds of delivering fourteen young women, five comely matrons and five able-bodied men to Lundy. In those cases, the right-hand columns, which were usually empty, held details of how the proceeds were distributed between the men and their captain.

'Here's the raid I told you about. Nineteen women,' said Bones, putting a forefinger on it. 'And there are the details of the payment. And there's something here about a payment for information supplied – yes, you were right about that, Magnus. We didn't get any shares for that, seemingly.'

Magnus was muttering and counting on his fingers. 'These

records *look* all right, except a lot are criminal. But they don't match up with all this treasure, no they don't!'

'He always said the pirates paid him in English money,' said Bones. 'Stolen from English ships, no doubt. His share of that is here, right enough, and our shares were in English money too. But we never saw a piece of Algerine or Spanish money, let alone any jewellery. Not as much as a pearl brooch or a couple of doubloons! If he was being straight with us, where the hell did all this come from?'

Clay, muttering again, was examining the jewellery. 'This b'ain't English work, not any of it. I were a goldsmith's apprentice once and I can tell. He got all this from Lundy all right but he never declared it to us.'

He stood for a moment, fingering a necklace of rubies, and then exploded, livid. 'Gawdstrewth! Judging by this here, he's been salting away riches what should of been ours! Doing himself well out of other men's gold! I suppose he reckoned most of us wouldn't know what he'd be likely to be paid but I learned a thing or two in Algiers. I've allus had my suspicions, as Mr Bones here well knows. Only, I never dreamed it'd be on *this* scale!'

'If the men see this . . .' said Bones.

'They'll see it, right enough. By heaven, they will!' Magnus was seething. 'My God, we'll have the old bastard swinging among his own sails for this. *If* they see this? They'll see it right enough. *Now!*'

There was some argument about who should be present when the crew were confronted with the way they had been cheated.

'Best you and Mr Brockley go back to your quarters. The ladies shouldn't come face to face with the crew,' Clay said. 'There's an inside door bolt for those passenger cabins; best use it. They're a wild lot and they'll be that angry.'

'Kate certainly shouldn't be exposed to them,' I said. 'She and Mistress Jester had best stay where they are, with Joseph to guard them. But I'm the one who opened the cabin and the box. Without me, no one would know about this. I want to be there.'

'No, madam,' said Brockley earnestly. 'It wouldn't be wise. Mr Clay is right.'

'Listen,' I said. 'If the crew mutiny, well, we women will be exposed to danger from them in any case. They might do anything – sell us on Lundy for their own benefit, maybe assault us women as well. But something might be done about that if . . . if they see us differently.'

'I don't understand,' said Bones.

I said: 'Up to now, hardly any of the crew – at least the ones on board now – have seen us at all. We're just . . . merchandise to them. *I'm* just merchandise. They've never seen me as myself, an individual, let alone as an individual who's done them a service. Also, let me remind you, if you don't already know it, I am the half-sister of her majesty Queen Elizabeth of England. I propose in fact, to appear as such, properly attended, by you, Brockley, as my manservant, and by Dale, since a queen's sister should not be without a female companion, and I will myself tell the crew what we have found.'

'Fran will be petrified!' said Brockley.

'She'll still do as I ask her. I know she will, if you urge her to it as well. Don't you see – on top of being the one who used the picklocks, I'll also be a member of the royal house. It might make just that extra difference. I would ask you, Mr Bones and Mr Clay, to put my part in all this very plainly to the men. If they still betray me and my friends after all, well, I suppose that would have happened anyway. At least Garnett will have got his deserts and even if we do end up in Algiers, well, who knows? Magnus here escaped; so may we, and God help Garnett and his crew if ever we do get free and come back home. I know about the brands, after all.' I saw the shock in the faces of both Bones and Clay, and hastily added: 'Not yours or Jacky's! I'd never mention yours. Don't worry about that.'

There was a little more argument, but an idea had begun to stir in my mind and I was fiercely persistent. Brockley's protests were the most insistent, but when I said, 'Very well, if you won't attend me or let Dale do so, then I'll have to rely on Sybil to give me countenance, and on these two gentlemen here to protect me, but I *will* be present at the confrontation,' he gave in.

TWENTY-ONE
Conspiracy

As we made our way back to our quarters to collect Dale, I said: 'Just what happens when you take captives to Lundy? Who goes ashore to talk to the pirates, and do they meet you when you land and settle the business then and there? I suppose not, since Mr Bones here says he has been into their living quarters. Does Captain Garnett deal with them directly? If so, then I take it that he goes to their head-quarters too?'

Bones swung his lantern so as to see my face properly. 'Why do you want to know?'

'An idea I've had. Exactly what *does* happen?'

'There's some formality. They're weird folk, those corsairs. They have their own rules of propriety – even of hospitality. They have lookouts – and cannon too, up on the cliffs – and yes, someone meets us when we land. We have to anchor some way out because it's a dangerous coast, so the captain has to be rowed ashore – he has his own shoreboat, a lightweight affair for him and two oarsmen. Mostly they're Myers and Leo but sometimes Garnett takes me and one of them stays aboard instead. There's an old half-ruined castle on the island and our customers have fitted some of it out as a fort, and believe me, they've fitted it out for princes. We're received by their chief in a room where he sits on a seat like a throne, all draped in luxury furs, and something called sherbet is served to us . . .'

'That's a cold drink with no alcohol in it,' remarked Magnus Clay regretfully. 'I tasted it in the galley, so I did. It's not so easy to get clean drinking water in the hot countries.'

'That's right. Well, we're shown hospitality. Refreshments, sociable conversation – the chief – Abdul Hussein, his name is – can't speak English but he has a couple of followers who

can, and they interpret. We take a meal with him and if it's
evening we stay overnight. I did that once and very comfortable they made us. We had a room with padded couches,
coverlets in silk and some kind of fur that I didn't recognize
but nice and soft. Then, eventually, Captain Hussein comes
out to the *Lucille* to see what we've got for him.'

He broke off to laugh and then said: 'He comes in his own
boat with an escort, plastered all over with cutlasses and
handguns. He keeps his boat in a boathouse by the little jetty
and the boathouse is kept locked. Once I asked the interpreter
why and the interpreter laughed at me and said that sometimes
his master's guests didn't appreciate his hospitality the way
they should and tried to escape. But if they do, they could
only escape on to the island. Grinning all over his face, he
was, when he said that. "They can't get away from the place,"
he said. "They can soon be rounded up again!" Obvious
enough, I suppose. Well, Hussein and those with him see what
we've got for them and assess their value and they take away
the ones they want. It's a steep climb up the cliff path from
the little beach to the top of the island where the fort is and
Garnett says that it's a waste of time and effort marching all
the slaves up there if some of them may have to be marched
down again and they'd have guessed what's ahead and be
gibbering with fright or else resisting, trying to fight or get to
our boats first and get away in them. These pirate folk are
quite particular and sometimes they reject some of what's
offered though Garnett is pretty good by now about making
sure he only snatches promising ones, that aren't too old or
too ugly. He won't take ones that are lame or deaf or can't
see properly. Only, when it's raiding by night . . . well, you
can't always tell. You'll be all right. You're kidnapped passengers and he had a good look at you before he decided to snatch
you. He doesn't snatch passengers often. The last batch we
had, we just took from Edinburgh to Dover as virtuous sailors
should because they were three overweight merchants in their
fifties with a couple of flabby menservants. No sort of a
consignment! We landed them all at Dover, good as gold, and
left them free to recommend our services. They were lucky.
The next bit is nasty.'

Like the rejected slaves, I had guessed what was coming and there was a cold clenching in my stomach.

'It's only happened once since I joined the *Lucille* and I didn't take part,' Bones said. 'Myers and Leo saw to it. Even this crew of miscreants mostly find it a bit too much.'

'I was a coiner,' remarked Magnus. 'I've never killed anyone in my life and don't want to.'

'Quite. Witnessing it was bad enough. I did witness it – it was done at dusk when we were sailing away. I was on deck, ordering the sail to be shortened and it happened right in front of me. There were two rejects – one man with a withered arm and one woman the pirates said was too old. That was horrible. She'd been an ordinary woman, a cottager – had a wedding ring, though the Lundy men took that off her – and she didn't seem to believe what was happening to her. She cried and called on Garnett to remember he was an Englishman, just as she was an Englishwoman . . .'

'Oh, my God!' I whispered. 'What was that *like* for her? To grow up in safety, have a family, have children, be a normal woman, and then, your hair goes grey and you lose your teeth and your joints start to ache, and you're grabbed from your home in the night . . .'

'Don't!' said Brockley. 'Madam, don't think about it.'

'She can't have believed it was real!' I said. 'She died in a nightmare! And you *saw* this, Mr Bones?'

'Yes, I saw it. There was nothing I could do. I suppose it was necessary. In a way. We can't just land rejects; by then they'd know too much and be able to recognize Captain Garnett and some of his men, and Garnett can't very well keep them as pets. So as I saw, it was a quick knife thrust all round and then the bodies went over the side, weighted. Myers did it as just one more task; Leo enjoyed it. One can tell.'

'Oh, my God,' said Brockley.

'We're pirates, same as the gang on Lundy,' said Bones. 'We don't have luxury furs and formal dinners, that's all. But the killing's a bit of the business that isn't popular with most of us, though it's rare. It keeps the gentry on Lundy just a wee bit wary of us, of course, which I suppose is a good thing. While Hussein is on the *Lucille* deciding about his purchases,

one of Garnett's escort has to stay in the fort as a hostage. I
was the hostage once. I was well treated, kept in a small room
but I had every comfort. If I needed to relieve myself, I had
a silver basin to do it in! But there were two guards at the
door, all cutlasses and lovely white teeth, just like Garnett has.
And their chief. He's got more teeth than any man I ever saw.
You hardly notice his eyes. They're just black pits. But those
damned teeth . . .!'

He stopped, and like a dog coming out of water, he shook
himself, as if to cast off bad memories. 'I was scared half out
of my wits,' he said. 'And if anything had happened to Hussein,
even by accident, I'd have had good reason. I remember
praying, actually praying, on my knees like a good Christian,
that he didn't fall in the sea while getting from his boat into
the *Lucille* or back again. Well, is that what you wanted to
know?'

'Who is present when Garnett settles terms with their
captain?' I asked.

'Ah. That's interesting. When I was there, it was always
with either Myers or Leo as the other man in Garnett's escort.
Garnett and Hussein go to Garnett's cabin, and take one of us
along but it's never been me. I reckon Myers and Leo are in
on his little deceit and get their share, whereas I'm not. Hussein
would have his interpreter and a fellow carrying a little chest.
The terms were settled and the money – or jewellery – would
change hands, away there in Garnett's quarters. The times I
was there, Garnett told me the total when he came back. Or
what he wanted me to believe was the total. Now look, Mistress
Stannard, what is in your mind?'

We were nearly at the door of our cabin. I stopped short,
and then, briefly, came to the point. Brockley at once protested.
'You can't rely on pirates to respond as you think they will.
You and they don't think alike.'

Here, however, Magnus Clay spoke up for me. 'Mistress
Stannard's idea might work, you know. I can tell you one
thing about the way they think. When I were their prisoner I
did see one or two renegade men from Christian lands among
'em but that were rare. A lot of they corsairs don't make
brethren of foreigners or what they call unbelievers. And I can

say this: they set a lot of store by loyalty. To each other, I mean – reckon they don't pay all the taxes they owe their rulers – but among theirselves, that's different. They call each other brothers.'

'Wait,' said Brockley. 'Let me think . . . look, the interpreters – can they read and write English as well as speaking it?'

'Yes,' said Bones. 'I've seen one of them write a receipt for Captain Garnett. Why?'

Brockley explained and Bones scratched a thoughtful nose. 'You mean, provide a letter to tell them just what they're getting. Yes, I see.'

'There's no guarantee it'll work,' I put in. 'But that would give it as good a chance as I can well imagine. And it could avoid some ugly and very dangerous scenes, if the men turn on their captain – and then get at the drink. They'll have time to quieten down.'

'There's no guarantee that the crew will like the notion at all,' said Clay, 'but I'd say it's worth a try.'

'It has a pleasing touch,' Bones agreed. 'Poetic justice. I rather fancy it myself.'

When it came to the point, of course, I was badly frightened. From what Bones had told me, it was plain that the crew weren't all complete ruffians but there was clearly a strong ruffian element among them. The scheme I had proposed was anything but foolproof. But I had gone too far to turn back now.

Once back in our cabin, we explained the situation to the others. Dale was horrified and shook visibly at the thought of what lay before us but Brockley told her he would be there and that he wanted her to do as I asked, and she finally agreed though she was trembling and her protuberant blue eyes were bulging with alarm. Kate and Sybil were only too glad to stay behind and Joseph promised to protect them as best he could if anyone tried to trouble them.

Clay went ahead to assemble the crew. After a few minutes, I followed with the Brockleys and Bones. Each of us carried one of Brockley's lanterns. Magnus had duly fetched all the men on deck, a surprised audience, visible enough in our lantern-light.

Bones stepped forward and held up his light to survey the

enquiring faces before him. I had only seen a few of them until now and as I studied them my heart failed me. What had I done? Perhaps it was the bad light, but to me they all looked villainous. The thought of addressing them terrified me. But Bones was forging ahead.

'I have with me,' Bones said, 'two ladies and a man who, for a very special reason, I have freed from imprisonment in the passenger quarters. One of the ladies is Mistress Stannard, who happens to be a half-sister to the queen herself, and has carried out some courageous tasks for her majesty. Tonight she has carried out another, for our benefit. With her, as befits a lady of such status, are her manservant Roger Brockley and his wife, who is her personal woman. I would not bring Mistress Stannard into your presence without being sure that she is correctly attended.'

This was greeted by some muttering and shifting of feet. But no one shouted or attempted to create any disturbance. Bones' dignified manner and measured speech were setting the right tone.

'You will be surprised to hear,' said Bones, 'that one of the skills which Mistress Stannard has used in her tasks for the queen is that of picking locks.'

There were more murmurs, and heads turned, peering round Bones to where I stood with the Brockleys. 'This night,' declared Bones, 'she has in my presence unlocked the door of the captain's cabin and opened his strongbox. I made use of her talents in this way because I think, as many of you think, that Captain Garnett has cheated some of us out of money to which we are entitled, and in my case, I am angry because he has branded my young nephew and is prepared, if the boy tries to leave the ship, to report him to the authorities as a wanted criminal, which he is not. And I can tell you now, that you have indeed been cheated.'

He paused long enough to let that sink in and then added: 'Will you, in a moment, choose two of your number to accompany us to Captain Garnett's cabin, where Mistress Stannard will once more open the door and the box and show you what is within. You are likely to find it most interesting. But before we do that, let Mistress Stannard address you.'

He beckoned us forward. We stepped up beside him. Brockley, tense and grim, was on one side of me, while Dale, shaking so much that I could feel it even though I wasn't touching her, was on the other. I was trembling too but hoped no one could see it. I must not show my fear. I must not show weakness.

No, I must not. I must hold fear at bay. I must remember that I was the sister of Queen Elizabeth and the daughter of King Henry, Eighth of that name, Great Harry of England. Something of what they were, was bred into me as well. I must hold up my head and keep my back straight, and be a sister, a daughter, of whom my royal kin would not be ashamed.

I must play the queen.

'I would say good evening to you,' I said, 'except that evening has gone, the morning hasn't come, and good night would sound ridiculous.'

A few of them laughed, which was my intention. 'Now,' I continued. 'To business. Since coming aboard, I have learned that as Mr Bones says, some and perhaps all of you suspect that you have not been paid money that you are owed. Some of you have other causes for complaint. I will say at once that your pasts are nothing to do with me. If you would like to be free of this ship and this captain, I am in complete sympathy with you. I would like the same thing! I will be happy to show you what, with Mr Bones' assistance, I have discovered. If it does interest you, then I have a suggestion to offer you. A very pretty revenge, if we can make it work. We would need to act together. But first, pick your representatives and they shall see what I have found.'

'What if cap'n comes back while we're seein' it?' someone shouted, but I had no need to answer because several voices at once retorted with exclamations such as *Don't be daft; does he ever come back till morning, once he's off for the night?* and *We don't have to let him aboard; leave him fending off till we're ready for him!* and *If he's been a-stealin' of our pay and we've got proof, haul him and them mates of his aboard and clap the gyves on* them *for a change!*

Bones took over again. There was some more muttering and some squabbling, and also a wary voice counselling caution and what if it was all a trick, to which Magnus Clay retorted indignantly that none of them had ever had aught against Bones and hadn't most of them been there when Bones' nevvy was branded and screamed like a soul in hell, and if he, Magnus Clay, felt angry about that, Lord knows what Alfred Bones was feeling like!

There was one dissenting voice after that, from the fellow with the hairy wen. He tried to say they'd all been branded and it hadn't killed them, but someone shouted: 'You bawled like a babby, when it was your turn, Dick Mitchell!' whereupon there was laughter and Mitchell subsided, growlingly.

In the end, accompanied by two crewmen chosen by the others, we all went back to Garnett's cabin where I repeated my earlier performance with my picklocks. Bones threw open the lid of the strongbox; Magnus lifted out a couple of bags and the ledger. They did it in a thoroughly histrionic manner, like showmen at a fair. *Come one, come all, see the five-legged pony! See the most daring acrobats in the world; brought here from far Cathay! See Dr Wondrous show you marvels with a pack of cards!*

There is no need to recount in detail the reaction of the two new witnesses. Once they had glimpsed the coin and the jewellery and grasped both their probable value and their virtually certain source, they were so angry that if the captain had walked in at that moment, he would have died then and there.

Eventually, they grew calmer and we took them back to the deck where the rest of the crew were impatiently waiting, and about to come in search of us. We left it to our two witnesses to explain what they had seen. Then there was an outcry so huge that Dale and I put our hands over our ears because we didn't want to hear any more of the things that his crew were prepared to do to their captain once they got hold of him. Finally, Bones raised his voice to a bellow, ordered them to be quiet and once more called me forward.

'Let Mistress Stannard tell you what she proposes. It has a certain – charm, shall we say? I recommend it,' he told them.

'As long as it works,' muttered Brockley.

'Amen to that,' I muttered, and then did as I was asked.

TWENTY-TWO
A Matter of Timing

Timing mattered. We wanted to arrive at Lundy as evening was approaching, and we must time it just right. Too soon and the transaction would be over too quickly: too late and he'd stay aboard the *Lucille* till morning. Either of those situations would make things more difficult. We needed the cover of darkness, to give us a head start.

The four days we spent on rounding the toe of Cornwall were as taut as lute-strings. We kept out of sight and kept our door bolted inside except when mealtimes were near. We heard, from Bones, that arguments several times broke out among the crew, and that more than once, the whole plan hung by a thread. We all slept badly and I sometimes heard Sybil crying on her pallet at night, and heard Brockley whispering words of comfort when Dale did the same thing.

But Kate did not weep. After her first outburst, Kate had to begin with been quiet, apparently stunned by her lover's shocking betrayal. But our plans seemed to have made her hopeful and after we left the Isle of Wight, she found some source of courage within herself. She tried to be cheerful, sometimes even made jokes. I began to like her more and more.

We rounded Land's End at last and then acquired an inconveniently brisk, fair wind. Bones, bringing one of our meals, said glumly that at this rate, we'd be there by mid-afternoon, which would be most inconvenient. 'We might have to get off-course, and risk Garnett's losing his temper with the helmsman,' he said.

He withdrew, limping artistically. To make sure that Garnett didn't take it into his head to have Bones in the shore party on this occasion, he had staged a fall down a companionway and declared that he had sprained an ankle. 'No one with a sprained ankle could manage that cliff path,' he told us.

Presently, Brockley, who had all along spent a good deal of time clambering on to barrels and peering out of the awkward windows, called the rest of us to look, and by handing each other up on to barrels as well, we all had our first sight of Lundy, standing out of the sea in the distance like the back of a monster whale, as Sybil said. As a child, she told us, she had had a tutor who had shown her pictures of whales.

'We'll soon see it more clearly,' said Brockley gloomily. 'We're getting there a lot too fast.'

Fortunately, however, the wind eased just after that. Providence was with us and we reached Lundy at just the right time, nearly dusk, but still light enough to give us a real view of the island.

'It doesn't look like a whale now,' said Sybil, slithering down from a barrel and shaking out her grubby skirts.

'It's more like a cake, with green marchpane on top,' Kate agreed. 'Except that marchpane isn't usually green.'

It was quite a good description. The island stood high, with dark, greyish cliffs rising sheer for at least four hundred feet, and on top, there was grass, vividly green, the kind of grass that is frequently and thoroughly watered. As the *Lucille* manoeuvred to her anchorage, we caught glimpses of the nearby sea, blue-green in colour and of an astounding crystal clarity. Seabirds bobbed in the water and wheeled round the cliffs, calling with cold, free voices that reminded me of the wild geese I had once been told I had an urge to follow. I was cured of that now, I thought, grimly.

Brockley, who on our various journeys had taken an interest in such things, recognized some of the birds. 'Those with the yellow necks are gannets and the squat ones with those coloured stripes on their beaks, that look like popinjays – they're sea-parrots. Some people call them puffins,' he said informatively, and Kate said gravely: 'This is a most educational voyage,' whereupon we all laughed, or tried to, recognizing one of her valiant jests.

We had the pleasure of watching as Captain Garnett, accompanied by Myers and Leo, set out for the shore in the captain's shoreboat. By now the light was fading rapidly, and according to Bones, who came to see us, along with Clay, it was a near certainty that they'd stay ashore till morning. Bones was thankful we had arrived safely and at the right time. 'It's been even more of a worry than I've let you know,' he told us. 'It's been hard on the men, too, even the ones who like our scheme best, trying not to show what they think. I've caught some of them giving the captain and Myers and Leo too, dirty looks, and making gestures behind their backs. Lucky no one was caught at it! And the way some of them have said *Aye aye, sir . . .* I heard insult in the very tone! What's saved us is that Captain Garnett is so sure of himself that he simply didn't notice it! Now, Master Brockley's plan about the letter, Mistress Stannard. I dare say you can write clearly. So while our captain climbs the cliff, maybe you could make a fair copy of this draft letter that Magnus and I have made. I thought I'd slip ashore and nail it to the chief's boathouse.'

He handed me a folded sheet of paper and Magnus, delving into a bag he was carrying, presented me with a writing set and some unused paper. I read the draft while my friends crowded round to read it too and Brockley laughed. 'Very good,' he said. 'That should make the point.'

To Abdul Hussein, commander of Lundy Island. We the undersigned herewith offer you three strong males, suitable for the galleys or the mines. They are Mr Garnett, captain of our ship, and his two close friends, known as Myers and Leo. Garnett has proved himself a faithless captain who has defrauded his men of pay to which they are entitled, and has shamefully misused men who have done no wrong. His companions have been his partners in these things. We seek no payment for their persons. The profit for selling them on is entirely yours.

'That should do it,' said Magnus. 'These gentry, they really do have their own laws and customs. They really do hold by loyalty and sticking together. A captain what cheats his men and mistreats them won't be invited to join them; no, he won't, nor his best friends neither.'

'We'll get the signatures or marks from the crew,' said Bones. 'But not yours, Master Brockley, or yours, Mistress Stannard. This letter is from the men of the *Lucille*. Do you agree to that?'

We all agreed. I wrote the fair copy and Bones took it away, saying that he would leave the cabin unbolted outside but it was best that we stayed there until he was back from taking the letter ashore and the ship was under way.

We waited restlessly. From time to time one or other of us would climb on to a barrel for whatever could be seen outside, but there wasn't much. We were anchored some way out because one of the pirates' own vessels was closer in and in our way. Before it was quite dark, we caught glimpses of it when the *Lucille* swung at her anchor. The pirates had two ships, Bones had told us, but the other was probably at sea, harassing respectable merchantmen or making uninvited calls on the coast of Cornwall.

I also caught glimpses of the tiny cove which was the landing place, and the pirate captain's boathouse that Bones had mentioned, a small stone building, well back from the sea and huddled against the cliff, but with what looked like a slipway leading down to the water.

The light had completely gone and we had lit our lanterns before we at last heard a boat being lowered, presumably for Bones. 'Our letter's on its way,' said Brockley. And then, causing us all to look at each other sharply, came the sound of approaching footsteps. A lot of them.

The cabin door was thrust open. Bones stood there. His thin face looked unhappy. Magnus Clay was a few steps back, his pugnacious countenance also oddly sad. Behind him, filling up the passageway, was what seemed like most of the crew.

'I'm sorry,' said Bones. 'Mighty sorry. But we can't take the risk. I mean, we can't risk freeing you. We can't sail away with you and put you ashore on the mainland and trust you not to tell the world what the *Lucille* is and how to recognize her crew.'

'*What!*' Kate screamed.

'Don't be too scared.' Magnus' voice was almost pleading. 'We won't hurt anyone. Your lives might be quite happy, somewhere in the sunshine.'

'But you have to see,' said Bones in a voice of real regret, 'that we can't just let you go.'

Brockley said grimly: 'Are we to understand—?' and was

cut short by Sybil, who cried out: 'But we *would* hold our tongues. We'd swear it! You know we would!' and Dale echoed her with: 'Yes, yes, of course we would!' in a voice that was hardly intelligible because it shook so much.

'You'd have to give some account of yourselves and where you'd been. You especially, Mistress Stannard, being who you are.' Bones sounded almost reasonable. 'You'd be questioned. It would all come out. This is the best we can do for you. Please, now, don't make it worse for yourselves. We shan't ask any money for you . . .'

'You're going to abandon us to slavery and you think that would make us feel better!' I shrieked.

'They're going to do *what*?' demanded Joseph. 'We're going to be handed over to these here slavers on the island?'

'I think so,' said Brockley in savage tones. Dale sank on to her pallet, her eyes bulging with terror.

Bones said: 'Let's get it over.'

He and Magnus stepped into the cabin and stood aside while the other crewmen poured in after them. They made straight for Joseph and Brockley and I saw that every man carried a bunch of ropes. Brockley was wearing his sword and tried to draw it, but he was overpowered and the sword was seized. He and Joseph swore and fought but they were overcome and their hands were bound behind them, it seemed, on the instant. No doubt, I thought bitterly, the crew had had plenty of practice at this sort of thing.

'Now,' said the unpleasing Dick Mitchell as he tightened the last knot, 'let's not have any trouble. We've got knives.' He produced one and caressed Brockley's left cheek with it, drawing a thin line of blood from the cheekbone to the jaw. 'If you ladies don't want your men friends hurt, you'll do as you're bid. Get your things together but hurry.'

'Put on cloaks; it's chilly on the sea,' said Magnus. 'And the beach ain't much better. Then we'll take you ashore.'

There was nothing to be done. Joseph and Brockley cursed; Dale and Kate wept; Sybil was now silent but moved stiffly as though half paralysed and I kept my mouth tightly shut because otherwise I would have burst into uncontrolled screams of rage and imploring wails both at once. We jumbled our things into our saddlebags and I made sure that Brockley's lanterns, tinderbox and candles were safely in his shoulder-bag.

'Pile it all together,' Bones said. 'We'll bring it. Now come with us.'

We were taken to the boat we had heard being lowered. Brockley and Joseph were made to board first. Each was untied while he negotiated the rope ladder, and secured again once he was aboard. Neither resisted because, each time, the other had a knife at his throat.

After that, we women were told to climb down. Joseph and Brockley were hostages for our good behaviour so we did as we were bidden, with difficulty because as well as cloaks we had skirts. Mine swung and struck the side of the ship, and the things in my hidden pouch made a muffled thud. I hoped to heaven that no one would notice and take them from me but Kate, who was just above me, was sobbing so loudly that probably no one could have heard it but me.

Bones and Magnus came behind us, bringing our belongings. Six more men followed. The boat was big enough to need three pairs of rowers – and in this case, two extra men to keep watch on us.

We were rowed towards the land, a slow and cautious business for there was no moon, although the sky was thick with stars, and it was just possible to make out the shore as we drew nearer.

We were landed at a little jetty. There were mooring bollards, and the captain's boat was tied to one of them. While the others were getting us ashore – they didn't untie Joseph or Brockley this time – Bones strode up to the boathouse with the letter I had so painstakingly written for him. We heard the tap of a hammer, a very small sound against the murmur of the sea, and then Bones came back.

'That's done. I know you have lanterns so if you don't fancy going up to the fort and presenting yourselves, you can see what you're about while you collect driftwood for a fire. There's driftwood in plenty. Though you might prefer to go up to the fort even if you have to carry all your belongings. Even with a fire, you'll find it a cold, wearisome night here on the beach, and you'll end up in the corsairs' hands anyway. It'll be quiet as well as cold. That Dick Mitchell had a notion that we might launch a cannonball or two at the pirates' ship that's anchored out there. He said it would annoy the pirates and make it doubly sure that they wouldn't feel kindly towards Garnett and his friends, but the rest of us said it would make too much noise and tell them up at the fort that something's wrong. As you well know, we want to be safely at sea before anyone realizes the *Lucille* has gone. So, though I'm sorry we can't take you up to the fort and carry your things for you like the knightly gentlemen we'd like to be, we must be off as soon as we can.'

I was speechless. Kate was still sobbing. There didn't seem to be anything any of us could possibly say.

'I'm sorry,' Bones said again. 'Really, desperately sorry. But there it is. We have to look after ourselves.' He studied our faces for a moment, then said: 'You have a dagger with you, have you not, Mistress Stannard?'

I nodded, wondering how he knew. I had thought of it but dared not touch it, for either Brockley or Joseph would probably be dead before I could make any use of it. 'I saw it when you got your picklocks out,' Bones said. 'Such useful things, picklocks. You can use the dagger to release your menfolk. Goodnight. Goodbye.'

'Good luck,' said Magnus, I think with genuine sorrow for he of all men understood the fate that lay ahead of us. We watched them go back to the jetty. Two of them took the captain's boat while the rest got into the larger craft. We heard the plash of oars as the two boats drew off to sea. The sound of Bones' voice, talkative as ever, drifted back to us. We saw that far away, the *Lucille* was showing lights so that the boats could find their way back.

'So now what do we do?' asked Sybil, finding her tongue at last. 'Shiver here all night and wait to be found in the morning, or go up to the fort and explain ourselves and hope we won't have to share quarters with Garnett and those others?'

'Neither, I think,' said Brockley, as I cut his wrists free with my dagger and then turned to release Joseph. 'I fancy, Mistress Jester, that with a little luck, we'll soon be on course for the mainland. Lucky that the wind has dropped. The sea should be fairly quiet.'

'What do you mean, Roger? We haven't any boats. They've taken the captain's one as well as ours,' Dale moaned.

'Well, we might still be able to conjure a vessel for ourselves,' said Brockley. 'Am I right, do you think, madam? Was Bones reminding you that you had picklocks with you?'

'I think so,' I said.

'What are you *talking* about?' cried Dale.

'Only Brockley and I heard this,' I said, 'but when Brockley and I were out of our cabin, getting at that strongbox, Bones told us that the pirate chief has a boathouse here. There – you can just make it out.' I pointed. 'Bones said it was kept locked but when he was hinting just now about picklocks, he sounded cheerful so I imagine that there's nothing too special about the kind of lock that's been used. Well, I do have my picklocks with me and I believe there's a boat in the boathouse. Come with me, everyone!'

TWENTY-THREE
Eyes In Shadow

B ones had tried to give us a chance. Despite the risk to himself and his fellow crew members, he had still tried to give us a chance. He must have struggled with his conscience over that. I could only be grateful that he had finally decided to offer us that glint of hope. Just a glint. He couldn't be more open with the others there. He couldn't rely on me remembering what he had said about the boathouse. He had, as it were, tossed a fateful coin for us, and left it at that.

As it was, we got out a couple of lanterns and lit them, and then I led my companions to the boathouse. It was just about visible and anyway, Brockley immediately tripped over the slipway. Even in total darkness, we could have followed that. As far as I could tell, from kneeling down to feel it, it consisted of wooden rollers, fastened together as if they were the rungs of a ladder, but lying flat, over a stone-lined trench, so that there was space below the rollers, to let them revolve. It was only a few yards long, and then we were in front of the boathouse. My lantern beam at once caught the letter which Bones had nailed to its door. It looked different somehow from the letter I had written out, and then I saw that another paragraph, in a different hand, had been added before the crew had signed it.

We also commend to you the captives that Captain Garnett intended to sell to you on this visit. We offer them to you freely, in thanks for relieving us of Garnett and his friends. There are two sturdy men, one young, one in middle years but still strong, and four serviceable women. The youngest we believe to be a virgin. They are all yours, for nothing. We only ask that you treat them well, for they have done no wrong.

Bones really had done his best for us, in more than one way. I left the notice where it was.

The boathouse was secured with a padlock that looked massive but as with Garnett's strongbox padlock, it was actually quite simple to open. I only took a moment or two over letting us in. Once inside, Brockley and I each held up a lantern and tried to make out our surroundings.

'There's their boat,' said Joseph. 'Funny looking thing, ain't it? Foreign, like.'

This was so, since the little vessel had a high curly prow which had been painted gold and shone when the light caught it. There were oars inside the boat, a coiled mooring rope, and what Brockley said must be a bailing bucket. 'I hope we don't have to use that!' said Dale. Brockley commented unenthusiastically that the boat wasn't much of a size for the open sea but it would have to do and now we had to get it to the water.

We fetched our baggage, threw it into the boat and set to work. Getting it out of the boathouse was the hardest part. The line of rollers extended right into the building and the boat was already on it, but at first we couldn't move it at all, until we found that it was fastened at the stern to a ring in the rear wall. Joseph borrowed my dagger and cut it loose and after that, with all of us heaving and shoving, we were able to inch the boat forward until it met the point where the slipway began a downward slant. After that, things were more straightforward, though not rapid for the descent to the water was not steep and the boat needed some manhandling. We all strove together, three each side. We were still only a yard or two clear of the boathouse when the quiet night was shattered by something that for a moment froze us all into horrified rigidity.

It came from the sea, and it was the boom and flash of a cannon. Followed by a crash and then shouts, distant but carrying easily over the water from where we knew the big pirate ship was anchored. Evidently, she had a guard on board. The shouts had a quality of fury rather than anguish; by the sound of it, no one had been hurt, but the vessel had probably been damaged.

'I could hazard a guess as to who arranged that!' said Brockley. 'That damned hothead Dick Mitchell!'

Joseph was squinting towards the sea. 'I think I can make

our ship out. I can see her sails against the stars. She's under
sail, moving. Oh, dear God!'

Another cannon had boomed, this time from the pirate vessel.
'Didn't get her,' said Brockley, peering seawards. 'The
bonny *Lucille*'s all right. Already out of range. Mitchell loosed
off at just the right moment. And I could kill him for it! Come
on, all of you, we've got to get launched and away. That
racket's going to bring every pirate on the island tearing down
that cliff path in minutes from now. Come *on*!'

He was perfectly right. As we dragged and pushed and
steadied and pushed again, we heard the sound of voices from
high above us, and Sybil said breathlessly: 'Lights! Top of the
cliff!'

But we were there. The slipway ran down into the water
and the boat went with it, sliding free of it to bob alongside
the jetty. There was plenty of room, since the boats that had
brought us and the captain's party were both gone. Brockley
dragged out the mooring rope we had found, and between
them he and Joseph fastened our vessel to a bollard. We all
scrambled over the side. In our haste, we made the boat rock
and Joseph nearly fell in. Sybil caught hold of him just in
time and yanked him to safety, with no more than one wet
foot.

'And one foot's enough! That water . . . cold as icewater
. . . fall into that and you wouldn't drown, you'd freeze!'
Joseph gasped as he seized an oar. The boat bumped ominously
as though it had touched bottom for a moment. The tide was
falling. A little later, and we would have had far more trouble
in getting on to the sea.

The shouts from the land were coming closer and we could
see lights on the cliff path, moving rapidly downwards.
Brockley leant over the side to loose us from the bollard and
then sat down, grabbing an oar for himself. He pushed off. He
and Joseph started to row. We lurched unsteadily out from
the jetty. 'Trim, trim!' Brockley barked at us. 'Sybil, Fran,
shift to the other side! *Quick!*'

His urgency was right, for that was the moment when a
crowd of angry pirates, brandishing flambeaux and a hair-
raising selection of weapons, reached the foot of the cliff and

came running across the little beach. They saw at once that the boathouse was open; for a moment they crowded towards it, and someone saw the letter and had torn it off the door and was shouting something – reading it aloud, perhaps. There were answering shouts in some foreign tongue. Then they saw us, just clearing the end of the jetty, and they poured after us, bellowing with rage.

'But *we've* not done anything to them!' wailed Dale.

'We're escaping merchandise and the ship we came on has just hurled a cannonball at theirs,' said Brockley tersely. He and Joseph were rowing with all their might. Kate and I seized another pair of oars and added our strength. None of us was practised at the work and the boat wallowed, refusing to get underway. The foremost man of the enemy was shouting something at the others. He was sprinting forward, leading the way. He plunged into the sea, determined to catch us before we were completely beyond their reach.

I made out that he had a jewelled turban and that, added to the way he had shouted commands and been obeyed, made me think that this was probably Abdul Hussein himself. He thrust his way forward till he was thigh deep in the sea, still carrying a flambeau in one hand, while in the other he brandished a cutlass. He almost reached us. But we were in deeper water by then and suddenly he lost his footing, stumbled and went under, dousing his torch. But not before the torch had lit up his face so that for a moment we saw it plainly.

It was a dark, bearded face, and as Bones had said, his eyes were shadowed, lost in a deep cavern under his black brows, and his teeth, bared in fury, were his most obvious feature, much as they were in the case of Captain Garnett. The two of them were alike, only with this man, it was worse. It was even worse than with Leo. One could at least *see* Leo's eyes, however disagreeable they were to behold. But this man's face was that of someone who had altogether ceased to come forth to meet the world of other people.

We strove at the oars. We saw Hussein break the surface and reappear, snorting and cursing, saw three or four of his followers dive forward and try to swim after us, saw his hand grab our gunwale. He was a powerful man and he moved fast, heaving his body out of the water and sliding over the side, levering himself up with one hand while the other still grasped his cutlass. Behind him, his reinforcements were shouting encouragement and they too had cutlasses.

Then Kate wrenched her oar out of the water, scrambled to her feet, and thrust the oar with all her might straight at Hussein's starlit teeth. It seemed that she disliked them as much as I did. His head jerked back and for a split second we saw blood spurt from his mouth and heard his snarl of fury and pain. The boat lurched under what was now wildly uneven rowing but Kate kept her balance and thrust again, shouting. He lost his grasp and fell back into the sea, and as he did so his cutlass sailed out of his hand and splashed into the waves. Kate sat down hurriedly and plied her oar once more. 'Thanks, Kate,' I gasped, and Joseph said: 'More than thanks! Reckon she's just saved us from God alone knows what.'

'Harder! Faster!' Brockley panted, plying his oar with all his might. Joseph matched him. Now the boat was responding and the gap between us and the enemy was widening. Behind us, the foe, cursing, was losing the race. Hussein had gone under and when he reappeared, spluttering and raging, he was a good way aft.

'They can't stay in this water long, anyhow,' said Joseph breathlessly. 'Too bloody cold, saving your presence, ladies.'

'You should hear the queen, sometimes,' I said. 'She can swear with the best.'

'Hope they all die of lung congestion,' said Joseph. 'Think you knocked a couple of his teeth out, Mistress Ferguson. Well done.'

'Amen to that,' said Sybil in heartfelt tones. And then, with a gasp of relief: 'They've given up!'

And so they had. Swearing and dripping, they were retreating now from the double menace of depth and cold. They shook their fists and one of them hurled what looked like a spear, but it fell short. 'Waste of a good weapon,' remarked Joseph.

'So now,' said Brockley, 'all we have to do is row for the mainland. It's likely to take us all night. Lucky the sea's calm.'

TWENTY-FOUR
Travelling On

At the time it was a dreadful struggle, although I now look back on it with pride. We had overcome one peril after another and we had got away. It provided us with the sort of memories that are good to recall, round the hearth on stormy evenings, in a safe, snug house, with a mug of ale or a goblet of good wine in one's hand.

Brockley had said the sea was calm but we soon learned that a sea that looks quite calm from a distance may not seem calm at all when you're bouncing over it in a small open boat. We battled along, navigating by the stars. We wallowed in the troughs between rolling waves, took in water and had to bail.

When dawn broke, we were well away from Lundy, and there was no ship in sight, neither the pirate vessel nor the *Lucille*. Dick Mitchell had perhaps done well by us after all, since he had possibly crippled the pirate ships, and the *Lucille* had presumably got away towards Land's End. She would have had to go round the end of the island to do so, but in the dark the pirates could not use their cliff cannon. We ourselves were aiming straight for the mainland. We were exhausted. The wind and the savagely cold spray seared our faces and made our whole bodies shudder, and Joseph's wet foot had seriously pained him until Sybil took off his shoe and his cloth sock, rubbed his foot hard with her skirt and helped him to unearth fresh socks and shoes from his saddlebags. We had nothing to eat or drink and no prospect of anything for the foreseeable future. And land, though visible, still seemed far away.

I think that after all, we might at last have been defeated by the Bristol Channel except that suddenly a ship came into sight. She was certainly not the *Lucille*. She was a big three-masted vessel, coming up the channel as though homeward bound from

a voyage. We stood up and waved, and after a time, we saw
men aboard her waving back. We made towards her. Within
half an hour, we were clambering stiffly up a rope ladder to
her deck, and our little boat was being hoisted up as well.

She was a merchantman, home from the Mediterranean,
laden with casks of red wine, bales of silk and stone jars full
of spices, and she was headed for Bristol. She had no passengers, her cheery and amiable Captain Cox informed us, but
she had accommodation for them, and he had a couple of
cabins we could use.

It was magical. Suddenly we were surrounded by friendly
faces. There were shocked exclamations when we told our
story, and then we were being shown to the cabins, one for
Joseph and Brockley and the other for the ladies; there were
woollen dressing gowns and soft slippers so that we could get
out of our soaked and salt-stained clothing; there were hot
drinks that tasted of honey; there were meat pies and freshly
made bread; there were bowls of warm washing water, and
comfortable bunks . . . there was warmth and sustenance . . .

And sleep, blessed sleep.

We were landed at Bristol the next day and Captain Cox
wouldn't let us pay anything for our passages. We had
presented him with a nice little shoreboat, he said, worth quite
a lot, and that would suit him very well. He said he would
name her the *Generous Gift* and she would be recompense
enough. He liked the curly gold prow. He'd have the prettiest
shoreboat in the whole of English shipping, he said.

In Bristol we found a hostelry. Brockley went off with
Joseph in search of a hiring stables where we could obtain a
wagon and horses for the journey to Hawkswood, which meant
travelling across most of the width of England. Hawkswood
it would have to be, I decided. I had a report to make for
Walsingham and Cecil but I wanted to go home so much that
I couldn't even contemplate going first to Hampton Court –
where I might in any case find that the court had moved
somewhere else, possibly even to Greenwich. Besides, I wanted
to give careful thought to the wording of the report. From
Hawkswood it could be sent by messenger.

After that I must take Kate back to Dover and retrieve the

horses we had left with the Fergusons, but for that purpose, Hawkswood was on the way; Dover would just be a continuation of our journey, after a break.

Our choice of transport was controlled by the strain of the last few days. Joseph and Kate said they were recovered and could manage on horseback, but I still felt too tired and stiff and I was quite sure that Sybil and Dale were worse than I was. No, it was to be four wheels for everyone. Brockley and Joseph found a stable that was part of a chain, providing wagons and changes of horses at regular intervals, all the way to London. Getting to Hawkswood meant veering away from London for the last leg, but we would get the horses back to their proper stables later. For the moment, our destination was Hawkswood, dear Hawkswood and home.

Wagon travel is never rapid. The journey took five wearisome days. I was glad, so glad, to arrive. Little Harry came running out to me the moment I was in the courtyard and to pick him up and put my arms round him was a joy for which I have no adequate words. Many others came out to welcome me, too; Adam Wilder and John Hawthorn beaming broadly, old Gladys, cackling with joy through her brown fangs.

Yet there was no chance yet for a real rest. On the following morning, I despatched Simon to drive the wagon to its London stable with Rusty, our remaining saddle horse, tied behind the wagon so that Simon could ride back. Netta didn't like the idea of him being away overnight but she would have to get used to these things, I told her, as patiently as I could. It was a worry to me that most of our horses were still in Dover. The sooner we got our equine belongings back from the Fergusons, the better.

So much still to be done. The report on our adventures for Sir Francis Walsingham and Lord Burghley came first; that was urgent. I must also write a separate letter to the queen, for my report would contain information which should lead to the seizure of the *Lucille* and all aboard her when next she put into an English port, and I wanted to plead for Bones and Clay. I wished them to be pardoned. There was nothing now that I could do for Christopher Spelton. He, poor man, was lost. But I must help those I could. If I could.

As well as pleading for Bones and Clay, I also wanted to protect Duncan Ferguson. I knew I must explain what had happened to Count Renard, but I must emphasize how justified Duncan had felt when he insisted on his illegal duel. And I would not, I thought, actually name the Fergusons. They had better be just *a Catholic household in Kent*. And I must write to Kate's parents, to tell them what had happened, but assure them that she was safe and that I would in due course bring her home. I had too much to do to leave for Dover at once. I decided that I must send someone to fetch our horses and the letter could go with him, or them. Probably them – there were six horses to retrieve. I'd take Kate home myself, when everything was settled. All the letters would need the most careful wording.

There was something further, nagging at the back of my mind. Wearied by my adventures, I didn't want to face it though I knew I must. I was not too surprised when, as I sat in the little room that Hugh had once used as his study, nibbling the end of my quill while I tried to assemble the words I needed, the door opened to admit Sybil and Kate.

'We're sorry to interrupt,' Sybil said. 'But . . .'

I laid down my quill. It had come. I had been too thankful to be back at Hawkswood with Harry and too overwhelmed with all the things that *must* be done forthwith to add this to my burdens straight away, but now it was to be added by others. 'Ambrosia,' I said.

'It's only a little more than two weeks since Ambrosia started her journey to Edinburgh,' said Sybil.

Just over a fortnight. It felt as though we had travelled to the moon and back since we left Dover, and as if we had lived through an eternity of danger in that time.

Sybil was continuing. 'We don't know how long her voyage took. She can only have been there for a short time. Even if they do try to marry her off, even if she gives in to them, she surely won't be married yet. There hasn't been time. Mistress Stannard . . . Ursula . . .'

'I know,' I said. 'It's been in my mind too. But even if we go to Edinburgh at once, we don't know the name of these Ferguson kinsmen. Are they called Ferguson too? And where do they live? How do we find her?'

'That is no problem. I'm a Ferguson,' said Kate helpfully. 'I know who they are and where they live. I can lead us straight to them.'

I was still looking at Kate as though she were some kind of betrayer, when the door opened and in hobbled Gladys, without knocking, which was normal in her case. 'I heard that, I did. Heard something about Edinburgh, too. I seen maps in Master Hugh's office, once or twice. That'll be a thousand mile away!'

'Four hundred, roughly,' I corrected.

Gladys snorted. 'Too damn far by half, and when you get there, *if* you ever do, the state you're all in, sleepin' late and creepin' about as if you're lamer than I am, it'll all be for nothing, you wait and see.'

'What do you mean?' snapped Sybil. 'What do you know? You can't know anything!'

'Just got a feeling,' said Gladys, maddeningly.

TWENTY-FIVE
Four Hundred Miles

'Sit down,' I said to them. They did so and we sat there, looking at each other.

'I'm sorry,' said Sybil at last, uncertainly. 'Sorry to worry you so, Ursula. I know how tired you are. We all are! All we've been through . . . riding to Dover, being prisoners on that ship, trying to row back to safety . . . being frightened all the time . . . I'm as tired as anyone else. But Ambrosia . . .'

'I know,' I said. 'I *do* know, believe me. When I thought I'd never see Harry again . . .' The very memory brought the tears to my eyes. 'But . . .'

It was true that I was tired. More than anything, at that moment, I would have liked to retire to bed and go to sleep for ever and ever. But I couldn't. I simply had too much to do, that must be done, as soon as possible. For Sybil's benefit, I recited the list aloud.

'We can't leave for Edinburgh immediately,' I said. 'I have this report to prepare for Walsingham and Cecil, and a letter for my sister the queen. When Simon returns, he'll have to go straight off again with those. Then Eddie and Joseph must go to Dover with a letter to Kate's parents, and to fetch our horses. They'll have to hire horses for the journey there – and how just two of them will manage to bring back the hirelings *and* our six, I haven't yet worked out. I might send Billington with them; he's got a pony. I can't even think about going anywhere or doing anything else until all that's settled. And do you really think, Sybil, that you can ride four hundred miles?'

'No, I know I can't, and nor can Dale,' said Sybil, 'but once the horses are back we could use our coach! Though if we've got to wait for them to come back . . . no, we need to start out *now*! If you can hire horses for the grooms who go to Dover, why can't we use hired teams to get to Edinburgh? We did that to get here from Bristol! Can't we use the same chain of stables again? Ursula, we need to act at once! We can't afford delay!'

'That chain of stables only exists in part of the south of England. We couldn't use it to get to Scotland. Delay can't be helped; I have all these other things to see to first. We can go, but not instantly. Surely you can understand . . .'

'I see,' said Sybil bitterly. 'Once again, you have made it plain that you don't want to bother about Ambrosia. Very well. Just as she set out alone to find me when she fled from her in-laws, then I will set out alone to rescue her from the Fergusons. I'll hire a horse for myself and pack my saddlebags and just go! Well, not quite alone. I'll need Kate with me; I'll need her to find the Fergusons and . . .'

'Sybil, you can't! You know you can't manage such a long ride, you've just said so yourself, and I certainly can't allow Kate to go with you. No, don't say anything, Kate. I am responsible for you until I can return you to your home and I must do that in person – I may be able to smooth your reunion with your father. I fear he's likely to be angry. You are not going to rush off to Edinburgh with Sybil and that's final. Look, Sybil, if we can just let things settle for a few days, and give ourselves some rest . . .'

'*No!*' Sybil shouted, and with that, fled the room.

'Oh, dear God,' I said feebly.

'She is so anxious for Ambrosia,' Kate said. 'She does have to go to Scotland and I must go too, to find the house. And besides, we don't know how they'll receive us, so surely it would help if I were there, since I'm a Ferguson. Things might be very difficult. My father said he wanted Mistress Wilde kept in Scotland for good, by any method, however drastic. Though he was going to try for a pardon for Duncan as well. He was in a muddle,' said Kate. 'Frantic with worry. Mrs Wilde was so desperate, so furious – she wouldn't stop crying and screaming and pounding things with her fists and shouting that she'd see Duncan hang for what he'd done; it was difficult to think, through all that uproar. My father was like someone trying to hold back a flood when a seawall's collapsing – trying to stop a hundred leaks at once.'

'I can imagine it,' I said seriously. I added: 'I suppose his Scottish relatives will heed his instructions? Yes, I can see that there could be great difficulties and I can see that you might act as a mediator. I know he sent a maid with Ambrosia and the maid had a letter for the Edinburgh Fergusons, explaining what he wanted.'

'Yes, she's my mother's maid. She'll come back when Mrs Wilde is settled,' Kate said. 'That's why Mother isn't replacing her and Amy's had to look after me and Sheila *and* Mother. And why it was so easy for me to run away.'

'I know,' I said. 'And I *do* understand, even though Mistress Jester doesn't realize it. But we just can't set out for Scotland *now* because I can't leave till I've settled all these other things, and you can't go without me. And that's that. Leave me, Kate. And you too, Gladys. I have to get this report written and that has got to come first.'

They went, and I dipped my quill anew and set to work. It was hard to concentrate. From Sybil's point of view, my report was meaningless. What were reports to the court compared to the plight of Ambrosia, cast away among strangers in the far north? In Sybil's place I would have felt as she did.

But I wasn't in Sybil's place and the report had to be written, and the letters to the queen and to Kate's parents.

I wrote them.

Sybil kept her room all the rest of that day, and the next morning too. I tried to make my peace with her through the door but she would not answer me. Phoebe took trays to her. Heavy-hearted, I sent Brockley to Guildford, where there was a hiring stables, to arrange horses for Eddie and Joseph for their journey to Dover. Then I played with Harry until Tessie was ready to give him his nursery dinner and as the sun was out, I went into the garden.

I was trying to think about Sybil. I felt weary and harassed beyond belief and the thought of a four-hundred-mile journey made me wilt, but I knew that somehow it would have to be endured, and Kate's return to her home would have to be delayed, for it was true that we would need her in Scotland to guide us and act as a link between us and the Ferguson family. She was in my care so I *must* be one of the party. I groaned aloud, imagining it.

Despite the sunshine, the bitter easterly that blows so often in March was finding its way through my cloak and making me shiver. I started back to the house. The moment I entered our courtyard, I saw Rusty tied out in the open while Eddie brushed him down, and knew that Simon was back. I also realized that once more we had uninvited visitors. Well, one, at least, for Rusty wasn't the only horse out in the yard. A strange horse was there as well. Arthur Watts was picking out its hooves.

'Whose is that?' I asked, walking up to him. Arthur looked round with a grin.

'Someone I think you'll be pleased to see, mistress,' he said.

'Who might that be?' I enquired.

The horse snorted and Arthur patted him. 'He rode in not half an hour ago. It's Master Christopher Spelton.'

'You got away!' I said as we sat sipping wine in the little parlour. 'You're safe! We tried to come after you, to warn you that someone was following you and intending to tell the French court about your secret mission. But we couldn't – we were prevented. I don't know how much you know . . .'

'Most of it,' said Spelton, stretching his feet to my hearth. 'I've been talking to Mistress Jester and that lass Katherine. Dear heaven, what a time you've had! It's a miracle that you're here, safe at home, and not halfway to Africa! My dear Mistress Stannard – what an escape! God was surely watching over you. I gather you'll be sending a full account to Walsingham and Lord Burghley? I reported to them after I got back to England and heard that no one knew where you were and there was much anxiety about you. That's why I'm here – I've been sent to see if there was news of you at Hawkswood. I've been told most of the background. I understand that word of some kind came to Walsingham about Pierre Lestrange, Count Renard's man. He's been brought in under arrest and is in the Tower now. It's known at court that you had set off to Dover in pursuit of Count Renard, and

that he had been spying for France, but since then, there had
been no word of you.'

So Tom Sterling had delivered my letter and Lestrange
had been duly collected. But in that case . . .

'I hoped that Walsingham would send men after us,' I said.
'If he had, we might never have set foot on the *Lucille*.'

'I can explain that. I've been well briefed,' said Spelton.
'There were diplomatic considerations. After all, England was
sponsoring a match between the queen's sister and the French
king's brother, the aim being to back up a treaty with France.
Walsingham felt that to be obliged to arrest the count for
spying would have been embarrassing.'

'So he did nothing, and left me to . . . manage alone?' I
said indignantly.

'It seems that he thought it best. If you caught up with the
count, there was a chance that you might persuade him to turn
back; also, you could pursue him into France more easily and
safely than Walsingham's men could. They might be viewed
as a breach of French sovereignty, but you, the count's prospec-
tive bride, Queen Elizabeth's sister, and also a private person,
would not. The French were most unlikely to harm *you*. They'd
find *that* an embarrassment in the circumstances.'

'This isn't the first time I've felt like a pawn on a chessboard,' I said. 'It's most unpleasant. In my letter to Walsingham,
I spoke of my anxiety about you. Was he also relying on me
to warn you, if the count couldn't be dissuaded from his
spying? Which I feel sure he couldn't,' I added. 'He'd already
broken off his betrothal to me.'

'Probably. In a way. Walsingham,' said Master Spelton drily,
'does not approve of women being involved in such matters,
but as a diplomatic bride, you were already involved and you
have proved yourself resourceful in the past. As for me, well,
if I couldn't be warned after all, it would be unfortunate but
secret agents are always expendable in the last resort. I believe
Lord Burghley protested but he was overridden.'

'I see,' I said.

I never did like Walsingham much.

I didn't ask whether the matter had been discussed in council,
or whether the queen had known of Walsingham's decision

and if so what she thought about it. Spelton might know the answers but I didn't wish to hear them. 'It was a near thing,' I said. 'More than once, we didn't think there ever would be word of any of us, ever again. But someone did warn you. How did that come about?'

'I have friends and contacts among the Huguenots, and there are some at the edge of court circles, even in France. Count Renard's chaplain made the count's report for him, and some of my contacts got to hear of it. I'd spent a night with them when I first got to France and they knew my plans. They knew I didn't mean to present myself at the court straightaway, because you asked me to make sure that this time, Matthew de la Roche really was dead. When I left my friends, I went to the chateau at Blanchepierre first. A messenger caught me up when I was there and then I made straight for Calais, believe me!'

He paused, studying me with kindly brown eyes. Stocky Master Spelton, plainly dressed as before, with his weathered face and fringe of greying brown hair round his bald patch, was in no way a remarkable man to look at, but there really was something steady, reassuring, about him. 'Matthew de la Roche *is* dead, Mistress Stannard. I have seen his grave and spoken to the lady who believes herself to be his widow, and is the mother of his youngest son. I mean *really* his youngest son – he's younger than your Harry. He is gone, mistress. That, this time, is the truth. I hope you are not too much distressed.'

I didn't know whether I was or not. I thought I had put Matthew away in the past, but what had been between us had been too intense for that. When I was alone, perhaps I would weep for him. If I ever had time! To Spelton, I said: 'In a way, it's a relief. Something is over and done with that should have been finished long ago. Thank you for the trouble you have taken.'

'It probably saved me from much unpleasantness,' said Spelton. He added: 'Walsingham will be sending out someone else to do my work for me. It will be someone apparently appointed to our ambassador's suite. One of the secretaries there has been instructed to return to England on a plea of

ill-health. His replacement will also be mine. I don't know
how Walsingham proposes to explain the count's death to the
French king, by the way. I fancy the truth will be imparted to
him but secretly. It will be a buried truth.'

'Literally. In the grounds of a Kentish house,' I said. 'Well,
the French don't wish for a quarrel with us, nor we with them.'

'What's this about Edinburgh?' said Spelton.

'How do you . . .?'

'Mistress Jester is fretting badly. She told me. So did Mistress
Katherine, who will have to go with her, I understand.'

'Who coaxed Sybil out of her room to see you?' I asked.
'Though I'm thankful that she has come out. She and I have
been at odds with each other.'

'So Mistress Katherine said. It was she who talked Mistress
Jester into coming out. When she did, she begged for my
support. But I can see you have a problem.'

'She's entitled to fret. She does have to go to Scotland and
she will need Katherine with her, but I am responsible for
Kate and if she goes to Scotland, I must go too. So I will,
only we couldn't start out yet and Sybil wouldn't understand.
It's all so complicated. I have had a thousand things to do that
couldn't wait and on top of that . . .'

I embarked on a confused, not to say incoherent explanation
about having to hire a coach driver because Arthur Watts was
past long journeys now and none of the other grooms could
be spared so I'd have to take Brockley to drive, and I'd need
Brockley anyway, but Dale, being his wife, hated him going
off without her, only I didn't think she could stand another
long journey, and we were all so exhausted and most of my
horses were still in Dover . . .

At that point, I realized that my voice had risen and acquired
an hysterical edge. I stopped.

'Yes, I see the difficulty,' said Master Spelton soothingly.
'I saw your coach when I was here before. Surely you ladies
can be comfortable in that?' He hesitated and I said: 'Yes?'

'It is only a suggestion. But if your woman can't face any
more travelling, even by coach, leave her and her husband
behind. You will have Mistress Jester and Katherine as female
companions. I will come as your male escort. I am on leave

from my court duties for the moment. I can drive a coach as well as any man.'

'Master Spelton!' It was as though a magical spell had been pronounced and a wand waved, and all my difficulties had vanished. 'If only you would!'

'But I have said that I will. And I can do more. I think I once told you that I am officially a Queen's Messenger, so I can use the royal network of remounts. We can rely on good horses all the way, for harness as well as saddle. Changing teams will present no difficulty.'

'How soon can we leave?' I asked him.

Sybil's gratitude was tearful; Kate was a mixture of nervousness and excitement but she made her preparations with a will. Actually, it took three more days to conclude the arrangements, fetch a hired coach team from Guildford, send Eddie, Joseph and Billington off to Dover, despatch Simon to court with my letters, and make sure that the coach was in good order. The bitter wind had at least made the ground dry, which would mean better roads on the long journey north.

When we set out, with Spelton holding the reins and the rest of us snugly settled inside the coach with hampers of belongings at our feet, Brockley and Dale stood in the courtyard to see us off, their faces sad and strained. It was so rare for me to go away without them. 'Back soon!' I called, leaning out of the coach window to wave.

I hoped it really would be soon. Kate had told me that the Ferguson kinsfolk in Edinburgh were cousins of her father, and that she had once accompanied her parents on a visit to them, and thought them very pleasant. But she had been the young daughter of visiting relatives, not a complete stranger foisted on them to protect a wild young man who had killed the man she hoped to marry.

Ambrosia, grieving and furious, would arrive virtually under guard, with instructions that she was to be kept in Scotland, not allowed to communicate with England, married off if possible to another Ferguson relative and if not possible, then just kept. She was unlikely to be pleasant to them and they might not feel inclined to be pleasant to her.

I didn't say what I was thinking to the others. I just hoped we could get Ambrosia away from them even if it meant a midnight escape like my long-ago elopement with Gerald. We would have to be very careful over our initial approach. I did say that much. Kate would have to introduce us, after all.

On the way, therefore, Kate and I rehearsed that introduction, with me taking the part of a very surprised Ferguson cousin, and reacting in various ways – puzzled, surprised, startled, indignant and *get out of my house this instant!* – so that Kate should be prepared for anything.

For a coach journey, we travelled fast, but we were six days on the road, even though Spelton knew and was permitted to use every royal remount stable along the way. Two teams were trotters and I began to feel that Hugh's dislike of them was not justified. They were all fine strong animals, capable of covering long distances at speed – and what speed! One team took us eight miles in half an hour.

As you go further north, the inns become fewer and wayfarers have to ask for shelter at private homes. I expected this and so did Spelton. We had both been to this part of the world before and knew about its tradition of hospitality. Sybil hated it, because although we always found a welcome somewhere, we usually had makeshift beds with straw mattresses, uninteresting stew for supper and salted porridge for breakfast and there were difficulties about talking to our hosts, because their accents were so broad.

We arrived in Edinburgh in the evening and just as I had felt when we first reached Dover, I considered it too late to inflict ourselves and our difficult mission on the Ferguson household. We needed a hostelry of some kind. Through an overcast dusk, we rode along a main street which I recognized from my one previous visit to the city. It was lined on either side by well-remembered tall houses, punctuated by archways leading into dark alleys.

We looked hopefully to right and left and then, to our relief, saw a sign proclaiming that at this address, bed, board and stabling were to be had. A painted arrow on the wall directed us into one of the dark lanes, and at the rear, we found a gate with a gatekeeper, and once we had made ourselves understood, we were admitted to a rear courtyard with the promised stabling, and a landlord who came out to meet us and was pleased to give us rooms.

We were made quite comfortable, though the beds appalled both Kate and Sybil, for they were in compartments like cupboards, and had doors which one was supposed to close. Spelton and I had been expecting this but Sybil had never been to Scotland before and Kate had forgotten this Scottish peculiarity. 'Warm against winter,' the landlord told us and the evening before had been cold enough to make the point. Nevertheless, I think all of us slept with our doors open.

In the morning, we rifled our hampers for fresh clothes, suitable for what we all feared would be a nerve-racking visit, and having fortified ourselves with another breakfast of salted porridge we left the building on foot.

It was cold again, but the air was fresh, smelling of salt from the nearby firth, and there was sunshine. Edinburgh in the morning was livelier than it had been the previous evening. Stalls were being set up, shoppers were already abroad, pony carts clip-clopped by, bringing supplies of goods to the stalls. 'Can you really remember where your relatives live?' I asked Kate. 'It's some time since you were here, is it not?'

'Yes, it is, but I think I can,' Kate was frowning, but nevertheless seemed fairly sure of herself. 'I think . . . we need to turn right just past that line of stalls and – yes – there's a corner after that, turning right again, and we go round that, and it's a house on the left.' She paused, and then said: 'Now we're here, I feel nervous.'

'So do I,' I assured her. 'But whatever reception we get, we have tried to prepare for it. Please just introduce us by name, very politely, and then I'll take over, explaining who Sybil is, but in a slightly louder voice in the hope that Ambrosia will hear us and be able to come to us . . . that's the best strategy, I think.'

'I just want to see Ambrosia! I shall want to call her name!' said Sybil, but Spelton said: 'Better wait until we've explained ourselves and we see what kind of welcome we're going to get.'

'Very well, but let's start out now!' pleaded Sybil. 'To think that my girl may be so near . . .!'

We had gone perhaps fifty yards along the street, among the early shoppers and the stallholders shouting their wares, when we came face to face with her.

I don't know about the others but I had been imagining Ambrosia in all kinds of circumstances, most of them depressing. I had among other things visualized her being thrust unwillingly into another unwanted marriage, by beating or a bread-and-water diet, or else dressed in drab, grubby clothes and reduced to the status of an unpaid servant, running dogsbody errands or pounding dough in a steamy kitchen.

What I had not visualized – and I doubt if any of the others had either – was that we would meet her sauntering through the market, basket on arm like any other Edinburgh housewife, smiling and talking cheerfully to the middle-aged maid trotting at her side. The maid, who had a cheery round face, pink from the sea-wind, was discreetly clad in brown; Ambrosia wore a stout plaid shawl against the cold but her peach-coloured split skirt and the dove-grey kirtle beneath it were surely of the finest wool. She looked prosperous, she looked happy . . . and as soon as she saw us, just as astounded as we were.

'Mother!'

'Ambrosia! Oh, Ambrosia, my daughter, my darling . . .!'

'Annie!' said Kate to the maid.

'Mistress Kate! And Mistress Stannard!'

'This is a delightful reunion,' remarked Christopher Spelton. 'But now that we are quite sure who we all are, can we find somewhere to sit down – and then I think we'd all like some explanations.'

TWENTY-SIX
All Too Much

'We can go to my home,' said Ambrosia blithely. 'It's not far. I'll shop later. Come.' She turned to lead us back the way she had come and as she did so, the sunlight flashed on a ring on her left hand. It was a wedding ring and it glittered as though it were new. We all followed her obediently, glancing at each other in bemusement.

As Ambrosia turned towards the doorway of one of the tall houses, Kate said to me: 'Well, my Ferguson cousins don't live here, not unless they've moved,' and then Ambrosia glanced over her shoulder and said, laughingly: 'Indeed they don't live here. This house belongs to James Hale. I am Mistress Hale now.'

Then the door was being opened by a manservant, and we were being ushered inside. Our cloaks were taken, and we were shown into a most attractive bow-windowed parlour, a lady's bower in every way, with cushioned settles, little tables, mats made of colourful patchwork. An embroidery frame lay on the wide window seat, with a workbox beside it; a half-finished game of backgammon and a book of verse lay on one of the tables. Best of all on that cold morning, there was a bright wood fire, which a maid was tending. We moved towards it in a body.

'Leave it, Mary,' Ambrosia said. 'It's burning nicely now. Come, everyone, be seated. Mary, will you fetch us some wine? Thank you. Oh, Mother! I am so glad to see you!'

While the rest of us sat down, except for Annie, who remained deferentially standing, Sybil and Ambrosia then did what they couldn't do in the street without attracting public attention, and threw themselves into each other's arms. Then, at last, Sybil stood back, though still holding her daughter by

the elbows, and said: 'But how do you come to be here? How
do you come to be Mistress Hale? I don't understand!'

'Nor do I!' I said. I had been mulling it over. It was barely
a month since Ambrosia had left Dover. And here she was,
settled in marriage and a home of her own. It was all too much
to take in.

'I don't suppose you do,' said Ambrosia, amused. 'Ah, here
is Mary with the wine – and thank you, Mary, how sensible.
See, she has brought some cinnamon biscuits too.'

Mary said something incomprehensible, in a powerful
Scots accent, bobbed a curtsey and left us. Annie began to
dispense the refreshments. Ambrosia began to speak again
but was interrupted by youthful shouts and running feet, and
seconds after Mary had closed the parlour door, it burst open
again, to admit four young children, a fair-haired girl of
about seven, two boys with dark eyes and thick dark brown
hair, who were obviously twins of around four, and a second
girl, fair like the other, no older than three and sucking her
thumb.

The girls hung back a little, but the two boys hurled themselves at Ambrosia, which was no surprise for I had already
taken in their long eyebrows and mouths, their wide nostrils,
and the brightness of their eyes, and knew who they were.
They, however, did not know who we were and clung to their
mother, crying out for reassurance.

'Who are they? Have they come to take us away again? We
won't go!'

'Won't go!'

'No, we won't!'

'If they try, we'll kill them!'

'Kill them, yes we will . . .!'

'Hush, hush, you noisy pair!' The little girls were staring,
in evident alarm, but Ambrosia was now laughing. 'No one is
going to take you anywhere! Here is your grandmother, who
is delighted to see you here with me, and these others are her
friends. Yes, Mistress Stannard, yes, everyone, these are my
sons. Meet Paul and Tommy – this one's Paul though I don't
suppose you can tell the difference! The girls are my step-
daughters. This is Lucy, who will be eight next month, and

this little sweetheart is May. My loves, this is your step-grandmother, my mother, Mistress Sybil Jester . . .'

'But . . .' I said and then stopped.

'Settle down,' said Ambrosia to her sons, who had now stopped threatening to kill us all and instead were clamouring to know if they could have a sip of her wine. 'Where is your . . . Oh, there you are, Tilly.'

A plump nursemaid had appeared, in a hurry, and out of breath. 'Tilly, my love, I shall come upstairs later and hear Lucy's lesson as usual, and play with the others, but my mother has come to see me, with her friends, and we have so much news to exchange. Now, let go of me, my darlings. Go with nurse and I'll come soon, I promise and no, my dears, you may *not* share my wine; you're still too young.' The nurse shepherded the children away and Ambrosia sat laughing and shaking her head.

'My boys missed me badly while we were apart. Whenever I go out, I think they fear that I won't come back and when I do, they behave as if they haven't seen me for years, and they are afraid of strangers, as you saw – and heard! Annie, will you go and send the kitchen boy to the printing works to tell my husband who has arrived to see me. He may want to come home at once and meet them. Now.' Ambrosia smiled round at us. 'You wanted explanations, I think. No wonder. Well . . .'

She was silent a moment and thoughtful, her eyes downcast. Then she said; 'When Count Renard was killed, I was frantic. And furious. I wouldn't listen when the Fergusons tried to tell me what the count had done and what he was. How he had spied for the French and tried to lead young Duncan Ferguson into spying for them as well, at peril of his neck if he were caught. I raged and swore and said I would report Duncan as a murderer . . .'

'Duels are officially illegal,' I told her, 'but juries hardly ever convict and in a case like this, I am as sure as I can be, that they wouldn't. If necessary, I will beg the queen for a free pardon but I probably won't need to. The count had tried to lead a respectable young man into betraying his country. Everyone's sympathy would be with the respectable young man!'

'I didn't know that,' said Ambrosia. 'I don't think the
Fergusons knew either. I was just . . . wild with rage and what
I thought was grief and I threatened – oh, I don't know what
– and cried and . . . well, as you know, I was shipped to
Scotland to get me out of the way. The wind was fair and it
took only three days to get to Edinburgh but in that time, I
had a chance to think. And I began to see . . .'

She stopped for a moment and then said: 'It's hard to explain,
but suddenly, Count Renard began to change. I mean, the
memory of him began to change. I began to see that he had
done wrong, very wrong, was dangerous to England and even
to the queen. He was a danger to Master Spelton here . . .' as
she spoke, she gave him a grave, apologetic glance '. . . and
who knew what other secrets, English secrets, he was carrying
back to France? It was as though I were waking from a bad
dream. He ceased to be real to me. I don't think I ever really
wanted to be a countess! That would be an alien world to me.
He had promised to get my sons back. That, perhaps, was why
I thought I loved him . . .'

'And then,' I prompted, 'you arrived here.'

'Yes. I was taken to the home of Master Hamish Ferguson's
cousin, Angus Ferguson. You'll meet him soon! He's quite
elderly, white-haired, and he has eyeglasses that fall off his
nose, so he keeps them on a chain so that they just stay dangling
like a pendant . . . he has a nice, fat wife called Marie, with
a jolly laugh, and their eldest son lives with them and has a
pretty wife and four children . . . they were all kind to me,
comforted me for my loss and for the shock they were sure I
had had when I found out the truth about the count. I was
exhausted, bemused. I took refuge in being polite, behaving
myself and trying to think. And then . . .'

She looked up at us and her eyes were dancing. 'The day
after I arrived, they had people to dine and one of them was
another cousin, not a Ferguson. He was called Master James
Hale – Mistress Marie Ferguson was born Mistress Hale. He
is a printer. He has a works two streets from here and he is
prosperous. He prints all sorts of things, books of poetry, books
about religion and history and travel . . . he is so well read.
That was one thing I liked about the count, you know; the

amount he'd read; the poetry he could quote. But so can James! He is only a few years older than I am, and good-looking. He talked to me a good deal that day. I gathered that his wife died a year ago and that he was lonely and worried about the best way to bring up his daughters . . .'

'Is he the man that the Dover Fergusons thought you might be persuaded to marry?' Sybil asked.

'Yes, though I didn't find that out for several days. But the Angus Fergusons had noticed that we liked each other and eventually Mistress Marie took me aside and asked if I could consider him as a husband. I said would he help me get my sons back and Mistress Marie said he and I must talk about that. So we did, and, well, ten days after I arrived here in Edinburgh, we became man and wife. I was thankful to marry him! I felt safe with him, secure. We set off for York at once, the very day we were wed. James said the journey should be our honeymoon; that we should enjoy it and get to know each other properly on the way. He was pleased to have stepsons, he said. He is so kind!'

Ferguson had been right. He had said he might well be doing Ambrosia a favour and so he had. It was confusing.

'We took one of the carts we keep, for deliveries to publishers and so on – and our best horse,' said Ambrosia, beaming. 'James insisted on using the fastest one. She's a trotting mare and the speeds she can do and the distances she can cover, you would hardly believe it . . .'

Hugh had definitely been wrong about trotters, I thought. They were clearly much more useful than he had given them credit for.

Ambrosia was still talking. 'It only took us two and a half days to reach York!' She laughed. 'I know where my sister-in-law lives and we went straight there and found the house in an uproar because my boys were having a tantrum, *both* of them. Being twins they do most things together and Eliza was slapping them and shouting at them to be quiet.'

'Oh dear,' said Sybil, distressed.

'I've *never* liked Eliza,' said Ambrosia. 'She has no idea how to care for children properly and she certainly doesn't understand my sons. They respond to people who are reasonable. They

take after their father, that way. John was always reasonable.
Dear John . . . but there, all that's in the past. Eliza was
relieved to see me. My offspring were disrupting her household! Her husband sometimes comes home for dinner from
the school where he teaches and he did so that day, and he
was relieved too! Now that I was married, no one could
push me into another alliance, and neither Eliza nor her
husband really wanted the boys anyway. Well, they gave us
dinner and handed the boys to us and were glad to do it.
We started for home the same afternoon. We were back here
about ten days ago. It amazes me, too! Barely three weeks
after I was loaded on to a ship at Dover, crying and angry
and threatening revenge, I was bringing my sons into my
new married home and introducing them to Tilly, the nurse
who was already in charge of my step-daughters. How life
can change!'

'How, indeed! The boy wasted no time in fetching me, my
dear. Here I am! And here, I take it, is your mother – and
perhaps you will introduce me to our other guests? Good day
to you all, anyway.'

Engrossed in Ambrosia's tale, we hadn't noticed the new
arrival. But Ambrosia broke off as he spoke, and her face lit
up with a wide, happy smile. 'Mother, my friends, this is my
husband James!'

I turned. Here was the explanation of the mystery. James
Hale was the kind of man who is immediately likeable.
Middling tall, well-knit, black hair with a healthy gloss on it;
a pleasant face, browned a little by the sea wind from the firth,
hazel eyes, a little darker than my own. Eyes that smiled, a
personality that came forth to meet you, that shook hands with
you while you were still several feet apart.

It had seemed unbelievable that Ambrosia, who had left
Dover raging and weeping over the death of the count, should
in such a short space of time have met and married this
amiable-looking man, and retrieved her boys. Now I saw how
it could have happened. It still made my head go round.

Spelton had taken on the task of introducing everyone. 'This
is Ambrosia's mother, Mistress Sybil Jester, this is Kate
Ferguson, daughter of the Dover Fergusons, this is Mistress

Ursula Stannard and I am Master Christopher Spelton, in her majesty's employ . . .'

My head really was spinning. Had it been the wine? Surely it wasn't that strong! Ambrosia was saying something else now, something about the lodge-keeper's son who had escorted her on the voyage, but was now on his way back home and had really been kind to her; he was a nice lad . . . yes, I dimly remembered Ferguson mentioning him, when was it now . . .? I was very dizzy indeed. An inky blizzard of black dots danced before my eyes. Someone was asking me something but I couldn't understand what they were saying. I really must pull myself together and . . .

I came round to find myself lying on one of the settles. Sybil was sponging my forehead with cold water and Kate was pushing a cushion under my feet. Ambrosia was outside in the passageway, calling for Mary. Annie was making up the fire. I tried to sit up but Sybil gently pushed me back. Ambrosia was now ordering Mary and Annie to go upstairs and make up a bed in the north-east gable room. Christopher Spelton and James Hale were standing beside the settle, looking down at me.

'You have exhausted yourself,' Spelton said to me. 'You have been through more than you can bear. Mistress Sybil has been borne up by the need to trace her daughter and Kate Ferguson is young enough to be resilient but you have only had responsibility. Master Hale, can we carry her upstairs?' To me, he added: 'Take your ease, Ursula. It's all over now.'

It had been over, of course, before we ever left Hawkswood, had we only known it. The only one who had guessed was old Gladys, who had said that our journey would be for nothing. *Just a feeling*, she had said. Gladys did sometimes have a trick of knowing things that on the face of it she couldn't know – and then being right.

She had more than once been arrested as a witch. Sometimes, I suspected that there was truth in that.

TWENTY-SEVEN
Saving Kate

I slept for a while in the chamber to which I had been carried, and woke with another blinding migraine. Sybil, however, had brought the recipe that Gladys used to relieve me, and Ambrosia had the ingredients. Before night had fallen, the pain was receding. It didn't, for once, end in nausea and before nightfall I was even able to drink a little broth. However, I spent the next two days in bed.

On the third day I was able to get up and go out into the salt-scented spring sunshine. On the fourth day, we made our farewells and started for England: Spelton, Sybil, Kate and myself. The maid Annie, who had been sent to Scotland along with Ambrosia, had decided to stay. She and Ambrosia, surprisingly, since Annie had originally been almost her jailer, had made friends and Ambrosia wanted to keep her.

There were tears at the parting of Sybil and Ambrosia, but not bitter ones. 'I am glad you're happy but I wish you weren't so far away!' Sybil mourned, holding her daughter tightly.

'But we shall meet again. One day perhaps we shall come to Hawkswood!'

'That we will. I've heard that much about it!' said James. He had a Scottish accent but it was not overly strong and he was easy to understand. Even during the short time I had spent in the house, I had realized that my first impression of him was right. Ambrosia had found a good man.

'Maybe there'll be new grandchildren for you!' Ambrosia said to her mother.

'I hope so. I hope so. And if there are, I pray that they shall come easily and safely. I shall pray for you every day.'

'And I for you. Here are the boys, come to say farewell . . .'

They tore themselves apart eventually. The journey home began.

We were bound first for Dover, to take Kate home. Spelton's privileged travelling arrangements proved a blessing, as ever, as did his purse. Our money was running low but he was well supplied and had no hesitation about spending it. We took it more easily this time, and took eight days. By late afternoon on the last day, under cool cloudy skies and a whirling canopy of crying gulls, we arrived at Whitefields.

All day, Kate had been very quiet. As we turned in at the gate, she said: 'Mistress Stannard, I'm frightened. My father is going to be so angry; I know it.'

'I've worried about that all along,' I said. 'But I had to bring you home. I'm here, Kate. I will try to smooth things for you. Don't be afraid. Even if he is angry, he'll probably be thankful to see you safe.'

'He knows I'm safe. You wrote to him before we left your house at Hawkswood.' Her eyes brightened. 'What a lovely place it is! But,' she added as the brightness faded, 'he'll have had time to feel relieved and then get over it and start wondering how he should treat me when I come home – and when I do, he'll be more angry than glad. I know. I know *him*.'

'I'll do what I can,' I said.

'We all will,' said Sybil.

We were expected, for Christopher – he and I were comfortably on first-name terms by then – had sent a courier ahead of us. Mr Hamish Ferguson was on the doorstep to meet us. Grooms came out to unharness the horses and push the coach into shelter, and the butler Morley was hovering with a couple of minions to take our cloaks and carry our baggage inside, but Mr Ferguson was standing rigid, like one of the Norman pillars in Hawkswood parish church, and he didn't smile.

He merely nodded an acknowledgement of our arrival, and then he turned and went in, leaving us to follow him. He led us to the hall, where a fire was crackling in the hearth, and where his wife and the younger girl Sheila had evidently been told to wait. There was no sign of Duncan.

Mrs Ferguson rose to her feet as we entered, and stood stiffly for a moment, but Kate's sister fell upon her instantly with hugs and kisses, and after a moment, Mrs Ferguson stepped forward and pushed her out of her way while she took

her errant daughter in her arms. Until a peremptory command
from Hamish made her step back.

'That'll do! Didn't I tell you? No tears!' There were tears,
I saw, on Mrs Ferguson's harsh countenance. 'If ever a daughter
betrayed her family, defied her parents, behaved in fact as
though she had never heard of family honour, then it is this
Kate you're clasping to your breast and sobbing over!' He
glanced round at the rest of us. 'Well, come along in, come
to the hearth, all of you.'

Mrs Ferguson let go of Kate, but stood close to her and
did not wipe her tears away. Sybil and I accepted the invita-
tion to warm ourselves, though nervously. Christopher
Spelton also moved towards the hearth, and he showed no
sign of nerves. When he shed his cloak and gloves at
Morley's behest, he had done so with the air of one who
has no doubt of a friendly welcome in this house and he
brought the same air into the hall. He warmed his hands for
a moment, and then, as two maids brought in the obligatory
tray of refreshments, turned to smile at them and helpfully
pushed a small table into a more convenient position for
setting the trays down.

After which, he turned his smile on to the stark figure of
Hamish Ferguson and said: 'Well, Mr Ferguson. We have
brought your daughter home to you at last. Aren't you going
to give her a kiss of greeting? I would, if she were mine. She
has been through such terrors; more than you can imagine.
She has been as brave as a lioness through it all. You have
surely told him of Kate's bravery, Ursula. I understand you
wrote to him when you first got home to Hawkswood.'

'Yes, I did,' I said. 'Mr Ferguson, during the anxious time
when we were travelling towards Lundy, all the time afraid
that the crew would lose patience and give our plans away,
Kate smiled through her fear, to keep our spirits up as much
as her own, and we were grateful. And when we were escaping
from Lundy in a small boat, and the pirate captain tried to
board us, flourishing a cutlass, it was Kate who struck him
down with an oar, just as he was about to climb aboard! She
was truly valiant!'

'I read your letter, madam. I must say that the thought of

a daughter of mine behaving in such a way, fighting, hitting out with a weapon as though she were a man herself, shocks me deeply.'

'The pirate captain had followers just behind him and they intended to seize us all and take us to North Africa to be sold as slaves!' cried Sybil.

Christopher said: 'If I had a daughter in such danger, I would be very proud of her if she defended herself so well. And not just herself. She saved her friends too.'

'Yes,' I said. 'He could have used that cutlass to take one of us hostage while his followers rowed the boat back to the jetty.'

That silenced Ferguson for a moment, and then he let out a deep sigh.

'The world has gone mad, it seems to me. I cannot endure it. Kate, I will give thanks to God that you are safe but I still cannot accept the things you have done, whatever your reasons. To run away from home, to a man like Garnett, to behave like a hoyden . . .! Your room is ready for you. Your mother would have it so for I yielded to her coaxing. But you will not occupy it for long, you may rest assured of that.'

'Are you going to send your elder daughter to Scotland as well? Just wash your hands of her, like Pontius Pilate? Just hand her over to someone else?' Mrs Ferguson's voice was bitter. 'Perhaps your cousin won't care to have another inconvenient person foisted on him!'

'What I do with a daughter who has misbehaved like this one is my business, madam. I yielded to your motherly weakness by saying that yes, she can stay here for a while, until I decide what best to do with her. But I will yield no further. The final decision is mine. I am master here.'

'And I am mistress!' Suddenly, we were in the midst of a savage domestic dispute. 'How dare you? I carried our daughter within me for nine months and bled and cried out and risked my life to bring her into the world. And you say her fate is not my business!'

'I shall ask if my cousin in the north will take her on, but if he won't, and I shan't blame him if so, then she can go out and earn her living alongside Bessie in the Safe Harbour!' thundered

Hamish. 'I certainly won't try any more to marry her off. She's no fit wife for any man!'

'I'll marry where you wish, Father,' Kate said pleadingly. 'I'll do anything . . .'

'I daresay you would, my girl, but it's too late. You've gone too far, much too far. I am disowning you!'

'I see. You are shocked when your daughter defends herself from defilement and slavery! But you can tolerate the thought of her working as a tavern maid! What kind of father are you? And though you are ready to send Kate to work in a tavern, you won't accept a decent innkeeper's girl as an honest daughter-in-law! You are unreasonable!' shouted his wife. 'When will I make you see it?'

It sounded as though this was a continuation of a quarrel that had been begun before we arrived. Mrs Ferguson now wrenched the conversation – if one could call it that – in a new direction. 'If anyone is wondering where Duncan is, he is on the way to Italy. But if and when he can come safely home again, I shall urge him to marry his Bessie as soon as she's willing – if she hasn't found someone else by then. He shall bring her home, and I'll see she's made welcome! And Kate will *not* be banished to the inn to replace her. I'll see to that, too!'

'I don't advise you to attempt anything so rash, madam.'

'Don't madam me! I have a right to protect my children.'

'I will protect them myself!'

'By casting your daughter off to serve ale and rabbit pie to all and sundry? By denying your son a man's right to choose his own bride?'

'My son will be fortunate if he is ever able to come home!' Ferguson turned angrily to me. 'Have you reported the way Count Renard died to the authorities? Will I soon have officers here, wanting his body exhumed so that there can be an inquest? He is buried, of course, here in my grounds, with Catholic rites provided by Morley, as I think you know was my intention. But where will that leave my son?'

'I have made a report of sorts,' I said. 'But I did not give your name. I did not identify Duncan. What I did do was describe the circumstances. Duncan issued a challenge, though he has no title – but the titled man he challenged was a murderer and a traitor to a country that had shown him kindness when he was exiled from his home. I doubt if there is very much for your son to fear, even if his name does come out. No jury with even normal common sense would condemn him for that, even if it ever came to trial. And as I said, I did not identify him.'

'I should hope not!' cried Mrs Ferguson.

'You sent Mistress Wilde to Scotland, hoping thereby to prevent her from ever reporting him to the law,' I said angrily to her husband. 'But we were merely despatched to France. Or was it *merely*? *Did* you know what Captain Garnett's intentions were?'

Garnett himself had already exonerated Hamish Ferguson, but I said it to take some of the aggression out of Hamish and it worked. He reacted with a mixture of horror and wrath.

'I certainly did not! When I received the letter that your grooms brought me when they fetched your horses, the letter that told me of his perfidy, I was appalled! Of course I didn't know! I simply wanted to get you off to France and out of the way while I got Duncan out of danger! The *Lucille* was there in the harbour and I knew Garnett would take you. I'd sometimes wondered if he did a bit of piracy on the side but I didn't *know* and if I'd had the least idea that . . .!' Words failed him.

We all murmured understandingly and his stiffness seemed to ease. 'I am glad that according to the letter your courier brought, Mrs Wilde is now contentedly remarried and is no threat to Duncan. I never wished her harm! I only wished to protect my boy. But now,' said Mr Ferguson grimly, 'we must return to the matter of my daughter Kate, except that I can no longer regard her as a daughter!'

'Father . . .' said Kate tremulously.

'Please!' Spelton intervened. 'Surely we can find an amicable settlement. If we could all sit down and talk this over . . .'

Kate was trembling from head to foot and now she looked at me piteously and said: 'Mistress Stannard, please help me!'

And I knew what to do. Suddenly, it was obvious.

'Mr Ferguson! Please listen to me. I like your Kate. It is quite usual for families to send their daughters to learn about the world in the households of others, who thereafter are responsible for their well-being and in due course their marriages. I have in the past cared for other girls, in that way. I will be happy to take Kate in, on those terms. If you wish her to leave your home, then could she not come to mine?'

Kate's unhappy face lit up with hope. Her mother said: 'Will you be kind to her? Will you promise to be kind to her?'

It occurred to me that Mrs Ferguson's air of harsh rigidity was probably a defence against her husband's even more rigid mind. I had seen such things before.

'I promise,' I said. 'Kate has suffered enough. Mr Ferguson, have you not grasped that Captain Garnett meant to sell us to the corsairs on Lundy? We would never have come home again and the fate in Algiers of a young girl such as your daughter doesn't bear thinking about. We have all been terrified, but Kate most of all, I think. And it was she, in the end, who saved us.'

There was a silence. Ferguson had after all more or less put himself in the position of a man who, when painting a floor, has found that he is now in a corner, standing on the only bit of floor still free of paint, and unable to escape without leaving footprints all over the work already done. He didn't really want to alienate his wife for ever, and probably didn't really want to throw Kate out of his house either. He had lost his temper and gone too far to turn back. I had offered him a way out.

Sheila said timidly: 'Father, it could be a solution. Couldn't it? It's true that people often do send their daughters to other houses as part of their education. No one would think it strange. There wouldn't be any *talk*.'

'There'd certainly be talk if people we know went into the Safe Harbour and were handed their ale by our Kate!' said her mother vigorously.

'Kate is a Catholic,' said Hamish. 'You, Mrs Stannard, are not. How will you deal with that?'

'The Safe Harbour isn't a Catholic household either!' snapped Mrs Ferguson.

'I will not interfere with Kate's religion,' I said. 'There is a decent Catholic servant in my house, a Master Flood, who can arrange for her to hear Mass now and then. Please don't worry about that.'

'Well . . .'

'We would all wish to be on our way tomorrow,' I said. 'Kate can come with us. I miss having a daughter at home, since my Meg was wed and went to live in Buckinghamshire. Kate will be most welcome, and perfectly safe.'

'Well . . .' said Mr Ferguson, again.

Kate opened her mouth as if to say *please* but I gave her a tiny shake of the head. Pressure of any kind might annoy her father. Silence, while he considered, was more likely to work.

It did. 'Don't unpack, Kate,' he said to her. 'Or not more than you need for the night. You will leave with Mistress Stannard in the morning. Express your thanks to her!'

Kate, for once, was obedient to him. She thanked me, on her knees. I raised her up, smiling at her. Kate, with that ferociously wielded oar, had truly saved us all. Now, I hoped, I had saved her in return.

In the morning, when the horses were harnessed and everyone else was in the coach, literally half a minute before departure, I said my farewells to the Fergusons. I kissed Mrs Ferguson goodbye and promised again to take good care of Kate. Then, to his visible astonishment, I kissed Mr Ferguson.

And whispered into his ear: 'I have met Bessie from the Safe Harbour. She is a good girl. If you let your son marry her when he comes home, I don't think you'll regret it.'

Then I stepped away, got quickly into the coach, closed the door, and tapped on the roof to tell Christopher to start. I didn't want Ferguson to take sudden offence and try to snatch his daughter back. As it was, when I waved a last farewell through the window, he was merely standing there, looking astonished.

I could only hope for the best.

TWENTY-EIGHT
Shaping the Future

Christopher was acquainted, I think, with nearly every town in England and certainly with Dover, and he knew where in Dover to find a courier service. Before we ourselves set off in earnest, he had hired a man to ride at speed for Hawkswood, to let my people know that I was on my way home, and then go to the court, to bring Walsingham and Cecil up to date with what I had been doing, and my whereabouts. Then, at the slower pace dictated by a coach, we took the road ourselves.

Many times, I had returned to Hawkswood after frightening adventures. This was just another, and yet it felt more intense than any that had gone before. The first sight of the chimneys was like a glimpse of Paradise. And not only to me. It brought tears to Kate's eyes, too, and a whispered prayer of thanks. I suppose that to Kate, as much as to myself, Hawkswood represented safety and also more kindness than her father had given her. By most people's standards, I knew, he had been a perfectly responsible father, even indulgent in some ways, but that harsh streak had been there all the same, and she had feared him. They would be better apart for a while.

'Take heart,' I said to her. 'Your father will come round one day, I'm sure of it. How Gladys will preen herself, after being proved right when she said we were going to Scotland for nothing. Good God!'

My exclamation had nothing to do with either Kate or Gladys. We were now entering the Hawkswood gateway and the courtyard before us was astonishingly congested, with two ornate coaches and a crowd of people, some of whom were heaving baggage about, and several saddle horses including a fine blue roan stallion, which was snorting and tossing his head as a groom I didn't recognize strove to remove his bridle.

'I know the coat of arms on those coaches,' I said. 'Walsingham! And that blue roan belongs to Sir Robert Dudley. We have distinguished visitors waiting for us!'

Arthur Watts and Simon came to meet me as I clambered out of our own more modest vehicle. 'You have guests, madam,' Arthur said.

'So I see! I take it that Wilder and Brockley are looking after them.'

Five minutes later, I had joined them in the great hall, and there was Sir Francis Walsingham, dark and stark as ever but not quite as stark as he sometimes was, for he smiled broadly as we entered. With him, as I had guessed, was Robert Dudley, Earl of Leicester. Brockley, Dale and Gladys were there too, and pounced upon me, all three wanting to embrace me at once. When the first transports were over, Walsingham cleared his throat and explained that Lord Burghley was laid up with gout.

'It plagues him sore,' Walsingham said. 'Or he would have come as well. Luckily, my own health, just now, is not too bad. We bring a letter from her majesty, Ursula, and other news too. Do you wish to refresh yourself before we settle down to talk, or . . .'

'I want all the news here and now,' I said. 'I don't know if Kate or Sybil, or Master Spelton . . .'

A chorus of voices assured me that they too could leave washing and changing for a while in favour of hearing the word from the court.

There was plenty of it. The queen's letter was a great relief to me, for I now knew that those I wished to protect were no longer in danger. I was duty bound, said her majesty, to reveal who the people were who had killed and buried Count Renard, but although there would have to be an inquest, a free pardon would be forthcoming if any were needed. The disgraceful nature of the count's attempt to suborn an honest young man had been noted. It also appeared that under questioning, Pierre Lestrange had admitted to the murder of Joan Flood, in accordance with orders given by the count. My suspicions were justified.

Under persuasion (I preferred not to enquire what kind of

persuasion), Lestrange had apparently come up with a good deal of interesting information. The queen and her council now knew of the many things the count had managed to learn that he ought not to have learned, and it was a matter of great regret that his chaplain had got away to France and must have passed this information on to the French court. It would do England no good, and various policies would now need rethinking. However, queen and council at least knew of the disaster and could set about mitigating it.

In addition, I need not fear for Alfred Bones or Marcus Clay, though this was not a matter of clemency. The *Lucille* had been seized when she recently put into Dover but Mr Bones, Mr Clay and Mr Bones' nephew Jacky were not aboard. According to the rest of the crew, the ship had first put into a French port, and the trio had gone ashore and not returned. All the crew said the same and there was no reason to disbelieve them. I could assume that though they might now be struggling with the French language, they were safe from arrest.

From what you have reported of the Lucille *and the crimes committed by her crew under Captain Garnett, the pardon you seek for these men might have been difficult to grant. As it is, they are out of our jurisdiction.* I was glad.

'You, Mistress Stannard, are commended,' said Walsingham, 'for bringing the *Lucille* to the attention of her majesty's officers. A scourge and a menace has gone from our seas.'

He gave me a sardonic smile. 'It is known that you once refused a proposal of marriage from Captain Yarrow, the Assistant Constable of Dover Castle. He was very downcast at your refusal, but overjoyed at the opportunity to take part in the capture and questioning of the *Lucille*'s crew. He sends you his warmest thanks and says that he forgives you.'

'Well, really!' I said.

Walsingham, blanking the amusement out of his voice and face, said: 'We intend to make a renewed effort to clear out the wasps' nest on Lundy. Your attempt to save Master Spelton, which brought you into such peril, is also commended. The queen is so very thankful that he made his way safely home after all.' I nodded. All of that was in her letter, too.

'We will have a feast tonight,' said Robert Dudley cheerily.

'We have our own cooks with us and have brought the necessary viands. There will be no expense for you.'

Perhaps not. Though once more, my temperamental chief cook John Hawthorn would probably sulk at the prospect of alien cooks in his kitchen. 'He's doing that already,' said Gladys with a knowing leer, when I said as much.

There was laughter. Later, there was feasting. My guests left, however, the next day. When, from Dover, we sent word ahead to Hawkswood and the court, we couldn't give a definite day for our arrival. Travel is too uncertain for that. Our guests had been fortuitously lucky to arrive only just before we did and said considerately that they had no wish to burden my household with themselves and their servants any longer than necessary. Christopher, though, asked if he could stay on for a few days.

'Even hardened Queen's Messengers and secret agents can get tired,' he said to me. 'What we've all gone through has been enough to wear anyone down. I have been granted some leave of absence from the court.'

'You've earned it,' I said.

A sunny April morning. There was new growth in the rose garden, but that day I chose to sit in the flower garden next to it, where the daffodils were out and tossing in the breeze. I was watching while Harry played ball with his nurse Tessie.

My household was returning to normal. I had soothed John Hawthorn's feelings and made a special point of telling Ben Flood in detail of the count's death. He was a downcast man after losing Joan, but he was a little comforted by knowing that the count was now under the ground himself. I promised him a rise in wages and agreed with him that when he went to the house where he occasionally heard Mass, Kate should sometimes go with him.

My guests had not left until the afternoon on the day of departure and before they went, I had talked with Dudley about horseflesh. He was, after all, the queen's Master of Horse. I had admired his blue roan stallion, who was called Blue Agate, asked his opinion of trotting horses and found that it agreed with mine and not with Hugh's, and discussed with him how best to find a first pony for Harry. Dudley knew of a breeder not far from Guildford who could provide a suitable animal.

'He trains them himself. You need a well-mannered pony, narrow enough for a young child. For all the old king's ranting about runts and scruffy ponies,' Dudley said, 'ponies are valuable. Children must learn to ride and you can't put them up on trotters or towering monsters sixteen hands high! Ponies make splendid pack animals, too.'

It was a comfortable, normal conversation, all the more enjoyable because I had called Brockley to join us and the three of us had sat in the little parlour, sharing a flagon of wine as we talked, the kind of practical, everyday talk that I missed when cut off from it.

Now as I sat in the garden, I had a notebook on my knee and a writing set on the bench beside me. I was making notes of some of the things we had discussed. Also, there were other plans I wished to make for the future. I wanted to extend the rose garden and – oh yes, indeed! – provide the grooms with bed-sheets. I had not forgotten the decision I'd made back on the *Lucille*. Between my notes and my benign glances towards Harry and Tessie, I did not notice Christopher Spelton coming towards me until he was actually there. Then I laid down my quill and smiled at him. 'Good morning to you, Christopher. You breakfasted early, I believe. You were gone before I came downstairs.'

'I was anxious to go out and walk, and think,' he said. 'I have something to ask you and I needed to decide on the right words.'

'Concerning what?' I moved the writing set to the ground. 'Do sit down.'

'That wouldn't be quite in order. Not for this.' For the first time since I had known him, I saw that Spelton was nervous. He was wearing a hat but now he swept it off and knelt down at my feet. 'Mistress Stannard, we have both been through some terrifying adventures and we have travelled far together. Of all the ladies I have ever known, I have never found one so courageous and full of endurance as you. You have filled me with admiration. Will you honour me by ceasing to be Mistress Stannard and becoming Mistress Spelton instead?'

I gaped at him, literally. I had never for one moment expected this. Nor did I want it. I had got rid of Captain Yarrow, it seemed, only to find Christopher Spelton in his place. I raised a hand to stop him, but he gently put it aside.

'Hear me out before you decide,' he said earnestly. 'I am a widower, these last three years. I have no children, no dependants. I have a home, near Kingston-on-Thames. It's just a small house, but it is pretty, with a view of the river and a pleasing garden. I have a married couple to look after it when I'm away, and to look after me when I'm there. You might not want to live there, as you have Hawkswood and Withysham, but I could let it and join you here. I have a good income from my work at court. You would gain, not lose, I promise. And the queen could never again try to use you as a substitute for herself, in a foreign marriage of convenience. You would be safe from that. What do you say?'

Staggered, I said: 'I have to think. I can't decide all in a moment. Give me two days.'

But I gave him my answer the following morning.

It was a close thing. I almost said yes, for Christopher was as nice a man as I have ever known. The woman who married him would have a good husband, just as Ambrosia now had. I would not have to leave Hawkswood and Christopher was right when he said that I could not be used again as a marital pawn on the royal chessboard.

But I had been married three times and it was enough. I would gladly have stayed with Gerald for ever but Gerald was gone and after him, I had known the heights and depths of passion with Matthew and found out that they were no guarantee of happiness. Then there had been Hugh, calm, loving Hugh, and that had gone so very deep that I did not think I could create anything like it again and a marriage that did not have that depth, could not now satisfy me. I didn't want, even with this likeable Christopher Spelton, the emotional strain of trying to form it. I didn't want another marriage. I didn't want upheaval, disruption, disturbance.

I didn't want any more children, either. I had had too many bad experiences of that business and though Harry's birth had been easy, it was the only one that was. Nor was I was getting any younger.

No. I wanted to stay where I was, and make plans. One of the things I had discussed with Dudley and Brockley was the idea of buying a couple of trotting stallions and making a business of it. I would move the trotting mares from Withysham to Hawkswood, where there was more space, and develop a stud. If I made a success of it, it would create a fine inheritance for Harry. And I would not have put myself at risk, providing siblings for him.

So Christopher and I parted as friends, with a handclasp and a long kiss, which, yes, was more than simply friendly, just before he mounted his horse.

But it went no further than that. I knew my decision was right because of the sense of relief I felt as I turned to go back indoors. I found that Brockley was beside me, and glanced at him.

He said: 'Madam, may I have a private word?'

In the little parlour, where, earlier that morning I had had my final interview with Christopher, Brockley and I stood face to face. 'Madam,' he said, 'perhaps I have no right to ask this, but did Master Spelton propose marriage to you?'

I never lie to Brockley. 'Yes, he did. But I have refused him. How did you know that he had proposed?'

'From a window, madam, I saw him go into the garden yesterday and kneel to you. And Tessie heard him speak to you of his circumstances . . . I think he told you that he was a widower and spoke of a house near Kingston. Those are such things as suitors tell the ladies they are courting, or the ladies' fathers.'

'Tessie must learn not to gossip about things she overhears.' I had been so haunted by eavesdroppers during the last two or three months that hearing of another made me indignant. I would take Tessie to task for this.

'Why did you refuse him, madam? I thought he would be a good match for you, far better than the count! And being married to him would protect you from any future counts.'

Dear Brockley. Dear, generous Brockley. We had never been lovers and we never would, but we loved each other just the same. It had not interfered with his marriage to Dale (though it had come near it); nor had it intruded on my marriages to

Matthew and Hugh. Hugh had known it perfectly well, but been sure enough of himself and me to ignore it. My feelings for my husbands had run like a river on a parallel course with my feeling for Brockley, close but separated by a strong, high dyke.

But Brockley was there, always there, at the back of my mind. To take Christopher would have been like betraying him, and I knew that, for all his generosity, he would suffer if I took yet another husband.

'I don't want any more emotional entanglements,' I said. 'I have had enough. If the queen offers me another count, I shall just say no. I mean it, Brockley. I am not a slave – though I now know what it feels like to be threatened with slavery. I know the queen had her reasons for asking me to make a political marriage for her. Time is going on. It's getting late for her to produce an heir. But I can't do that for her, anyway, and it *is* possible to sign a treaty without backing it up by a marriage. I want to be here at Hawkswood, in peace. I only want a quiet, domestic life.'

'Humph!'

'Brockley?'

'Madam, I think all here at Hawkswood would heartily agree with you. We would all enjoy a quiet domestic life. But I sometimes wonder if you are capable of such a thing!' said Brockley.